NEW YORK REVIEW BOOKS
CLASSICS

BOYS ALIVE

PIER PAOLO PASOLINI (1922–1975) was born in Bologna and spent a peripatetic childhood following his father, a soldier, from one posting to the next. During World War II, Pasolini lived with his mother in Friuli, moving with her to Rome in 1950 after being charged with "corruption of minors and obscene acts in public places." It was in Rome, while working as a teacher at a private school, that Pasolini began to write *Boys Alive* (1955)—a novel that was hailed as a masterpiece by prominent Italian writers and condemned as pornographic by Marxist critics and the conservative judiciary of Milan. In the decades that followed, he published many more novels, books of poetry (in both Italian and Friulian), essays, and plays. He also became a screenwriter and filmmaker, collaborating with Federico Fellini on *Le Notti di Cabiria* (1957) and *La Dolce Vita* (1960) and directing *The Gospel According to Saint Matthew* (1964), *The Hawks and the Sparrows* (1966), and *Theorem* (1968), which Pasolini had first published as a novel earlier the same year. A figure of controversy due to his antiestablishment political views and homosexuality, he was brought to trial at least thirty-three times. He was brutally murdered under mysterious circumstances on the beach in Ostia, on the outskirts of Rome.

TIM PARKS has written eighteen novels, including *Europa*, which was short-listed for the Booker Prize, and, most recently, *Hotel Milano*. He is the author of many works of nonfiction, most notably *Italian Neighbors*, *Teach Us to Sit Still*, and *Out of My Head*, and has translated the works of Alberto Moravia, Giacomo Leopardi, and Niccolò Machiavelli, among others. He is a frequent contributor to *The New York Review of Books* and the *London Review of Books*. He lives in Milan, Italy.

BOYS ALIVE

PIER PAOLO PASOLINI

Translated from the Italian by
TIM PARKS

NEW YORK REVIEW BOOKS

New York

THIS IS A NEW YORK REVIEW BOOK
PUBLISHED BY THE NEW YORK REVIEW OF BOOKS
207 East 32nd Street, New York, NY 10016
www.nyrb.com

First published in Italian under the title *Ragazzi di vita* by Garzanti Editore.

Library of Congress Cataloging-in-Publication Data
Names: Pasolini, Pier Paolo, 1922–1975, author. | Parks, Tim, translator.
Title: Boys alive / by Pier Paolo Pasolini; translation by Tim Parks.
Other titles: Ragazzi di vita. English
Description: New York: New York Review Books, [2023] | Series: New York Review Books classics | Identifiers: LCCN 2023007829 (print) | LCCN 2023007830 (ebook) | ISBN 9781681377629 (paperback) | ISBN 9781681377636 (ebook)
Subjects: LCSH: Street children—Italy—Rome—Fiction. | Gangs—Italy—Rome—Fiction. | LCGFT: Novels.
Classification: LCC PQ4835.A48 R313 2023 (print) | LCC PQ4835.A48 (ebook) | DDC 853/.914—dc23/eng/20230224
LC record available at https://lccn.loc.gov/2023007829
LC ebook record available at https://lccn.loc.gov/2023007830

ISBN 978-1-68137-762-9
Available as an electronic book; ISBN 978-1-68137-763-6

Printed in the United States of America on acid-free paper.
10 9 8 7 6 5 4 3 2 1

INTRODUCTION

RAGAZZI di vita. Pier Paolo Pasolini's original title for his first novel—literally, "Boys of Life"—brings together youth and vitality. But in Italian a *donna di vita* is a prostitute. So what are we to expect in these pages? Call boys? Hustlers? The title of Pasolini's second novel would again include the word "life": *Una vita violenta.* And again there is a dark side, as if life could hardly be separated from sinister and dangerous forces.

Both novels are set in Rome, both feature adolescents from the underclasses housed in the sprawling developments that sprung up around the city during the Fascist era and in the years immediately after the Second World War. Characters invariably speak the fierce and distinctive Roman dialect, whose mannerisms, blasphemies, and obscenities spill over into the more literary third-person narrative. In an essay published posthumously, Pasolini described this dialect as the only "revenge" of the common people, "depository of a view of life that is ... virile: uninhibited, vulgar, cunning, often obscene, free from any moral ballast." And he gives two examples of this ethos: "When I told a boy it was hardly polite to spit on the floor in a pizzeria, he shrugged and with his blond baby-Cain face told me: 'I do *my life*; I don't give a damn about anyone else.'" On another occasion, when the author complains about an old drunk urinating on the sidewalk, a young friend observes: "It's life."

Ragazzi di vita was published in 1955. Pasolini was thirty-three. He had not grown up in Rome and was not a native speaker of its dialect. The elder of two sons, his father a Fascist army officer and compulsive gambler, his mother a schoolteacher, he was born in

Bologna. But the family moved about with his father's military post-ings, and for one period, when his father was jailed for gambling debts, they went to live in his mother's home village, Casarsa della Delizia, some fifty miles northeast of Venice. It was here that Pasolini would later escape, again with his mother, when Allied bombing targeted northern Italy in 1942. His father at this point was a prisoner of the British in Africa; his younger brother, Guido Alberto, had joined the partisans fighting against Fascism. But Pasolini pursued his literary studies for the University of Bologna, researching a thesis on the nineteenth-century lyric poet Giovanni Pascoli. He was also intensely active writing poems in the dialect of Friuli and short stories that were rural, lyrical, and sentimental, as well as joining his mother in offering free schooling to pupils in the wartime circum-stances. In the summer of 1943, at the age of twenty-one, he began to talk explicitly to friends about his homosexuality and fell in love with one of his pupils.

The move to Rome, a turning point in Pasolini's life, was more a desperate escape than a career choice. In 1945 his brother had been murdered along with several of his comrades by a rival group of partisans aligned with Tito's Yugoslav forces and opposed to working with the Americans and British. "My mother and I were half-destroyed by grief," Pasolini remembered. Shortly afterwards, his father returned from the war paranoid and alcoholic: "He drove us mad, he roared and fretted." Father and son fought: "The battle was ferocious: if a man were to fall ill with cancer, then recover, he would have the same memory of his illness that I have of those years." By this time, Paso-lini was teaching at a state school, intensely active in the local Com-munist Party, and already the published author of four small collections of poems. However, on August 29, 1949, returning from a village fair, he involved three underage boys in some kind of group masturbation. When the story got out he was pursued by the local anti-Communist authorities and put on trial. He lost his teaching job and was expelled from the Communist Party. In January 1950, he and his mother abandoned his father and set off for Rome.

The impact of Rome, its lively, aggressive dialect, its postwar squalor and violence, thus occurred exactly as Pasolini found himself forced to acknowledge that the path of respectability was no longer open to him: "Like it or not, I was tarred with the brush of Rimbaud ... or even Oscar Wilde." Urgently looking for teaching work, walk-on parts in films, literary journalism, anything to achieve independence and security, he was immensely attracted to the young men of the underclass around him who cared nothing for bourgeois values, who lived intensely, carelessly, refusing to be hampered by scruple and convention. As early as 1950 he published the story "Il Ferrobedò" which, much reworked, would become the first chapter of *Ragazzi di vita*: during the last lawless days of the German occupation of Rome, a young boy, fresh from his first communion, joins the crowds looting the Ferrobedò, a huge factory producing reinforced concrete.

Ragazzi di vita would be accused of not really being a novel. "It's impossible to summarize the plot decently," Pasolini confessed to its eventual publisher, Livio Garzanti, "because there is no plot, in the conventional sense of the word." Simply, the narrative would follow a group of boys, principally Riccetto (a nickname that means "curly") "from the chaos and hopes of the first days of the Liberation through to the reaction of 1950–51." During this time the protagonists would pass "from infancy to early youth, or rather ... from a heroic, amoral age to an age that is already prosaic and immoral."

Pasolini follows this brisk description with a number of reflections on the responsibility of Fascism for having built "those concentration camps that are Rome's outlying housing developments" and again of the postwar government "which hasn't solved the problem." He even goes on to speak of framing his narrative with two parallel incidents, one in the early pages where the young Riccetto generously saves a drowning bird, the other toward the end where he does nothing to rescue a drowning boy, trapped as he is in "the selfishness and sordidness of a morality that is no longer his."

Reading the novel, one can't help feeling that this reassuring account of its underlying values was little more than an alibi, a false passport that would enable the author to get his writing before the public. The literary and movie scene of the time was dominated by what came to be known as neorealism, bleak, haunting stories of urban and rural deprivation which tended to suggest that suffering was largely a question of political corruption and capitalist greed; the prevailing mood was socialist and it was important to appear concerned about the underprivileged. Such sentiments never emerge in *Ragazzi di vita*. On the contrary, Pasolini revels in the vitality of the squalid world he so lavishly and energetically evokes. The lyricism and literary allusion of earlier efforts is now bent to conjuring up an urban *inferno* as vast and hideous as it is colorful and dynamic. One has the impression of a writer who has finally found his subject and style and is rejoicing in it, delighted to throw all caution and respectability to the wind. The only occasion when his characters show any class consciousness comes when the two losers, Begalone and Alduccio, find themselves too broke to pay for a prostitute and see a sports car drive by: "Fucking poverty, what shit!" Begalone declares for the benefit of the neorealists. "You think it's fair, him all spiffed up with that sweet pussy, loaded with cash, and us: zilch? Big-shot bastards! But their time is up. The world's changing!" Socialist revolution will mean always having the price of a whore.

If there is no grand plot, nevertheless a clear organizing principle soon emerges: Pasolini's narrative voice moves like a heat-seeking missile, infallibly locking on to situations of great intensity, conflict, and comedy. Possessing nothing, his young characters fight to survive and to live. At all costs they must have fun; boredom is death. And if food and fun must be paid for, then money will be found: looting, hustling, scavenging, stealing. Once found it is immediately squandered on smart clothes and smart shoes, or it is drunk away, gambled away, or simply lost. In everything the characters are both accomplices and antagonists. They need one another, perhaps care for one another, and compete ferociously. Every boy aspires to be the toughest, the shrewdest, the most unscrupulous punk on the block. Boasting and exhibitionism are the norm. Each must be the best swimmer, have the biggest dog, wear the sharpest clothes. Challenge and mockery abound. Bullying is rife. Schadenfreude is a constant consolation. To be cheerful and in the money is also to possess a weapon, to make

someone else feel down and defeated. As each new episode begins—
a warehouse heist, an evening's gambling, a search for sex—the reader
can only tremble, waiting for disaster to strike, which perhaps it does,
and then again perhaps it doesn't, but in any event never where or
when or how you expected. Nothing is predictable.

This is partly because our characters' days and nights are so very
long. The novel may unfold over five years, but in these pages it is
always summer, as if Pasolini were not interested in his protagonists
when they were, so to speak, "hibernating," perhaps at school or forced
by the cold to stay home; only in the interminable scorching emptiness of the Italian summer when the call to live and to live intensely
is most powerful. The weather plays its part, inducing states of extreme
irritableness, or sunstruck stupor, driving the boys to water, to the
crowded beach at Ostia, the filthy banks of the Tiber, the dangerous
currents of the Aniene, forcing them to live mainly at night, indeed
all night, roaming the city in search of action, any action, hanging
on to the platform of a first tram in the gray dawn light so as not to
pay. Then the heat explodes in apocalyptic downpours; lightning
plays over the tenement blocks, weirdly illuminating the chaos of
ruins, shantytowns, and building sites. Pasolini is in his element: "his
love of summer" he wrote in a poem about himself, "was perhaps the
most powerful feeling in his life."

Meantime, any possible drift toward the symbolic or the surreal
is held at bay by constant and extremely precise topographical refer-
ences; streets, districts, schools, hills, factories, parks, and apartment
blocks are all and always rigorously named. Follow the action on
Google Maps, if you will. At the same time these names often gesture
to other ancient narratives: Via Donna Olimpia, Monte di Splendore,
Via Nomentana—the contrast between antique glory and contemporary decadence could hardly be starker. The characters' nicknames—
when speaking in dialect Italians frequently use nicknames—also
bring in other suggestions and ideas: Guaio means trouble, Picchio
is a thump or a woodpecker, Caciotta is a cheese, Lupetto a young
wolf, Borgo Antico the title of a popular song. Songs abound. When
happy, Pasolini's characters cannot resist singing, usually at the top

of their voices. There are quotations from Dante and from Gioachino Belli, a much-celebrated eighteenth-century dialect poet. Sometimes it seems Pasolini's text is as busy with literary hints and allusions as his characters are intent on cheating, seducing, and doing harm to one another

Which brings us to the issue of translation. "Mimicking a dialect infiltrated with literary prose is the riskiest, most exhausting and exasperating writing endeavor you could ever take on," Pasolini remarked. On the other hand, when his publisher Garzanti worried that some readers might find his text too difficult, he explained that "the dialect words are absolutely essential for me...they give me the fun I need to grasp and capture my characters." For the translator there is the problem that the postwar dialect Pasolini was using is not only near incomprehensible at times but that it locates the characters' speech in place and time. One cannot transfer his characters' dialogues into the demotic of, say, New York's Bronx or London's Whitechapel, since the action is very specifically taking place in Rome, not New York or London, and in the late 1940s, not in our own time. To use a specific British or American idiom would be a distraction. Even the frequently described gesticulation of the characters is a specifically Roman gesticulation. All the translator can do is feel for a mix of the fiercely colloquial and the evocatively literary that is as generic and non-place-specific as possible, trusting that Pasolini's insistence on Rome and his lavish descriptions of its districts and street life will do the rest.

There remains a further issue with the status of the Italian text itself. When Pasolini sent his finished manuscript to Garzanti, the publisher lost his nerve and insisted the author remove obscenities and graphic descriptions of sex, and tone down the dialect. "So I'm in the midst of a half-dead text to correct and castrate," Pasolini despaired. Offensive words were reduced to an initial letter followed by suspension points, whole scenes were cut, others were doctored and neutered. In recent years, since the original manuscript still exists, there have been calls to republish the novel in its original form. But Pasolini clearly took advantage of this unwanted edit to refashion and rewrite many aspects of the text that had not proved problematic for Garzanti. It thus becomes hard to say which text might be considered "definitive." On just two occasions, where the cuts Pasolini made were so radical and so poorly hidden that the reader cannot help sensing that something is "missing," I have taken the liberty of translating from the earlier version; these moments are signaled with footnotes that offer the version normally published.

Despite all this self-censorship *Ragazzi di vita* provoked a scandal and its author and publisher were put on trial for obscenity, thus guaranteeing the book notoriety and sales. "Perhaps," observes the Italian critic Vincenzo Cerami, "what really upset people was not the strong language, but the very idea of...giving a literary dignity to the lowest of the low." Eventually absolved after many celebrated intellectuals had testified on his behalf, Pasolini went on to become one of the foremost intellectuals, cultural critics, novelists, and film directors of his time, writing scores of coruscating analyses of Italian public life. Interested readers wishing to savor the milieu conjured up in *Ragazzi di vita* might usefully look up his movie *Accattone* (Scrounger), an adaptation of the novel *Una vita violenta*—the extraordinary urban landscape of suburban Rome in this period, the vitality of Pasolini's characters and the urgency and precariousness of their existence is conveyed with an immediacy that one can then fruitfully take back to reading the novels.

Continuing to associate with Rome's underclass, Pasolini's own existence was also necessarily precarious. On the night of November 2, 1975, at the age of fifty-three, he was murdered on the beach at Ostia, a place he describes in *Ragazzi di vita* and where he regularly went for sex. The murderer was never identified and the motive remains obscure. But turning back to his first novel one is bound to notice just how many deaths there are in its pages, how much collateral damage around this thirst for intensity, as if life were hardly life without the risk of death. And then how little pathos accrues to the unlucky victims, how little reward or credit is afforded to anyone who seeks to save another human being. At the end of *Una vita violenta* the wayward delinquent hero, recovering from TB, dives into the turbulent waters of a flooded building site to rescue a drowning girl, and as a result dies himself. At the end of *Ragazzi di vita*, called on to play the hero and save a younger boy, Riccetto reflects that "to dive in the river under the bridge was tantamount to saying you were tired of life, no one could survive it." "I love you, Riccetto, you know!" the young man assures himself a moment later, in one of the very rare occasions when the author allows his character a moment of introspection.

It is in this sense that Pasolini is indeed a moral writer: the world and experience are presented in such an uncompromising and disturbing way as to force the disoriented reader to reexamine the values underpinning his or her own life.

—TIM PARKS

BOYS ALIVE

1. THE FERROBEDÒ

And beneath Mazzini's monument...*
—Popular song

IT WAS a hot, hot day in July. Riccetto, who was supposed to be taking his First Communion and getting confirmed, had been up since five; but walking down Via Donna Olimpia in his long gray pants and white shirt he looked more like a kid dressed up to pull girls down by the Tiber than a churchgoer or a soldier of Christ. With a bunch of other boys, all like him, all in white, he went down to the Church of the Divine Providence where Don Pizzuto gave him Communion at nine and the bishop confirmed him at eleven. But Riccetto was dying to be off. Monteverde down to Trastevere station was one long din of traffic. You could hear horns and engines attacking the slopes and hairpins, filling the city's outskirts, already simmering in the early morning sun, with a deafening roar. As soon as the bishop was through with his little sermon, Don Pizzuto and a couple of young altar boys took the kids into the courtyard for photographs; the bishop walked along with them blessing relatives who knelt as he passed. Just being there was a torment and Riccetto decided to dump the lot of them; he slipped out through the empty church but ran into his godfather at the door: "Hey, where do you think you're going?" "Home," Riccetto said, "I'm hungry." "You're coming to our place, right, you little son of a bitch," his godfather yelled after him, "we've got lunch waiting." But Riccetto paid him no mind and ran off on asphalt that was scorching in the sun. The whole of Rome was

*Giuseppe Mazzini (1805–1872) was a visionary political thinker and one of the chief architects of Italian unification.

one great roar, except that up here it was quiet, but a quiet primed like a bomb. Riccetto went to get changed.

The Granatieri are pretty close to Monteverde Vecchio: you just cut across Prato and between the apartments they're building along Viale dei Quattro Venti: landslides of garbage, unfinished houses already in ruins, muddy excavations, escarpments full of crap. Via Abate Ugone was a minute's walk. The crowds coming down from the peaceful, well-paved streets of Monteverde Vecchio were all heading toward the Grattacieli;* you could already see the trucks as well, endless lines of them, jeeps too, motorbikes, armored cars. Riccetto joined the crowd hurrying to the sheds.

Below him the Ferrobedò† opened up like a huge courtyard, a fenced field, sunk in a hollow, the size of a plaza or a cattle market. There were gates along the fence, rows of wooden huts at one end, all the same, then sheds at the other. Riccetto, moving in the pack, crossed the length of the Ferrobedò, everybody yelling, and reached one of the huts. But there were some Germans there and they weren't letting people through. By the door was a small table turned upside down; Riccetto grabbed it and raced for the gate. Outside he ran into a young guy who said, "What you up to?" "Taking it home," Riccetto answered. "Come with me, dummy, we'll get some better stuff."

"Right," said Riccetto. He chucked the table and someone walking by grabbed it for himself.

With this new guy he went back in the Ferrobedò, pushing his way into the sheds; they grabbed a bag of cables. Then the guy said, "Come here and get these nails." So between cables, nails, and other stuff, Riccetto went back and forth to Donna Olimpia five times. The sun was scorching, at its postlunch hottest, but the Ferrobedò was still full of people along Trastevere, Porta Portese, the Mattatoio,

*_Grattacieli_, translated literally, means "skyscrapers."
†The nickname for a large factory, the Ferrobeton (literally, "Ironconcrete"), that still produces steel-reinforced concrete for major construction projects. The company was founded in 1908. Much of Pasolini's novel is set around the sort of building sites and high-rise apartment blocks that companies like Ferrobeton made possible.

San Paolo, vying with the trucks to fill the burning air with noise. Back from the fifth trip Riccetto and this other guy saw a horse and cart between two huts near the fence. They went close to see if maybe they could grab it. Meanwhile Riccetto had found an arms cache in one hut and slung a machine gun over his shoulder, stuck two pistols in his belt. Armed to the teeth, he climbed on the horse.

But a German came and chased them off.

While Riccetto was hiking back and forth between Donna Olimpia and the sheds with bags of cables, Marcello was hanging out with the other boys at the Buon Pastore. The pool was thrashing with kids swimming and yelling. On the dirty grass all around others were kicking a ball.

Agnolo asked, "Where's Riccetto got to?"

"Went to Communion," shouted Marcello." "Bless his little soul!" said Agnolo.

"I guess he'll be eating with his godfather," added Marcello.

Up there by the water in the Buon Pastore they still had no idea. The sun beat in silence on the Madonna del Riposo, Casaletto, and Primavalle behind. When they came back from their swim they went through Prato, where the Germans were camped.

They stopped to look around, but a bike and sidecar came by and the German in the sidecar yelled, "*Rausch*, infected area." The Military Hospital was nearby. "Who gives a fuck?" shouted Marcello. The bike had slowed down; the German jumped out of his sidecar and gave Marcello a slap that sent him staggering. Mouth swollen, Marcello twisted like a snake and, slithering down the steep slope with his friends, blew the man a raspberry. Running off, laughing and yelling, they ended up right in front of the Casermone,* where they found some other friends. "What are you up to?" this lot said, all tousled and dirty.

"Why?" asked Agnolo, "What's there to do?" "Go to the Ferrobedò, if you want to see something." They set off at a rush and as soon as they were there headed straight through the crowd to the workshop.

---

*The word *casermone* literally means "big, ugly apartment block."

"Let's take the engine apart," shouted Agnolo. But Marcello went out and found himself alone in the mayhem, right by the tar pit. He was on the point of falling in and drowning like an Indian in quicksand when a yell pulled him back: "Hey, Marcè, watch out, Marcè!" It was that son of a bitch Riccetto with his friends. So he joined up with them. They went into a shed and ripped off a bunch of grease pots, lathe belts, and scrap iron. Marcello took a ton of the stuff home with him and dumped it in a little yard where his mother wouldn't see it anytime soon. He hadn't been home since morning and his mother gave him a whack. "Where've you been, you rascal?" she shouted, slapping him. "Went for a swim," said Marcello, hunched and lean as a cricket, "honest I did," trying to fend off the blows. Then his older brother came and saw the stuff in the yard. "Asshole," he shouted, "stealing this stuff, son of a bitch." So Marcello went back to the Ferrobedò with his brother and this time they took some car tires from the back of a truck. It was coming on evening already and the sun was hotter than ever; the Ferrobedò was leaping, worse than a market, you couldn't move. Every now and then someone yelled, "Run for it, run, the Germans are coming," to get the others to clear off so they could steal more easily themselves.

Next day Riccetto and Marcello, who were getting into it, went to the Caciara, the general markets, which were closed. Masses of people were milling around and there were Germans walking up and down, shooting in the air. But the people really stopping you from getting in, the ones generally making a pain in the ass of themselves, weren't the Germans but the African Police.[*] The crowd was growing bigger and bigger, heaving at the gates, roaring, hollering, cursing. When the stampede came, even those bastard Italians gave up. The streets around the markets were crawling with people, the markets themselves empty as a cemetery under a sun hot enough to split stones; no sooner were the gates forced than the place filled up.

---

[*]The Italian African Police was a militia formed to police the Italian colonies of North Africa but redeployed in Rome toward the end of the Second World War. The force was made up of Italians, not Africans.

Inside there was nothing, not so much as a cabbage core. The crowd started wandering around the warehouses, under the open sheds, in the outlets; no one wanted to leave with empty hands. Finally a group of youngsters found a basement that looked full; through barred windows you could see heaps of bike tires and inner tubes, tarpaulins, canvas, and, on the shelves, whole cheeses. Word got around fast; five or six hundred people rushed after the first group. They broke down the door and everyone lunged in in a great crush. Riccetto and Marcello were in the thick of it. Sucked through the door, feet barely touching the ground, they were swallowed up by the pull of the crowd. You went down a spiral staircase, the crowd behind pushing and women half-suffocated yelling. The staircase was overwhelmed with people. A thin iron handrail gave way and a woman fell screaming and banged her head against a step at the bottom. The people outside went on pushing. "She's dead," shouted a man at the bottom. "She's dead," some women started shrieking, terrified; you couldn't get in or out. Marcello was still going down the stairs. At the bottom he jumped over the corpse, rushed into the basement, and filled his bag with tires, along with other boys grabbing everything they could. Riccetto was nowhere to be seen, maybe he'd gone out. The crowd had broken up. Marcello climbed over the dead woman again and hurried home.

At Ponte Bianco he ran into the militia. They stopped him and took the stuff. But he didn't move on, just stood off to one side feeling forlorn with his empty bag. Pretty soon, Riccetto turned up, climbing from the Caciara to Ponte Bianco. "What's up?" he said. "I'd grabbed myself some bike tires," Marcello told him gloomily, "and this lot robbed me." "Who do these assholes think they are, why don't they mind their own fucking business!" Riccetto yelled.

There were no houses beyond Ponte Bianco, just a huge building site, and at the end of that, either side of the deep canyon of Viale dei Quattro Venti, the dusty white expanse of Monteverde. Riccetto and Marcello sat there in the sun on the sparse black grass watching the African Police taking people's loot. After a bit, though, the guys with bags full of cheeses turned up at the bridge. The militia stopped them, but this lot took them on; they really went for them, looking so mad the militia thought better of it and gave up; they left the boys with their stuff and when Marcello and others gathered around getting loud they gave them back their stuff too. After a little victory dance, trying to work out how much they could sell the stuff for, Riccetto and Marcello headed down Donna Olimpia and all the others went off too. At Ponte Bianco the militia were left with the stink of garbage simmering in the sun.

On the muddy ground beneath Monte di Splendore, a knoll around ten feet high that blocked your view of Monteverde, the Ferrobedò, and the horizon line of the sea, one Saturday, when the kids were fed up with playing, some of the older ones gathered around the goal with the ball at their feet. They made a circle and began to pass the ball about, kicking with their insteps to keep it low, not bending it, just stroking it about clean and sharp. After a while they were all soaked in sweat, but they didn't want to take off their smart jackets or their blue woolen tops with the yellow or black stripes because of the relaxed, jokey way they had started playing. But since the smaller boys hanging around might have thought they were crazy, playing under the hot sun dressed like that, they started laughing and making fun of each other, so as not to give the younger kids a chance to make fun of them.

Passing and trapping the ball, they called to each other. "Damn, but you're gloomy today, Alvà!" shouted a dark-looking kid, hair slicked back with grease. "Women," he added, going for a bicycle kick. "Fuck off," Alvaro told him, face so bony it seemed full of dents, and with a head so big a flea would have died of old age before making the journey right round. He tried a smart back-heel but miskicked and the ball rolled off toward Riccetto and the others who were sprawled out on the muddy grass.

Agnolo, the redhead, got up and, taking his time, kicked the ball back to the youngsters. "Doesn't want to overdo it, you know," shouted

Rocco, nodding to Alvaro, "tonight there's going to be tons of stuff to carry."

"They're after pipes," said Agnolo to the others. Right then the Ferrobedò and the other factories farther off toward Testaccio, Porto, and San Paolo sounded their three o'clock sirens. Riccetto and Marcello got up and went off without a word down Via Ozanam, and taking it easy under the burning sun, one stretch of road at a time, made their way to Ponte Bianco to hitch a ride on a 13 or a 28. They'd started with the Ferrobedò, gone on with the Americans, and now they were after cigarette ends. True, Riccetto had had a job for a while: a mechanic servicing jeeps in Monteverde Nuovo had taken him on as a dogsbody. But then he'd stolen five hundred from the boss, who sent him packing. So they idled away the afternoons, at Donna Olimpia or on Monte di Casadio, among the other kids playing on the small sun-blanched knoll, and later the women who came to spread their laundry on the scorched grass. Or they went to play football in the clearing between the Grattacieli and Monte di Splendore, amid hundreds of other boys fooling around in the sun-drenched tenement yards or on the parched grass beside Via Ozanam or Via Donna Olimpia, outside the Franceschi Elementary School, which was full of evacuees and evicted families.

When Riccetto and Marcello hopped down from the tram buffers at Ponte Garibaldi, the bridge was deserted under an African sun: but between the pilings beneath the bridge the Ciriola bathing barge was leaping. Alone on the bridge, chins resting on the scorching hot railing, Riccetto and Marcello spent a while looking down at the river folk soaking up the sun on the barge, or playing cards, or swimming across the river. Then after arguing a while over where to go, they grabbed onto an old half-empty tram that, scraping and squealing, took them toward San Paolo. At Ostia station they drifted here and there between the café tables, near the newspaper kiosk and the market stalls, or where people stood in line at the ticket office, picking up cigarette butts. But they were already fed up; you could hardly breathe for the heat, and God knows what it would have been like without the faint breeze coming off the sea. "Hey, Riccè,"* said Marcello half pissed off, "why don't we take a swim ourselves?" "Let's do it," said Riccetto through twisted lips, and he shrugged.

Behind the Paolino Park and the golden facade of San Paolo, the Tiber ran under a big embankment plastered with posters; and it was empty; no bathing barges here, no boats, no swimmers, just a bristling of cranes to the right, antennae and smokestacks, a gasometer huge against the sky, and, on the horizon, beyond all the scorched and filthy escarpments, the whole neighborhood of Monteverde with its old houses like so many little boxes fading in the bright light. There were the pilings of an unfinished bridge in the river here, with dirty water eddying all around, and on the San Paolo side the bank was thick with reeds and scrub. Riccetto and Marcello rushed through the reeds to reach the first piling, down by the water. But they didn't swim until they were a few hundred yards downstream, where the Tiber begins a long bend.

Riccetto lay naked on the weedy grass, hands under his head, looking up in the air.

"Ever been to Ostia?" he suddenly asked. "Christ's sake," Marcello answered, "didn't you know I was born there?" "Well, fuck,"—Riccetto looked him over with a grimace—"you never told me that!" "And so?" "Ever been on a ship out at sea?" Riccetto asked, curious. "Course," said Marcello smugly. "Where to?" asked Riccetto. "Christ's sake, Riccè," said Marcello, enjoying himself, "what a lot of stuff you want to know! Can't remember, I was barely three, wasn't I!" "Reckon you've been to sea about as often as I have, idiot," said Riccetto, disgusted. "Fuck you," Marcello shot back, "I was out there every day on my uncle's sailboat." "Give me a break!" Riccetto clicked his tongue. "Whoa," he said then, "junk!" He was looking at the water. "Serious junk!" Some flotsam was drifting by, a waterlogged crate and a chamber pot. Riccetto and Marcello went to the edge of the oil-black

---

*Most names and nicknames have diminutives that involve a shortening and a shift of accent. So Riccetto becomes Riccè; Marcello, Marcè; Alvaro, Alvà; and so on. Their use can be affectionate, ironic or mocking.

water. "Damn but I'd like to go on a boat trip!" said Riccetto with a sorrowful air, watching the crate drift off to its destiny, bobbing in the filth. "You know the Ciriola rents out boats?" said Marcello. "Right, and who's going to give us the cash," Riccetto said gloomily. "Dummy, we can lift a few pipes as well as anyone else, can't we," said Marcello, all fired up at the idea. "Agnoletto's already got himself a wrench." "OK," said Riccetto, "I'm up for it!"

They stayed until late, stretched out with their heads on their shorts, which were stiff with sweat and grime: it just seemed such an effort to get up and go. All around, the place was thick with dry reeds and bushes, but underwater there were stones and gravel. They passed some time chucking stones in the water, and even after they decided to leave and were half dressed, they went on tossing stones high in the air, toward the other bank, or at the swallows skimming the surface of the river.

They threw whole handfuls of gravel as well, yelling and having fun; the little stones clattered down on the bushes all around. But suddenly they heard a shout, like someone was calling them. They turned and in the already darkening air saw a black guy nearby kneeling on the grass. Knowing at once what was going on, Riccetto and Marcello sneaked off, but as soon as they were at a safe distance, they grabbed handfuls of gravel and chucked them right at the bushes.

Tits half out, seriously pissed off, the whore jumped up and started screaming at them.

"Ah, shut your face," Riccetto called wryly, cupping his hands, "you're dripping like a duck, dirty bitch." But the black man sprung up like a beast, and came after them, holding his pants in one hand and a knife in the other. Riccetto and Marcello skedaddled, shouting "Help," through the bushes, to the bank, up the steep slope. At the top they found the courage to turn and look back a moment, seeing the black guy at the bottom waving his knife and yelling. Riccetto and Marcello went down the other side, still running; looking each other in the face, they couldn't stop laughing; Riccetto even started rolling around in the dust, sniggering up at Marcello and shouting, "Oh my God, have you had a stroke or what, Marcè?"

The dash had brought them out on the road by the river near the facade of San Paolo, still glowing faintly in the sun. They went down to the Paolino Park, where the low trees at the other end were leaping with workers and off-duty soldiers from the Cecchignola barracks, then skirted around the church on a stretch of empty, dimly lit road. A blind man was begging with his back against the wall, legs sprawled across the sidewalk.

Riccetto and Marcello sat on the curb to catch their breath and the old man, sensing someone was near, began his misery spiel. His legs were spread wide, a beret full of coins between. Riccetto nudged Marcello with his elbow and pointed. "Take it easy," muttered Marcello. When they'd stopped panting, Riccetto nudged him again, he seemed riled, gesturing with his hands as if to say, "So, what are we going to do?" Marcello shrugged to tell him he was on his own and Riccetto sent him a look of pity, flushing with anger. In a low voice, he said, "Wait for me over there." Marcello got up and went to wait on the other side of the road, in the trees. When Marcello was gone, Riccetto waited until no one was walking by, went up to the blind man, grabbed the handful of coins from his beret, and ran off. As soon as he was safe, he counted the money under a streetlamp; there was almost five hundred.

The following morning, the nuns' convent and other buildings in Via Garibaldi had their water cut off.

Riccetto and Marcello had found Agnolo in Donna Olimpia outside the Giorgio Franceschi Elementary School, kicking a ball around with some other kids and nothing but moonlight to see by. They told him to go get his wrench, and Agnolo didn't have to be asked twice. Then all three went down San Pancrazio, toward Trastevere, looking for somewhere quiet, which they found in Via Manara. The street was deserted at that hour and they were able to set to work around a manhole cover without anyone coming to bother them. They weren't even worried when a door banged open on the balcony above and an old woman, half-asleep but all made-up, started yelling: "What're you doing down there?" Riccetto looked up a moment and told her, "Hey, lady, it's nothing, just the mystery of a blocked drain!"

They were already done; they took hold of the manhole cover from above and below and Agnolo and Riccetto carried it, slow and quiet, toward a derelict house beneath the Gianicolo, a ruined old gym. It was dark, but Agnolo knew the place; he found the sledgehammer in a corner of the big room and they started to smash the manhole cover into bits.

Next thing was to find a buyer; but once again Agnolo was on it. They went down Vicolo dei Cinque, which, aside from a drunk or two, was completely empty. Under the ragman's window, Agnolo cupped his hands around his mouth and called, "Hey, Antò!" The ragman looked out, then came down and opened his shop, where he weighed the cast iron and gave them two thousand seven hundred lire for the hundred and fifty pounds in weight. Now that they'd got the hang of things, they wanted to clean up. Agnolo ran to the gym to get the hatchet and they set off toward the Gianicolo steps. They opened a drain and clambered down inside. With the handle of the hatchet they crushed the pipe to stop the water, then cut off five or six yards. They stamped on it in the gym, breaking it up into small pieces that they stuck in a sack and took to the ragman who paid them seventy-five lire a pound. Loaded with cash, they climbed back to the Grattacieli around midnight pretty pleased with themselves. There they found Alvaro, Rocco, and some other guys playing cards at the bottom of the stairwell, crouching or slouching in silence on the landing outside Rocco's apartment, which opened onto one of the many courtyards inside the block. To get home Agnolo had to go through the development and Riccetto and Marcello were keeping him company. So they stopped to play cards with the older boys. Barely half an hour later they'd lost all their money. Luckily enough they still had the five hundred stolen from the blind guy to go and have fun in one of the Ciriola's boats; Riccetto had hidden it in his shoes.

"Here comes the baby mob!" said one young man on the barge, seeing them hurrying down the burning-hot sidewalk. Riccetto couldn't resist the temptation to have a go on the swing, but he jumped down soon enough to catch up with the others who had already crossed the gangway and were handing their fifty lire to Orazio's wife in the bathing station that floats on the waters of the Tiber. Giggetto was hardly welcoming: "Sort yourselves out here," he said, pointing to a single locker for all three. They hesitated. "So, what are you waiting for?" Giggetto snapped, stretching an open hand in their direction as if to suggest how hopeless they were. "Or do I have to come and undress you myself?"

"Fuck him," Agnolo muttered and pulled his T-shirt up over his head without further ado. But Giggetto was still at it: "Little kids, pains in the ass...the hell with you all, you and whoever sent you..." Crestfallen, the three pains in the ass undressed and stood naked, clutching their clothes. "Well?" yelled the lifeguard, "what now?" They didn't know the score. Giggetto grabbed the clothes from their hands, chucked them in the locker, and turned the key. His young son was watching and sniggered. The other youngsters, hanging around naked or in sagging underpants, combing their hair in the mirror or singing, checked out the new arrivals with sidelong glances as if to say, "Damn, what a lively lot they are." Knotting their floppy underpants at the hip, they dashed out of the changing room and got together at the iron railing around the big barge, but were immediately chased away from here too. Orazio himself came out of the middle part where the bar was with his withered leg and bloodshot face. "Fuck you," he yelled, "how many times do I have to tell people you can't stand there or you'll bust the railing?" They hurried off past the big shower mat with Orazio still bawling them out for a good ten minutes from where he was sitting on his wicker chair. Inside, some youngsters were playing cards while others sat with their feet up on wobbly tables, smoking. At the top of the gangway between the barge and the bank, Agnolo's puppy was waiting for them, tongue hanging out, happy as could be. This cheered up the three rascals and they ran off along the big wall with the dog racing after them. They stopped a while near the diving platform, then went on running toward Ponte Sisto.

It was still really early: not even one thirty, and Rome was all hot sunshine.

From the dome of Saint Peter's behind Ponte Sisto to Tiber Island beyond Ponte Garibaldi the air was stretched tight as the skin on a drum. In the silence, between big walls that stank of piss in the heat, the Tiber flowed yellow, as if driven by the refuse it bore down in plenty. Six or seven office workers who'd spent the whole time on the barge sunbathing eventually left, after which the first to come along, around two, were the tousle-haired crowd from Piazza Giudia, then the Trastevere lot, from beyond Ponte Sisto, long lines of them, half-naked, yelling and laughing, always looking for someone to beat up on. The Ciriola filled up, outside, on the dirty little beach, and inside, in the changing rooms, the bar, on the barge. A maggots' nest. Scores of kids were gathered around the diving platform. They dived head-first, feetfirst, did somersaults. The platform was only about five feet high, so even the six-year-olds were having a go. People crossing Ponte Sisto stopped to watch. On the big embankment too, where the plane trees hang over the wall, a few kids who didn't have the money to join in were sitting with their legs over the edge, watching. But most people were still lying on the sand or the patch of rusty grass clinging on beside the wall.

"Last in's a loser!" yelled a dark, hairy little boy to the others sprawled all around. But only Nicchiola bothered, setting off with his hunched shoulders and twisted back, flopping into the yellow water with legs and arms splayed wide so his buttocks splashed hard. The others clicked their tongues unimpressed and told the dark boy to clear off. Then, a bit later, lolling and listless, they got to their feet and drifted off like a bunch of sheep toward the patch of sand under the swing, opposite the barge, where they watched Monnezza lifting dumbbells, a hundred pounds' worth apiece, feet burning in the sand, face red with the strain, surrounded by a whole regiment of kiddies. Only Riccetto, Marcello, Agnolo and a few others were still at the diving platform, along with the dog, everyone's darling. "So?" said Agnolo to the others, a threatening look on his face. "Fuck you," said Riccetto, "in a hurry or something?" "Go fuck yourself," said Agnolo, "what did we come here for?" "To take a swim," said Riccetto, and went to end of the platform to look at the water.

The puppy went after him. Riccetto turned: "You coming too?" he said, cooing cheerfully. "You coming in too?" The dog watched and wagged its tail.

"Want to try headfirst, do you?" said Riccetto. He grabbed the creature by the fur and pushed him to the edge, but the dog pulled back. "Afraid, huh," said Riccetto, "well, I'm not going to force you to dive, don't worry." The dog was still watching him with anxious eyes. "What you looking at me for?" Riccetto went on reassuringly, bending down. "You naughty, dirty little doggie!" He stroked it, scratched its neck, put his hand between its teeth, tugged at it. "Dirty, dirty little dog!" he cried fondly. But the dog, feeling itself pulled, got frightened and jumped back.

"No, no, no," Riccetto said, "I'm not going to chuck you in the river!" "Hey, Riccè, you going to do this dive or what?" called Agnolo ironically. "Lemme take a piss first," said Riccetto and ran to pee against the wall; the dog went after him and watched with shining eyes and twitching tail.

Then Agnolo took a run up and dived. "Fucking hell!" shouted Marcello, seeing him fall all sideways on his belly. "Shit!" yelled Agnolo, head coming up in the middle of the river, "What a belly flop!" "Watch, I'll show you a proper dive!" shouted Riccetto, and threw himself in the water. "How did I do?" he cried, coming up to Marcello. "Legs splayed," said Marcello. "Let me have another go," said Riccetto, climbing out on the bank.

Just then the bunch milling around Monnezza and his dumbbells moved over toward the diving platform, all sure of themselves, grinning and joking and spitting, the smaller kids prancing around the others or rolling about, fighting on the walkway. There must have been more than fifty of them and they completely took over the patch of dirty grass around the platform. Monnezza went first, blond as straw, full of red freckles, and did a perfect pike with frills; then Remo, Spudorato, Pecetto, Ciccione, Pallante. Then the little kids as well, who weren't bad at all, in fact Ercoletto, who lived in Vicolo dei

Cinque, was maybe the best of the lot. He ran along the platform on tiptoe with his arms out wide, lightly, like he was dancing. Riccetto and the others backed off in a sulk, sitting on the scorched grass, watching in silence. They were like breadcrumbs in an ant's nest; it riled them to be left out while the others were kicking up a storm. Everyone was on their feet, with muddy legs, underpants clinging to their skin, pulling sarcastic faces as they looked at each other and yelled, "Up Yours." With his tough-kid face, round as an egg, Ciccione set off, slipped on the edge of the board, and let out a fierce laugh as he went down in the water yelling, "Fuck that!" On the bank, Remo shook his head and muttered cheerfully, "Fucking force of nature, you are." Beside him on the walkway, Bassotto was sniggering too when a lump of mud landed in his curls. "Bastard!" he yelled turning around in a rage. But he couldn't figure out who'd done it, with everyone looking toward the river laughing. Couple of moments later another lump splattered on his head. "Fuck and fuck," he yelled. He went to square up with Remo. "What's got into you?" Remo was offended. "Fuck you and your fucking granddad!" But a moment later the air was full of hundreds of lumps of mud; someone in the slime up to his knees was tossing whole handfuls of them as hard as he could from down below, throwing up showers of sludge all around; other guys were sitting coolly off to one side throwing muddy lumps on the sly, making them whistle like whips. "Fucking dickheads!" yelled Remo, caught in the middle of the action, furiously pushing his fingers into one eye and rushing off to jump in the water and get the mud off his eyelids. Seeing him go, Monnezza ran after yelling, "Last in's a loser," and dived, with a tuck and a somersault so that his back, knees, and elbows smacked down hard on the water. "Hell of a guy!" laughed Spudorato screwing up his forehead. He set off and did exactly the same. "Pallante!" he yelled. "Are you joking?" said Pallante. "Wimp," yelled Spudorato and Monnezza from the water.

"Fuck 'em all," muttered Riccetto sitting out of it. "So, what are we doing here?" asked Agnolo angrily. Marcello was the only one of the three who could row, so it was up to him to start the stunt. They went to sit on the pile of broken old rowboats. "So, Marcè," said

Agnolo, "we'll wait here, go for it." Marcello got up and moseyed around Guaione who was hanging around half-drunk the other end of the barge doing something with his penknife. "How much for a boat?" he asked straight up. "Hundred and fifty," answered Guaione without looking up. "You going to give us one?" said Marcello. "When it comes back. It's out." "Will it be long, Guaio, what do you think?" Marcello asked after a moment. "For fuck's sake," said Guaio, show-ing the whites of his drunk's eyes, "what the fuck do I know? When it's back." He glanced upriver to Ponte Sisto. "There it is," he said. "I pay now or later?" "Now's better." "I'll go get the cash," shouted Marcello. But he'd reckoned without Giggetto. The lifeguard was nice enough with the older folks, but when it came to the kids he'd just as well they all drown. Marcello spent a while trying to get him to listen, but Giggetto wouldn't play ball. Flustered, Marcello went back to the pile of boats. "How the fuck am I supposed to get the money," he said. "Ask the lifeguard, asshole!" "I did," said Marcello "but he wouldn't listen." "What an asshole you are," snapped Agnolo, furious. "See this," Marcello answered, voice quivering, reaching an open hand toward him, the way Giggetto had done a while back with them, "why don't you try?" "Go right ahead and start punching each other," said Riccetto with philosophy. "I'd give that asshole a punch anytime," said Agnolo. "I told you, why don't you try, Mr. Smartass!" Agnolo went off to confront Giggetto and was soon back with the hundred and fifty and a cigarette between his lips. They headed to the railing to wait for the boat and as soon as it reached the landing and the other kids were out, the three clambered in. It was the first time Riccetto and Agnolo had been in a boat.

At first the thing wouldn't move. The more Marcello rowed, the more the boat stayed put. Then very slowly it began to float away from the barge, zigzagging about like a drunk. "Oh, loser," shouted Agnolo at the top of his voice, "so you know how to row, do you?" The boat seemed to have gone crazy wandering at random, upstream, down-stream, a bit toward Ponte Sisto, a bit toward Ponte Garibaldi. But the current was taking it left toward Garibaldi, even though by pure chance the bow was turned the other way; then Guaione came to the railing of the barge yelling till the veins in his neck were fit to bust. "What an asshole," Agnolo went on shouting at Marcello, "they'll be coming to get us at Fiumicino!" "Get off my ass," said Marcello, fighting the oars that either smacked up off the water or plunged down into it up to the handles, "you try, go on." "I'm not the one from Ostia, am I!" yelled Agnolo. By now the Ciriola was way off, lurching beyond the back of the boat. Beneath the green of the plane trees, the embankment wall began to appear in all its length from Ponte Sisto to Ponte Garibaldi, while the kids along the bank and on the swings, around the diving platform, or on the barge, were getting smaller and smaller, voices all fading into each other.

The Tiber was pulling the boat toward Ponte Garibaldi like one of the wooden crates or dead animals floating downstream; and beneath Ponte Garibaldi you could see the swirl and froth of the water through the rocks and shoals of Tiber Island. Guaione had seen and was bawling away in his hoarse, throaty voice from the barge; the boat was already level with the enclosure where kiddies who couldn't swim splashed about inside a barrier. Roused by Guaione's screaming, Orazio and a few other loafers came out of the main hut to watch. Orazio started to wave and shout too; the youngsters laughed. Riccetto was watching Marcello, eyes wide and arms folded. "Planning to make fools of us, are you?" he said. But Marcello was getting a grip. The boat was pointing more or less steadily toward the other bank and the oars were beginning to bite the water. "Let's go over there," Agnoletto said. "What do you think I'm doing?" Marcello answered disgusted, sweating streams.

While the Ciriola bank was taking the full blaze of the sun, this side was plunged in a weary gray shadow; thickly coated with filth, the little black rocks were covered in weeds and low green brambles amid pools of stagnant water full of flotsam that barely stirred. At last they came alongside the rocks and since there was almost no current here, Marcello was able to row the boat back toward Ponte Sisto, except his left oar kept banging against the rocks, and it was a struggle to keep it from breaking or floating off on the stream. "Let's go in the middle, damn it," Riccetto kept saying, totally unimpressed by the effort Marcello was making. He wanted to be in the middle of the river so he could feel he was surrounded by water, really out there, and it annoyed him that if he looked up, just a bit even, it was to find Ponte Sisto close by, gray against the gleaming surface of the water, and the Gianicolo, and the dome of Saint Peter's, big and white as a cloud. Slowly but surely they passed under Ponte Sisto where, by the piling on the right, the river widened and slowed, deep and dirty and green. Since there was no danger of being carried off by the current here, Agnolo insisted on having a go rowing himself, but the hell if he could get anywhere; the oars flailed in the air or splashed down hard sending water spraying all over them. "Fuck!" yelled Riccetto indignantly while the exhausted Marcello stretched out on his back in the warmish water filling up the boat. Seeing Agnolo killing himself for nothing, two boys fishing from the steps by the Fontanone started taking the piss and laughing. Panting, Agnolo yelled, "What you looking at!" The kids shut up a minute, then shouted, "Who learned you to row? Can't you see even the walls are laughing?"

"Who learned me to row?" retorted Agnolo. "The fuck!"

"Fuck yourself!" the boys came back.

"Up yours!" screamed Agnolo, pepper-red.

"Asshole!" shouted the kids.

"Son of a blowjob!" yelled Agnolo.

And all the time he was fighting with the oars without the boat's moving so much as an inch. At the base of the other piling, to the left, there were more scumbags lying in the grooves in the stone, like big lazy lizards half-asleep and sunning themselves. The cries of the kiddies woke them. They stood up all white with dust and crowded together on the edge of the piling facing the boat. "Hey, you," one of them shouted, "wait for us!" "What's he after?" said Riccetto, worried. Another boy climbed the rungs halfway up the pillar and dived headfirst with a scream; the others jumped in where they were and they all started swimming across, heads up. A couple of minutes and they were right there, hair in their eyes and sly grins, hands grabbing onto the side of the boat. "What do you lot want?" said Marcello. "To get in," they said. "Aren't we welcome?" They were all older kids and our lot had to shut up. They climbed in and right away one said to Agnolo, "Enough," and took the oars from him. "Let's go to the other side of the bridge," he added, looking Agnolo in the eyes as if to say, "OK with you?" "The other side of the bridge it is," said Agnolo. At once the boy started rowing flat out, but the current near the pillar was strong and the boat was loaded. It took a quarter of an hour to do just a few yards.

"Ancient town / from your gray roofs under a hazy sky / I entreat you..."* sang the four kids from Vicolo Bologna, sprawled in the boat, belting it out at the top of their voices so that people on the banks and Ponte Sisto could hear. Overloaded, the boat sank to its gunwales.

Riccetto was still lying down, paying no attention to the new arrivals, sulking in the water at the bottom of the boat, his nose barely above the side, and still pretending he was out at sea, with no land in sight. "Pirates!" yelled one of the boys from Trastevere, hands making a megaphone around his old thief's face, on his feet in the bow; the others went on singing raucously. All at once Riccetto propped himself up on an elbow to get a better look at something that had grabbed his attention on the water near the bank, close to the arches of Ponte Sisto. He couldn't figure it out. The water was rippling and making scores of little circles, as if a hand were stirring it; in fact, in the middle you could just make out what looked like a small black rag.

"What's that?" said Riccetto, getting to his feet. Everyone looked that way, where the water was almost still, under the last arch. "It's a swallow, for fuck's sake," said Marcello. There were any number of swallows, flying close to the walls, swooping under the arches of the bridge, out on the open river, breast feathers skimming the water. The boat had drifted back a bit on the stream and now you could see it really was a swallow, and it was drowning. It beat its wings, jerking itself upward. Riccetto was on his knees on the gunwale of the boat,

*The lyrics are from "Borgo Antico," a sad love song written and sung by the great Italian singer and actor Claudio Villa (1926–1987), who is alluded to in various other parts of the book.

his whole body leaning out. "Asshole, can't you see you're going to turn us over?" said Agnolo. "Look," yelled Riccetto, "it's drowning!" The boy rowing held the oars up out of the water and the stream pushed the boat slowly back toward the struggling swallow. But a moment later the boy lost patience and started rowing again. "Hey, you," Riccetto shouted, stretching his hand toward him, "who told you to row?" The other shook his head in scorn and the biggest of the boys said, "What the hell do you care?" Riccetto looked at the swallow, still thrashing about, with little fits and flutters of its wings. Then without any warning he plunged into the water and started swimming toward it. The others started yelling after him and laughing, but the boy with the oars went on rowing upstream in the opposite direction. Riccetto was farther and farther away, pulled along by the powerful current; they saw him getting smaller and smaller as he swam close to the swallow, where the water was still, and tried to catch it. "Hey Riccettoooo," yelled Marcello with all the breath in his lungs, "why don't you grab it?" Riccetto must have heard, because, very faintly, they caught his shouted reply: "It's pecking me!" "Well fuck you," yelled Marcello, laughing. Riccetto was trying to grab the swallow that kept escaping him with a flap of its wings and meantime both were being dragged toward the pillar where the current was stronger and full of spiraling eddies. "Riccetto," his friends shouted from the boat, "forget it!" But right then Riccetto steeled himself and grabbed the bird, then swam one-armed to the bank. "Let's go back, come on," said Marcello to the boy rowing. They turned around. Riccetto waited, sitting on the filthy grass of the bank with the swallow in his hands. "What d'you save it for," said Marcello, "it was great watching it die!" Riccetto didn't answer at first. "It's wet through," he said after a moment. "Let's wait for it to dry off!" It didn't take long; five minutes and the bird was back in the air with its companions, flying over the Tiber; already Riccetto couldn't tell which one was which.

2. RICCETTO

Summer 1946. On the corner of Via delle Zoccolette, in the rain, Riccetto sees a group of people and sidles slowly up to them. In the middle of this group of thirteen or fourteen people with gleaming umbrellas there was one unusually large umbrella, black, open, with three cards placed in a row on top: the ace of coins, the ace of cups, and a six. A Neapolitan was shuffling the pack and people were betting, five hundred, a thousand, even two thousand. Riccetto stood there half an hour or so watching them; one man playing impulsively lost every bet while some of the others, also Neapolitans, lost some and won some. When the group broke up it was already late. Riccetto went up to the Neapolitan who was shuffling the pack and said, "Hi, can I say something?"

"Sure," said the other pushing out his chin.

"You're from Naples, right?

"Yes."

"And you play this game in Naples?"

"Yes."

"So how do you play?"

"Well ... it's tricky, but with time you can learn."

"So, can you learn me as well?"

"Yes," said the Neapolitan, "only..."

He began to laugh with the air of someone doing a deal and thinking to himself, "Well now, let's see what I can tell you!" He dried the rain off his young, furrowed face, lips hanging slack like a duck's ass, then looked Riccetto in the eyes: "Sure I'll learn you, course I will,"

he said, seeing the other was silent, "but I'll need something for it."
"Course," said Riccetto, all serious.

Meantime another group was starting to gather around the umbrella; among them were the same Neapolitans as before. "Hang on,"
said the Neapolitan with a wink while he lined up the cards on the
umbrella. Riccetto stepped back and started watching them play
again. Two hours went by, the rain eased off, and it was almost dark.
The Neapolitan finally decided to call it a day, closed the umbrella,
put the cards in his pocket, and glanced at his companions, two of
them, one blond, half-toothless, the other a small guy with a big
tartan jacket, Jewish-looking. They listened amiably to their friend
who was telling them he had stuff to do, and, went off happily enough
with their umbrellas, nodding goodbye to Riccetto as well.

"Let's go," said the Neapolitan. Riccetto was in the money so they
took the tram, got off at Ponte Bianco, and in a few minutes were in
Donna Olimpia. Sitting in the middle of the one room that made up
her home, with four beds at the four corners and walls that weren't
even walls but partitions, Riccetto's mother looked at the two of them
and said, "Who's this?" "Friend of mine," said Riccetto sharply, boss-
ily, hardly giving her the time of day. But since she stayed right where
she was and wouldn't stop bothering him—she was such a busybody,
she never shut her mouth—Riccetto went to look in the next room,
where Agnolo lived with his family, to check if the grown-ups were
all out. In fact there were only two or three of the smaller kids, whining, snot-nosed. So he took the Neapolitan in there and they sat on
the bed that Agnolo and his younger brothers slept on, head to foot,
leaning back on a blanket full of scorch marks from ironing. The
Neapolitan began his lesson: "There are five of us," he said, "one does
the cards and the others gather round pretending to be just passing
by. Let's say I'm the one with the cards and I begin to play, and my
friends round the umbrella make up the group. People start coming
to look and when that happens one of the friends quits, opening up
the group, and someone takes his place . . . At first the guy's not sure
if he wants to play or not. A friend lays a bet, a thousand, or two
thousand, whatever; while he's pulling out the cash, the one dealing

the cards, me, changes his card, but putting the good card for the friend and the bad one in the middle. Not understanding the game, you can't see that I've changed it, so you lay a bet too. And I say, 'If you lose, guys, it's none of my business,' but the friend goes for it— winning card, losing card, winning card, losing card—'OK, show your cards, both of you.' So the friend wins and the other loses. When the dummy has lost a lot, the friend joins in again and stakes, say, a thousand..." The Neapolitan went on a while explaining how the game worked and Riccetto sat beside him, listening to him going on and on and not understanding a damn thing. When the Neapolitan had finished, Riccetto said, "Hey, look, I don't get it at all! Could you, like, be so very kind as to go back and start over, if it's not too much trouble, eh!" But right then Agnolo's mom came back. "Sorry, Signora Celeste," said Riccetto, leaving, with the other in tow, "I had to say a word to this friend of mine." Dark and hairy as a clump of dog's cabbage, Signora Celeste didn't reply. The two ran off down the stairs and went to sit on the steps of the Franceschi School. The Neapolitan started over with his explanation, getting more and more excited until he was red as a plate of pasta; he stood up, facing Riccetto, who kept saying yes, looking him in the eyes with an expression of anger almost as the man went on talking and talking, then staring even harder when he left off a moment to give more weight to what he'd just said, half questioning, half inspired, standing with his knees bent, legs apart, stomach pushed out, hands raised and fingers spread like a goalkeeper waiting for a high ball.

But then he mouthed "Oh fucking shit" with his big, poor bum's, Porta Capuana lips, as if the profound reflection illuminating his skull ought to be enlightening Riccetto as well.

All this just to earn himself five hundred. And once again Riccetto hadn't understood a fucking thing. Meantime it was getting dark; in the Grattacieli thousands of rows and diagonals of windows and balconies were lighting up, radios were blaring, and a noise of plates and women scolding or fighting or singing spilled from the kitchens. By the step where the two were sitting, crowds of people were going about their business, some heading home bedraggled after a day's drudgery, others already dressed to the nines and setting out to have fun with their friends.

"Let's go have a little drink, what do you say," said Riccetto generously, as if he were a man of thirty who knew his customer through and through, imagining, with reason, that he must be thirsty. At this the other bucked up and, carried away by his enthusiasm, after responding to the proposal of a drink with an almost apathetic "Let's go," launched into his explanations again as if nothing had changed, so that as they walked toward Monteverde Nuovo, he mimed a whole show of how the guy who laid out the cards on the open umbrella had to behave toward the group, or toward the shill who placed the bets, winning some, losing some, or the dummy, who was a jerk of course, but sufficiently stacked to be worthy of respect, since of all those who joined in, he was the one who chose to gamble big time, staking a thousand, two thousand even ... The Neapolitan—actually from Salerno—mimicked his movements and expressions to a T, and with a certain deference to boot.

They were headed to Monteverde Nuovo because Riccetto didn't want the people in Donna Olimpia to know what he was up to; they were sickening snoops, every last one of them. "Soon as they see you, they're watching you," he said, acting knowledgeable for the Neapolitan to justify the walk up the hill, first on a stretch of road, all heaps of junk and broken asphalt, then along a path through trodden grass with the barracks for the homeless at the top. There too, and again in Monteverde Nuovo, it was all pretty wild, everyone in high spirits, Saturday night bedlam. They went into a little bar, right on the big market square, which was also the tram terminus, just beyond Delle Terrazze. The bar had a pergola, surrounded by a bamboo screen, where it was already quite dark. They sat on rickety benches and ordered a half liter of Frascati. Just a few sips and they were already feeling tipsy. The Neapolitan launched into his explanation for the fourth time, but by now Riccetto had had enough and he was damned if he was going to listen to any more and the Neapolitan was fed up with saying the same things over and over. As he spoke Riccetto looked at him with a small smile, half resigned, half sarcastic, and gradually the Neapolitan gave up; so quite happily they began to talk about other stuff. They were both shrewd movers and had plenty to tell each other, about life in Rome and Naples, about Italians and Americans, with much reciprocal respect, crediting what the other said, while at the same time, deep down, missing no chance to take little digs at each other, and underneath it all each of them thinking the other dumb; each was content to do the talking and irked to have to listen to the other.

But the more he drank, the stranger the Neapolitan became; by the time he'd drained the second glass it was as if someone had sand-papered his face, rubbing out his features: it was no more than a piece of burnt meat, eyes half-closed as though blinded by a bright light from God knows where and big lips glued together and sagging down. When he spoke he produced a sort of lamentation belied by steady smiling eyes, which seemed in stark contradiction to the serious, intensely felt things he was saying. By this point he was speaking exclusively in his own dialect. He sat there, hunched, his neck sunk between his shoulders, streaming sweat, face mushy and swollen, staring at Riccetto from eyes that shone with brotherly love. "Listen," he said, "I gotta confess something to you!"

"What do you want to tell me?" asked Riccetto, who was pretty far gone himself.

But the Neapolitan offered only a sad smirk, shaking his head, and falling silent for a while. Then he said, "It's something extremely important. I want to tell you because you're a friend!" This declaration left them both quite moved. The Neapolitan fell silent again, and Riccetto, all serious and dignified, offered words of encouragement: "So tell me what you have to tell me, but only if you want, eh! I'm not going to insist, am I."

"I will tell you," the Neapolitan said, "but you'll have to promise me something."

"What?" Riccetto asked eagerly.

"Not to speak about it to anybody," said the Neapolitan solemnly, totally tanked.

Riccetto understood the situation; getting even more serious, he puffed up his chest and put a hand on his heart: "Word of honor," he said.

The Neapolitan, as if feeling revived—eyes still laughing of their own accord, deep in their slits—began to tell his story. He said it had been him had killed an old woman and her two spinster daughters in Via Chiaja, with an iron bar, then burned the bodies. It took him a quarter of an hour and then some to get through this bullshit, repeating everything at least twice and muddling everything. Riccetto wasn't at all impressed, realizing at once that it was just drunken bragging; but he sat there listening carefully, sympathetically, pretending to believe it, so as to have the right then to tell his own stories. And what a lot he had to tell, all the stuff that had happened those two years after the Americans came!

In those two years Riccetto had become one hell of a son of a bitch. If he wasn't quite like the young friend of his who one day when they were at Delle Terrazze together heard someone call, "Hey, wassyername, hurry home cause your mom's really bad," then next day when Riccetto asks, "How's your mom?" says with a little grin, "Dead." "What?" asks Riccetto. "She's dead, dead," confirmed the other boy, laughing at Riccetto's surprise. If he wasn't quite like that guy, in short, he was getting there. At his age he'd already hung out with hundreds of people of every kind and condition, to the point that they were all the same to him: he could almost rival the guy who lived near the Rotonda and one day with a friend had beaten up a queer to get a thousand lire off him, and when his friend said, "Shit, maybe we've killed him," without even bothering to check, says "What the fuck do I care."

Riccetto was wallowing in a sea of memories; and when the Neapolitan fell silent, moved by his own confession, with that roasted dog's face of his, it was Riccetto's turn to spin some stories. Except he was telling the truth. Since earlier they'd started talking about Americans, Riccetto went back to the subject: "Listen to this one!" he said, all bright and breezy. And he began to tell a few stories, each one peppier than the next, all about the time when the Americans were there, and all starring him, the coolest son of a bitch there ever was.

The Neapolitan was watching him dreamily, nodding, smiling a tired smile. Then suddenly, puffing up his chest and with no change of expression, still staring at Riccetto, he began to say, "I must make amends!" then on and on, it was his turn again, for another quarter of an hour, hamming up the farce of his supposed murder. Riccetto let him sound off for a bit, fair enough, even looking at him, laughing. Then as soon as the Neapolitan lost his way and began to stutter, he dived back in:

"The Americans were nice guys! . . . They wound me up a bit, but they suited me just fine! Still, the fucking Poles were mean, but really mean, you know! Whoa, I remember once, I was at Torraccia, we were going to grab some stuff from the Poles' camp. We were walking along, near the caves, and we hear someone scream, we go nearer, it was two whores fighting with these Poles, wanting to be paid. So one of the Poles comes out of the cave and we hide, and one of them is still inside with the two whores. And maybe the whores thought the other guy had gone to get the cash. Instead, he comes back with a can. Before going in the cave he unscrews the cap. Then he pours it into a trash bin, then calls his buddy, the other Pole, and right at the mouth of the cave they chuck the gasoline over the two whores. Then he strikes a match and sets them ablaze. We're hearing screams and more screams and we go in there and see these two whores all on fire."

Then it was the Neapolitan's turn again, but now he was so smashed he couldn't keep his eyes open. "Same again?" asked Riccetto wryly. Right, maybe the Neapolitan hadn't even heard; he just chuckled a bit. "In luck today, or what?" asked Riccetto, cheerfully, ready to go now. They were both fed up of sitting there yapping. It was Riccetto who made the move: "Hey . . . what's your face," he said, "how about we head off?" The Neapolitan sniggered again, eyes down, then stumbled to his feet and set off in a great hurry straight toward the exit in the bamboo wall. It was already dark; everyone had eaten and come out of their houses to enjoy the cool of the evening. Youngsters on motorbikes were racing each other around the big square, from Delle Terrazze, all lit up at the end, to the half-empty tram shelter. While Riccetto was paying, the Neapolitan diligently performed various complicated maneuvers: he sneezed, blew his nose between his fingers, and pissed; then the two went to stand under the shelter to wait for the tram that would take the Neapolitan back to Rome.

"So where do you live?" asked Riccetto, waiting with him. The Neapolitan flashed a shrewd, diabolical smile but said nothing. Riccetto kept trying: "Don't you want to tell me?" he asked, looking a little hurt. The Neapolitan took his hand and held it between his own hot, swollen palms. "You're a friend," he began solemnly, and off he went once again with a bunch of assurances of his friendship, oaths, and declarations. Riccetto was hardly overwhelmed with enthusiasm, being so hungry and sleepy he could barely stay on his feet. In the end the Neapolitan's situation was this: he and his buddies had only been in Rome a few days, on the make. Which was why the Neapolitan had agreed to accept Riccetto's offer for just five hundred. Otherwise, never in a million years. The card trick was a real money-spinner, you could make millions. Meantime, he and his friends were sleeping in a cave along the Tiber embankment, in Testaccio. Riccetto guessed which and pricked up his ears. "So you guys," he said, sensing a big opening, "will be needing someone to give you a bit of a hand . . . show you some better places."

The Neapolitan gave him a hug, then tapped his nose, inviting Riccetto to say no more, all was clear. He liked the gesture and did it again, twice, then took Riccetto's hand in his own again, and once more launched into his oaths of friendship, sketching out certain confused and solemn general principles that Riccetto, who had a much clearer idea and a far more practical plan in his head, was at a loss to follow. "Yeah, sure!" he said. One tram had gone by and now another; when the third came, the Neapolitan, with his five hundred in his pocket, finally climbed on board and they agreed to meet next day, repeating the details two or three times, down at Ponte Sublicio.

Riccetto had finally found a profession for himself, not like Marcello, who had taken up bartending, or Agnolo, who was working with his brother as a house painter; no, something much better, something that took him up in the world, to the point that he felt on a level with

Rocco, for example, and Alvaro, who had moved on from stealing manhole covers to more demanding and responsible jobs, though in the end they never had a penny in their pockets and looked even more beat-up than before. These days he was hanging out more with these guys than with rookies of his own age, kiddies getting on fourteen who could hardly afford to go around with someone who was always loaded, not having a penny in their pockets themselves, or at very best a couple of hundred lire. To tell the honest truth, even Rocco and Alvaro were sometimes clean broke, more than sometimes, but that was a different matter altogether! Just how different, Riccetto was to find out the Sunday he went with them to Ostia absolutely flush with cash.

At first the card trick hadn't gone badly at all. Riccetto and the guys from Salerno would find themselves a nice little place around Campo dei Fiori, or Ponte Vittorio, or in Prati, or later, when they'd managed to replace the umbrella with a table, and the cards with three nicely smoothed pieces of wood held together by an elastic band, two without cards and one with a card slipped inside the elastic, they might move upmarket to Piazza di Spagna or some such place; then they would cheerfully lure the passersby until they had a good group of people, all well dressed and well heeled. Riccetto was what they called "the kid," the one who held on to the table, though in fact he had a trickier job and earned himself a thousand a day and sometimes more. But one Saturday evening, in early June, after they had got together a group in Via dei Pettinari, the police launched a sudden raid, running down the street from Ponte Sisto. Riccetto was first to see them and shot off down Via delle Zoccolette. One of the policemen shouted, "Stop or I'll shoot." Riccetto turned and saw the guy really did have a gun in his hand but thought, "Hopefully, the last thing he wants is to kill me," and kept running till he got to Via Arenula and was able to disappear down the alleys behind Piazza Giudia. But the other three got caught. They were taken to the police station and sent back to Salerno next day with an expulsion order, which was the end of that. In any event, that same Saturday evening Riccetto had gone down to the cave in the Ponte Sublicio embankment, actually the cellar of some old building of centuries ago, passed over the heap of rags that were all the clothes the three losers had, and went straight to the few bricks covering the hole where they'd hidden a month's worth of savings: fifty thousand.

Which is why Riccetto was so loaded and lighthearted that first Sunday in June.

It was a fine morning with the sun burning blithe and cheerful through miles and miles of blue sky, pouring down its gold every which way, on the fresh clean Grattacieli, on the brightly enameled knolls of Monte di Splendore and Casadio, on the sidewalks and the facades of the apartment blocks and the yards inside the blocks. And in the midst of all that golden freshness, people in their Sunday best were swarming around the center of Donna Olimpia, outside the doors of the tenements, and around the newspaper kiosk.

Riccetto had left home early, all dressed up, and with the back pocket of his pants bulging nicely. Right away, among a bunch of youngsters arguing and shouting outside Case Nòve, he saw Rocco and Alvaro. They were in their work clothes, since they hadn't washed yet, canvas pants loose at the crotch and tight at the ankles, their legs moving inside like flowers in a vase, or crossed the way soldiers cross their legs in photographs, their faces up top like exhibits preserved in oil in a museum of crime. Riccetto went over to them, ignoring the small fry his own age lower down the slope kicking around a ball they'd stolen from a kid who was crying. Seeing him, Alvaro turned a face so bruised and beaten that when he smiled it was like all the bones were moving of their own accord, and said carelessly, "Life treating you well, is it?"

"For sure," said Riccetto, equally nonchalant.

He was so cheerful and sure of himself that Alvaro looked at him with new interest.

"What you up to today?" Riccetto asked.

"Nothing much," said Alvaro, playing for time, his expression somewhere between tired and insinuating, mysterious.

"What about heading for Ostia?" said Riccetto, "Happens I'm loaded."

"Well, well!" said Alvaro, all the miserable bones in his face shifting up and down. "Meaning you've got a couple of hundred."

Rocco was listening carefully now too.

"Yeah, right, a couple of hundred!" said Riccetto all fired up.

"I've got fifty grand," he said after a moment. "Fif-ty grrrand!" he said again, lowering his voice and putting a megaphone hand around his mouth.

Alvaro was overcome by a fit of laughter, then Rocco too, until Alvaro laughed so hard he had to sit and almost tumbled down the steps. Riccetto waited a bit, smiling, until Alvaro had got over it, then took hold of his shirt collar to pull him close and said, "Come with me." They went round a corner and Riccetto showed them the fifty grand. The two friends said, "Whoa, you really have!" then put on a resigned look, as if to say, "Lucky you!"

"So, are you coming to Ostia?" Riccetto said.

"To Ostia it is," Rocco answered.

"First we should wash up and change, though," Alvaro said. "Go ahead, I'll wait," said Riccetto. The others exchanged glances. "Well," said Alvaro after a moment, hesitating, broken bones settling in satisfaction under his thick skin, "Riccè, what do you reckon if we have a fuck, in Ostia?" Riccetto was immediately up for it: "Sure," he said, "if you bring a girl!" "We'll bring one, we'll bring one," said Rocco. "In half an hour, back here then," said Alvaro. They went off into the courtyard of Case Nòve, but instead of heading home, or going to get the five hundred for a bathing cabin, they went out through the smaller door to the right that led into Via Ozanam, then into a tobacconist's where there was a phone. They sidled up to the receiver with an official air; Alvaro dialed and Rocco, slipping in fifteen lire, followed the conversation with intense interest.

"Hello," said Alvaro, "could you call Nadia for me, please? Right, Nadia, it's a friend of hers." Whoever had answered the phone went to call Nadia and meanwhile Alvaro winked at Rocco, leaning his shoulder against the flaking plaster and assuming an air of concentration.

"Hello," he said then, in a polite voice, "is that you, Nadia? Listen up . . . There's a bit of business . . . Do you have time today? . . . to come to Ostia. Ostia, yes. What? . . . Me, a big mouth? . . . It's a sure thing, a sure thing! . . . Wait for us at Marechiaro, got it, Marechiaro . . . Where the dance floor is, opposite . . . Right, yes, same as last time . . . At three, three fifteen . . . OK . . . see you, all set!" He hung up and left the tobacconist's with Rocco behind, beaming all over.

Nadia was lying on the beach, motionless, face set in hatred for the wind, the sun, the sea, and all the people who had come to settle on the sand like flies on a table after you clear the dishes. Thousands of them, in all the various bathing establishments along the beach from the Battistini to the Lido, the Lido to the Marechiaro, the Marechiaro to the Principe, the Principe to the Ondina, some stretched out on their backs, some on their stomachs, though these were mainly older folks; the youngsters—boys in sagging underpants, or maybe in tight ones showing off all their attributes, and girls, the dumb ones that is, in their supertight skimpy costumes under avalanches of hair—were walking up and down nonstop as if they had some nervous tic. And all calling to each other, shouting, yelling, teasing, playing, running in and out of the cabins, calling the attendant, there was even a boy band from Trastevere, with sombreros on their heads, playing accordion, guitar, and castanets outside the main building; their sambas got mixed up with the rumbas from the Marechiaro sound system booming out over the sea. Nadia was lying in the midst of it all, in her black costume with quantities of body hair, black as the devil's, that coiled in sweaty curls under her armpits; and the hair on her head was black too, black as coal, and likewise her eyes, burning with venom.

She was pushing forty, a big woman, solid tits, and thighs stacked in rolls of fat so tight and shiny they looked pumped up. And she was pissed off, fed up with hanging around in this fanatics' pandemonium since there was no way she was going in the water herself; she'd taken a bath that morning in Sister Anita's tub at the Mattonato. Riccetto, Alvaro, and Rocco had scarcely been there ten minutes and she was already eager to be off on her own.

"What's eating your ass, Nadia?" Alvaro asked calm as could be, seeing she was wired up. She spat it out in one: "Let's go and do what we have to do, keep it quick, and have a nice day! What are we hanging around here for, for Christ's sake?"

"Whoa, what the fuck's the rush?" Rocco said. She pulled an angry face and turned on him like a viper, mouth drawn down, eyes glassy with rage and gray as a heart-attack case: "You want a poke?" she demanded furiously glaring at Alvaro. "What do you think?" said Alvaro. "So let's go, what are you waiting for?" she wound up, fiercely, mouth red as a crack in hell. Alvaro went on looking at her, merry eyes shining with friendly irony: "Looks to me like you haven't taken a delivery yet today," he said, making as if to press something with the palm of his hand. "You look hot for it!" he added cheerfully.

"Oh, go fuck off and die," she hissed, in a rage, foulmouthed as a drudge in a slaughterhouse.

"We'll keep you happy, don't worry," Rocco promised, taking his cue from Alvaro. "We've got a couple of rolling pins ready, really we have!"

"Riccetto as well," said Alvaro, "He might look just a kiddie, but you gotta see the punch he packs, you gotta see it."

Riccetto gave no sign of any response, kneeling on the sand with his legs a little apart; he was wearing a sombrero too, tipped back behind his ears so that his forehead frothed with curls, and tied tight under his chin with a string.

"OK then, let's go," Alvaro finally agreed, with a sly tilt of his chin toward the changing rooms. She disguised her pleasure with a look that combined dignity and disgust; then pushing her hands into the ground and turning over so she was ass upward, bit by bit she started to lift the masses of fat distributed here and there in packs and parcels from tits to calves.

"You guys wait!" Alvaro ordered. "I'll go first." He got up and went off, disappearing among the sunshades, deck chairs, and sizzling flesh of the bathers. After a while, Nadia struggled to her knees, finally got vertical, and set off after him, planting her fat feet in the burning sand.

Riccetto and Rocco stayed put, waiting their turn. Rocco lay back, head on his hands, the usual vacant look on his face. Since the whole morning had gone by without either him or Alvaro even talking of taking a swim, just sprawled out with their backs against the huts, leering at all the pretty pussy served up from Trastevere and Prati, Marranella and Quarticciolo, Riccetto finally asked, "Hey, Rocco, know how to swim?"

"Me, know how to swim?" said Rocco, unfazed. "Check me out in the water, I'm a fucking fish."

"So while we're waiting, let's go swim, come on!" said Riccetto.

"Don't feel like it," said Rocco, yawning, "you go on your own, if you want."

"Think I will," said Riccetto, making up his mind, with a touch of emotion. He took off his sombrero and ran to the water, then stood there thinking about it for half an hour, putting one foot in and pulling it out again, then the other, in and out, then going in till the water was up to his knees, jumping every time a wave came, like someone had given him a kick in the ass. In front of him the water was so full of people there was hardly room for them all, a lifeguard's skiff bobbing up and down among all the heads. Finally he made up his mind and plunged in like a duck. His swim amounted to hanging around shivering with the water up to his nipples, watching a bunch of other boys scraping their hands and legs to climb a pole and dive back in from the top.

When he got back to their spot at the Marechiaro the others were both done. So it was his turn, but he sat down again, pulled the sombrero over his head and said not a word. Alvaro spoke up, shifting his jaw from side to side: "Hey," he said, "Riccetto, my friend, before you go, don't you think you should maybe offer us something here . . . not that I would ever insist, like . . . but you must have seen we only had just enough cash for the train and the cabin . . ." "Course," said Riccetto. He ran to the cabin, took the wad of notes from the pocket of his pants, slipped out one, went back outside, and waved for his friends to come. They got up and all three went to the bar for a Coke.

The sun was already lower in the sky and the pandemonium even louder, the sea gleaming like a sword beyond all the seething flesh.

The cabins and changing rooms boomed with thousands of shouting voices and the showers were full of youngsters, boys and girls, like carcasses crawling with ants. The band was playing as loud as they could and the Marechiaro's gramophone was deafening. "Hey Riccetto," Alvaro said after a bit, "it's your turn now."

Without saying anything, Riccetto jumped up at once, ready to go to the cabin with Nadia. The others laughed, Nadia included. Sitting at the table, she had brightened up a bit. "Pay first, maybe," said Alvaro breezily, kindly even, not wanting to take advantage of Riccetto's mistake. "God, I forgot," Riccetto excused himself, laughing, but inside he felt bad; he paid and went on ahead, same as Alvaro had. The cabin was even hotter now that the air and sand outside had cooled a little; it felt like an oven. His clothes smelled a bit, especially the socks, but there were good smells too, of hair oil and salt. After a while, as Riccetto got used to the gloom in there and already had a hard-on, Nadia scratched at the door and Riccetto opened. She slipped in, hauling her fanny behind, butt cheeks so big that when roving hands at the Arenula or the Farnese gave them a pat she would feel them wobbling over the edge of a chair like the coils of a python. Riccetto was right there with his sombrero on his head. Without a word she undid the top and bottom of her bikini and slipped them off her sweaty flesh while Riccetto, watching, took off his underpants. "Get to work then," he ordered in a low voice.

But while they were doing what had to be done and Nadia had the boy tight in her arms, his face buried in her tits, very slowly she slid a hand across his pants hanging on the wall, sneaked into the back pocket, pulled out the wad of notes, and stuffed them in her bag that was hanging beside.

Riccetto lived in the Giorgio Franceschi Elementary School. Climbing up from Ponte Bianco, there's a steep bank to the right with the tenements of Monteverde Vecchio at the top, while on the left, down in a deep hollow, you can see the Ferrobedò; keep walking and you're in Donna Olimpia, also known as the Grattacieli, and the first building on the right, as you arrive, is the school. Above the cracked asphalt rises an even more seriously cracked facade, with a row of square white columns in the middle and four big, solid structures, two or three stories high, like turrets, at the four corners.

First the Germans had occupied it, then the Canadians, then the evacuees, and finally families that had been evicted elsewhere, like Riccetto's.

Marcello, on the other hand, lived in the Grattacieli, a little farther on, tall as a mountain range, and with thousands of windows in rows, circles, or diagonals looking out over streets, courtyards and stairways, north or south, in bright sunshine or in shade, closed or wide open, empty or flapping with laundry, silent or loud with the din of women and the whining of children. Empty fields stretched into the distance all around, full of knolls and humps, packed with little kids playing half-naked or in snot-stained school smocks.

On Sundays these kids were the only ones around. Not the older kids and teenagers, who were off having fun in Rome, nor anyone flush with cash, like Riccetto, who would have gone to Ostia, to do some living! Flat broke and left all alone in Donna Olimpia, Marcello was dying of boredom, poor guy. He came sidling along, hands in pockets, through the courtyards of the Grattacieli where he'd been playing cards with a bunch of eight- and nine-year-olds, but they were soon fed up and went off to play cowboys and Indians at Monte di Splendore. Now he was the only person in the whole of Donna Olimpia, in the big plaza between the high blocks with the sun burning down. He crossed the road, rushed up the four broken steps of the school, and slipped into the stairway of the building on the right. Riccetto's family didn't live in the classrooms, like the evacuees, or the people who'd gotten there first, but in a corridor with doors opening off into the classrooms partitioned into lines of small rooms with just a narrow strip under the windows overlooking the courtyard for people to get past; and that was where Marcello came running right now. Inside these makeshift rooms you could see bunks and beds freshly made, since with all the children they had, the women didn't have time to tidy up till after lunch, and then rickety little tables, stools with the straw hanging out, stoves, boxes, sewing machines, kiddies' clothes hung to dry on strings. There was hardly anyone in the school right then, no youngsters for sure, and the older men were down in the bar in the semi-basement under the Grattacieli, which left only one or two older women.

"Signora Adele!" shouted Marcello, hurrying along the strip of corridor under the big windows, "Signora Adele!"

"What is it now?" shouted back Signora Adele through the partitions, already impatient. Marcello went to a flapping door.

"Is Riccetto back, Signora Adè?" he asked.

"No," said Signora Adele, irritated because it was the third time in an hour Marcello had come asking after her son. She was sitting on a battered stool, sweating, newspaper fallen at her feet and backside sagging all around, combing her hair in front of a mirror propped up against the sewing machine.

She had a center part and two waves of singed, curly hair, hard as boards, on each side. She tugged the comb gloomily, frowning, hair clips clamped between her lips, as if it were a girl's hair and she could afford to be impatient and treat it badly; she was dressing up to go to the pizzeria with her friends. "Bye then, Signora Adele," said Marcello, already leaving, "when he gets back tell Riccetto I'm downstairs." "It'll be tomorrow before he's back, my fine lad," grumbled Signora Adele.

Marcello went back downstairs and once again found himself in the empty street. He felt out of it, pretty well ready to burst into tears, and vented his frustration kicking the cobbles. "What a bastard," he thought, almost speaking out loud, "where's he got to, that's what I want to know, where's he got to, without saying anything to anyone ... What kind of a way to behave is this? What kind of a way to treat your friends ... ? Makes me so mad I'd blind him in three eyes with two fingers, the son of a bitch!" He sat down on a step where there was a patch of shade; all around the only objects available to his miserable gaze were four or five kiddies sitting in the dirt at the corner of the school on the Ferrobedò side playing with a penknife. Eventually Marcello got up, went over to them, and stood watching with his hands in his pockets. They barely noticed him and went on playing without a word. After a bit one looked up toward Monte di Splendore and, staring hard with his eyes shining, started yelling, "Look, Zambuia!" They all looked the same way, jumped to their feet, and set off at a run toward Monte di Splendore. Marcello followed, more slowly. He reached the small knolls of the Monte, beyond the excavations, and found the others crouched in the shade of some scaffolding on the slope, with the whole of Monteverde Nuovo visible to the right and, farther down, half of Rome as far as San Paolo. They were crouching around Zambuia and each kid had a puppy on his knee, Zambuia watching the animals' every move with an expert eye. The kids were quiet, on their best behavior, just laughing, not too loudly, when one of the puppies did something funny. Every now and then Zambuia picked one up like it was a bundle of rags, turned it every which way, opened its mouth, then plopped it back down on the ground between one of the kids' knees. The puppy under examination would stretch itself a bit, let out a little yelp, then prance about on its crooked little legs around the boy's bare knees, or maybe set off boldly to explore the hill. "Hey, where's the little son of a bitch off to?" shouted the kids, delighted. One got up and, prancing about just like the puppy, went to bring it back, then played with it, trying to hide the rush of affection the animal roused, blushing a bit with embarrassment. "Whose puppies are they?" asked Marcello, stepping up, acting superior, though with a certain interest, a certain sympathy for the puppies. "Mine," said Zambuia sulkily. "Who gave them to you?" "You blind?" said Zambuia, scratching one animal under its tummy. "Can't you see their mama?" The kiddies laughed. The mother was lying between their legs, a tiny thing, keeping very quiet. "Come on then," announced Zambuia. He gathered all the puppies, picking them up from between the kids' legs, and pushed them against their mother's tummy. At once they all went for a teat and started sucking like so many fat little piglets, with the kids crowding around them, excited and amused, urging them on, laughing and making comments. "Can you give me one?" asked Marcello, making out he didn't care. Busy trying to keep some order among the feeding puppies, Zambuia looked at him: "Oh, right," he said. And after a moment: "You got five hundred?" "You crazy?" said Marcello, laughing and tapping two fingers to his forehead, "I suppose you realize that at the zoo they'll give you a German shepherd puppy for free?" "Oh, fuck off..." said Zambuia, busying himself with his dogs again. The kiddies were all ears. "Really, a German shepherd?" Zambuia asked after a bit. "No, I'm just bullshitting you, of course," Marcello said quickly. He'd been expecting the question. "Go ask Obberdan,* the shoemaker's boy, he'll tell you whether it's true," he added. "What the fuck do I care," said Zambuia, "if it is, it is, and if it isn't, my ass." Two of the puppies had started snarling at each other like two wild beasts, biting at each other's noses, grabbing the attention of the kids, who started laughing and rolling around on the grass like the puppies. "Let's make it a hundred," said Marcello then. Zambuia didn't answer, but you could see he was ready to accept. "OK?" Marcello pressed him. "As you like," Zambuia muttered. "I'll take this one," said Marcello at once, having made up his mind while they spoke; he pointed at a fat black creature, the meanest, that wanted to suck all the milk himself. The kids looked at him with envy and tried to get the black puppy to go on biting the others' noses. Marcello took one of two hundred-lire notes from his wallet. "Here," he said. Zambuia didn't say anything but reached out a hand and slipped the note in his pocket. "I'll be right back, wait here, OK," said Marcello, and went back down the slope to the school. "Hey, Signora Adele," he yelled again in the corridor, "Signora Adele."

"OK, OK," she shouted, having just finished dolling herself up. "Still here, are you?" she said, appearing at the door squeezed like a sausage into her best dress. "For God's sake," she added, impatience morphing into good humor, "if I were in your shoes, darling, you know where I'd have sent that lousy son of mine by this time? What

---

*On this occasion Pasolini spells Oberdan with a double *b*, which is incorrect, to suggest the boy's accent and ignorance. Throughout the novel, names of both people and places are spelled inconsistently, sometimes correctly, sometimes not, for the same reason.

is he, made of gold or something?" "We were supposed to be going to the cinema," said Marcello simply. "If I know anything," said Signora Adele, putting a hand on her breast with an expression at once shrewd and despondent, so that for a moment her chin was lost in the fat folds of her throat, "he won't be home before midnight! If you knew what a sly one he is, and the hidings he gets from his dad, but to no end!" "Tell him I'll be back," said Marcello, in a slightly better mood now, consoling himself with the thought that he had an even better puppy than Agnolo. "Bye, Signora Adele!" Fat flesh packed into a gray dress that looked like it would burst any moment, bangs stiff as brushes to each side of her part, she went back into the room to powder her face and pick up her handbag. Marcello raced down the blackened, broken stairs, past twisted pipes spilling from the walls and down into the street; but he had barely crossed the threshold when he heard a huge bang, loud as a bomb, and felt a sharp blow to his back, as if someone had thumped him from behind. "Son of a bitch!" thought Marcello, falling face forward, a great roar in his ears, blinded by a cloud of white dust.

Riccetto had been left with barely enough change to buy himself a couple of cheap cigarettes and pick up the tram. He walked, miserably alone, as far as the Cerchi, where he waited for the 13, which was half-empty because it was still early, bright and hot as midafternoon, but not even six o'clock. Riccetto went to the end of the car and hung out of the window to be alone with his gloomy thoughts, and as the tram followed the mostly deserted riverbank, then Viale del Re, the breeze ruffled his curls into one big tuft on his forehead and glued others around his ears while his shirt flapped out of his pants. He stared, unseeing, at the facades slipping by, totally gutted, face scorched by the sun and eyes shining with tears. At Ponte Bianco he slipped off the tram like a thief, but then stopped dead, struck by an unlikely scene. Around the mini obelisks that decorated Ponte Bianco, on the grassy areas, between the building sites of Quattro Venti where normally you never saw anyone and along the road that climbed from the Ferrobedò to the Grattacieli where the only walkers were people who lived up there and had no issues with corns or tight shoes, the whole area was packed with people. "What's up?" Riccetto asked a man beside him. "No idea," the man said, looking around to work out what was going on. Riccetto hurried on, through the crowd and down the bank that took him to a level crossing then steeply up again, turning toward the Ferrobedò. But now the sound of sirens came from the Gianicolense ring road near Trastevere station. Riccetto turned round, shoved his way back through the swaying crowd, and was on Ponte Bianco again just in time to see fire engines and an ambulance heading toward Monteverde Nuovo at top speed. Their wailing faded slowly among the building sites and apartment blocks.

Riccetto hurried back down toward the level crossing but ran into Agnoletto, who was wheeling his bike. They started pushing through the crowd together. "What's going on?" Riccetto asked another by-stander, overcome with curiosity. "Must be a fire at the Ferrobedò," said the man with a shrug and a grimace. But when they shoved their way through to the level crossing they found a line of police blocking their way. Agnolo and Riccetto tried to get the men to hear reason, insisting that they actually lived at Donna Olimpia, but the police had orders not to let anyone through, and they were turned back like everyone else. They tried to get down the embankment under Viale dei Quattro Venti, taking a narrow path workers had made that came out beyond the level crossing. But the police were there too. So now the only way to get to Donna Olimpia was to circle right round through Monteverde Nuovo. Agnoletto and Riccetto went back to Ponte Bianco, where the crowd was even bigger now, and set off up the Gianicolense ring road, taking turns to ride on the crossbar, then walking for long stretches when the road was too steep. It was a good mile and then some to Monteverde Nuovo, then another quarter of a mile downhill across the grass, through the building sites and the barrack sheds where the homeless lived, to get to Donna Olimpia on the other side. Riccetto and Agnolo finally arrived as evening was falling. They hurried down the hill along the first stretch of road, then, once again, had to stop. Just before the Grattacieli they ran into a big crowd, moving along the street under Monte di Splendore and through the courtyards of the apartment blocks. There were shouts and cries and with being so crammed together people's voices sounded muffled, choked. Riccetto and Agnolo got off the bike and started pushing through the throng. "What's happened, what's happened?" asked Riccetto when he saw some people he knew. They looked at him and didn't answer, veering away in the commotion. Then as Riccetto pressed on, white as a sheet, someone grabbed Agnolo's sleeve and said, "Didn't you know the school collapsed?" As he spoke the sirens started wailing again from Monteverde Nuovo and a moment later more fire engines came rushing down the hill, forcing their way through the crowd and coming to a stop beside the others in the middle of the crossroads at Donna Olimpia. When the last siren fell silent the cries and comments of the people all around seemed louder. On the right-hand corner where the school building had been was a huge, still-smoking ruin with a mountain of whitish rubble and chunks of cement on the road beneath blocking the way and preventing you from seeing the white columns that were still standing in the middle of the facade. The fire brigade already had a crane mounted over the ruins and twenty or thirty men digging with picks, as the evening air grew darker and darker, shouting orders and calling to each other. The police had cordoned off the whole area and the crowd was standing at a distance watching the firemen intently; in the lighted windows of the building opposite women were shouting and crying.

Still white with dust like a floured fish, Marcello was taken to the hospital in an ambulance and found to have two broken ribs. They put him in a ward that overlooked the gardens where convalescents were sitting in the sunshine and gave him a bed between an old man with a liver problem who chattered away and laughed and complained about the nuns, like he was always drunk, and another middle-aged man who said not a word in the two or three days before he was taken away to die in the appropriate room across the corridor. The following morning they brought another old man to take the dead man's place; this newcomer moaned night and day, something that drove the other man mad and had him childishly making faces and mimicking him. Marcello wasn't unhappy with the situation. He spent the days mostly waiting for mealtimes; not that he was really hungry—in the end he almost always left food on his plate, but because he liked eating; his face would brighten when he heard the clatter of soup-filled pans down the corridor, a nun pushing them along on kind of trolley. At once his head turned that way and with a connoisseur's gaze he would study what was on offer, watching the ladle that came brimming out of the pan to fill the metal plates of the patients in the first beds. They would start eating, meticulously, rattling the medicine bottles on their white bedside tables. You could see their jaws moving, their eyes narrowing and gleaming with ill-concealed gratification. All the same, most patients would grumble about the food, playing picky, always finding something to criticize, swallowing a few mouthfuls with an air of resignation. Marcello was no different, and the thing he talked about most when his family came during visiting hours was precisely the hospital food, as if his parents didn't know what he usually ate at home. He would leave almost everything on his plate, then justified this lack of appetite by saying the food was bad, and badly cooked, and that the nuns gave him the worst portions on purpose to spite him, while the truth was that he left it on his plate partly because with his broken ribs even the smallest of movements was extremely painful and partly because he really wasn't hungry, and any food, even the restaurant food he used to dream of, would have made him feel sick.

As the days passed, the pain in his ribs and his loss of appetite got worse, not better. He grew paler and thinner every day, until he was barely able to move under the sheets. Even moving his eyes made him feel faint. But he thought nothing of it and put up with both pain and weakness without complaining much.

Meanwhile in Donna Olimpia one way or another they had piled up the rubble against the school wall, reopened the road, buried the dead, and with the help of the mayor found homes for the homeless. One says "found homes"; in fact they had crowded a dozen families into one large room in a monastery in Casaletto and the others into barracks or shacks for the homeless in the outlying estates of Tormarancio and Tiburtino.* Two Sundays later, life in Donna Olimpia was back to normal. The young people went to town to have fun, the old sank their liter's worth of wine, carafe after carafe, in the bars, and an army of children invaded the courtyards and grassy spaces. Marcello's father and mother, with their six or seven other children, had gone to visit Marcello at the San Camillo Hospital, choosing to walk, since in the end it was barely a half hour away, climbing to Monteverde Nuovo and then down again along the Gianicolense ring road. Husband and wife walked slowly in the sunshine down Via Ozanam beside the elder daughters, no one talking, heads down, while the smaller kids ran around needling each other and bickering in low voices. One after the other they walked behind the Grattacieli, passing Monte di Splendore, where some boys had begun to play football among the garbage in the small open space. Agnolo and Oberdan were there too, all dressed up and taking care not to mess up their pants on the sparse patch of grass they sat on; they were watching the others, but already fed up, when Agnolo saw Marcello's family walking by and, prey to a sentiment that was already making him feel important, gave Oberdan a nudge:

"Hey, why don't we to go and see Marcello too?" "Let's do it," said Oberdan at once, since in the end they didn't know what to do with themselves, and he jumped up with a righteous expression on his face, all fired up with good intentions. The two set off right away from the small field with its hillocks and hollows; but some friends coming from Monteverde Nuovo stopped them. "Where you off to?" they asked, with the idea of getting them to go somewhere else instead. It was quite a temptation. But, assuming a serious expression, Agnolo answered, "We're going to see Marcello in hospital." "Marcello who?" asked Lupetto, who didn't know him. "Marcello the tailor's son,"

---

*Tiburtino is a new suburban development, while the Tiburtina, or Via Tiburtina, is a major road dating back to Roman times and built to connect Rome with Tivoli (ancient Tibur) twenty miles to the east. The same is true of Prenestino, a new district, and the Prenestina, an ancient road connecting Rome and Palestrina, then known as Preneste. These names recur frequently, bringing the antique past and the industrial present together.

someone explained. "You know he's going to die?" Agnolo said. "What do you mean, die?" the other asked incredulously, "he's only broken a rib, you don't die of a broken rib, do you?" "Fuck you," said Agnolo, "his sister told me a rib got into his liver, or something, his spleen, I don't know." "Come on, Agnolè," said Oberdan quickly, "or we'll be left behind." "So long," Lupetto and the others said, hurrying on toward Donna Olimpia. Agnolo and Oberdan set off running to catch up with Marcello's family, who had reached the path across the field that led to the plaza at Monteverde Nuovo, and without saying anything they walked close behind them under the hot sun through deserted Sunday-afternoon streets until they reached the hospital gates.

Marcello was more than happy to see them. "They didn't want to let us in," Agnolo told him at once, still furious with the guards. Marcello didn't pass up a chance to give his opinion: "They're all shifty here!" he said. "The nuns worst of all, believe it or not."

The effort to speak turned him whiter than his sheets, but he didn't care.

"Have you seen Zambuia at all?" he asked quickly, looking at Agnoletto and Oberdan, eyes gleaming with curiosity.

"Why would we?" Agnolo said with a certain disdain, not knowing about the puppy.

"If you see him," Marcello insisted, a bit riled, "tell him to treat my puppy nice and I'll give him another hundred. He'll know what I mean."

"OK," said Agnolo.

"Pipe down a bit, will you," said Marcello's mother, anxiously, seeing her son growing feebler and paler the more he talked. Marcello shrugged, almost laughing.

"And did you know," he demanded of his friends even more vehemently and pleased with himself, ignoring his father and mother who were watching from the foot of the bed, "that they'll be giving me insurance?"

"What insurance?" asked Agnolo, who hadn't heard anything about it.

"Broken-rib insurance, didn't you know there was insurance?" Marcello explained cheerfully.

His face had taken on a little color at the thought of what he would do with the insurance money; he'd already settled it with his parents. With shining eyes he announced, "I'll get myself a bike better than yours."

"Damn," said Agnolo, raising his eyebrows.

At this point the old guy on the right began to fret, the same low moan, over and over, a hand on his belly. The old guy on the other side, who'd been unusually quiet so far, suddenly woke up, turning around with a toothless grimace and starting to copy him, going "uuuh, uuuh, uuuh," half as a joke and half because he was seriously fed up. Then he went back to fiddling around with his things, sitting up in bed. Marcello gave his friends an amused look, as if to say, "See?" then in a low voice: "They're always at it."

But saying this he must have had a moment's giddiness, because the words slipped out in a low moan just like his neighbor's. His mother came to the head of the bed, pulling up the sheets: "Will you keep quiet or what?" she said. The sisters, who hadn't been paying much attention, came close too, and his little brothers, already bored with the place, stopped winding each other up and grabbed hold of the bed rail.

"And Riccetto, what's he doing?" Marcello asked as soon as he'd recovered from his fainting fit.

"No idea," said Agnolo, "he hasn't been around for a couple of weeks, I reckon!"

"So where's he living now?" Marcello asked.

"Tiburtino, I think, Pietralata, around there," said Agnolo.

Marcello thought about this for a moment: "And what did he say when he heard his mother was dead?"

"What'd he say," Agnolo said, "he burst out crying, what do you think?"

"Oh God," said Marcello, grimacing as the pain stabbed more sharply in his side. His mother took fright and reached for his hand, wiping the sweat off his neck and forehead with a handkerchief.

What with the pain and his general feebleness Marcello had almost passed out; and his parents knew that the doctors didn't think he could hold on for more than two or three days now. Seeing him so pale, his father went to call one of the nuns and his mother dropped on her knees leaning against the bed, holding her son's hand tight and crying silent tears. His father came back with the nun, who looked at the boy, put a hand on his forehead and, turning away, eyes blank, said, "You'll have to bear up." At which his mother lifted her head a bit, looked around and began to cry more loudly: "My boy, my boy," she sobbed, "my poor boy..."

Marcello opened his eyes and saw his mother crying and moaning and the others around the bed either crying or looking at him strangely. Agnolo and Oberdan had pulled away now, at the foot of the bed, to leave the space nearest Marcello to his family.

"What's wrong?" said Marcello in a whisper.

His mother wept all the more fiercely, she couldn't help herself, trying to smother her sobs in the sheets.

Marcello looked around more carefully, as if he was thinking hard.

"Oh," he said after a moment, "so I really have to go, do I!"

Nobody answered. "So then," Marcello repeated, staring at the people around his bed, "I really have to die..."

Agnolo and the other boy scowled, tight-lipped. After a few minutes' silence Agnolo plucked up courage, went to the bed and put a hand on Marcello's shoulder: "We'll say goodbye, Marcè," he said, "we have to be off now, we arranged to see friends."

"Goodbye, Agnolè!" said Marcello, his voice weak, but steady. Then after a moment's thought he added, "And say goodbye to everyone at Donna Olimpia, if it's really true I won't be coming back... And tell them not to be too upset!"

Agnolo gave Oberdan a nudge and without more ado they set off through the ward, which was almost dark now.

3. A NIGHT IN VILLA BORGHESE

ON THE overpass above Tiburtina station two boys were pushing a cart with a couple of armchairs on top. It was morning, and up on the bridge the old buses, to Monte Sacro, to Tiburtino III, and to Settecamini, as well as the 409 that turned just below the bridge down Casal Bertone and Acqua Bullicante toward Porta Furba, were grinding their gears in the crowd, among the three-wheelers and the junk dealer's barrows, the kids' bikes and the red carts of the peasants trundling slow and calm back from the markets to their vegetable plots in the outskirts. The cracked sidewalks each side of the bridge were packed too: hordes of workers, layabouts, respectable mothers who'd got off the tram at Portonaccio, under the high walls of the Verano cemetery, dragging bags stuffed with artichokes and pork rind toward the rundown estates along Via Tiburtina, or to some high-rise recently thrown up amid the rubble and surrounded by building sites, scrap-iron and timber yards, and the big Fiorentini and Romana Compensati factories. Right at the top of the bridge, amid the stream of cars and pedestrians, the two boys, who had been dragging the cart a tug at a time, careless of the jolts it was taking in the potholes and moving as slowly as they could, stopped and sat on the thing. One found a cigarette at the bottom of a pocket and lit up. The other, leaning against the arm of a chair upholstered in red-and-white stripes and waiting his turn to take a drag, untucked his black T-shirt from his pants. It was getting hot. But the other went on smoking without paying him any mind. "Hey," he said at last, "are you going to give me a smoke or what?" "Take it and shut up," said the other, passing the cigarette. With all the traffic on the bridge they could barely hear each other. Now there was a train as well, whistling as it raced under the overpass without slowing at the station below where a tangle of tracks led off into the thick dust, and in the distance the sun picked out the thousands of houses they were building in the low ground behind Via Nomentana. Taking a drag on the cigarette his friend had passed him, the boy with the black T-shirt pulled himself up onto one of the armchairs on the cart and stretched himself out, legs wide apart, curly head on the back of the chair. Then he settled down to suck happily on the inch of cheap tobacco he had between his fingers while all around, here at the top of the bridge, the back-and-forth of cars and people intensified with the approach of noon.

The other boy climbed on the cart too and stretched out on the second chair with his hands on his crotch. "Damn," he said, "I feel so weak I could die, I haven't eaten since yesterday morning." But through the din came the sound of two long whistles from the end of the bridge. Sprawled on their armchairs, the two boys recognized the sound and shifted onto their sides to look; sure enough, at the bend in the tram tracks at the far end of the Portonaccio plaza, weaving cheerfully through the cars and buses that poured onto the bridge, were two other delinquents like themselves, sweating hard as they pushed a barrow uphill toward them. Aside from whistling they were shouting and waving at the two boys sprawled on their armchairs. They stopped right beside them, barrow full of garbage and stinking like a sewer. They were all ragged and filthy, with a thick layer of dust and sweat on their faces, though their hair was carefully combed, as if they'd just this minute come out of the barber's. One was a slim, dark youngster, handsome even in his present sorry state, eyes black as coal and fine round cheeks a blend of olive and pink; the other was something of a redhead, with a sickly face full of freckles. "Hi cuz, keeping sheep now, are we?" asked the boy with the black T-shirt of the first of the new arrivals, without moving an inch from where he was sprawled on his armchair, hands on his stomach, and cigarette butt glued to his bottom lip. "Fuck off, Riccè," said the other. Riccetto—our son of a bitch in the armchair—allowed his eyes to glaze over, wrinkled his forehead, and tucked his chin into his throat with the shrewd look of someone who knows what he knows. Caciotta, the other boy on the cart with Riccetto, got to his feet and with childish curiosity went to see what was in the barrow their friends were pushing. His face creased in disgust and he burst out in a forced laugh. "Ha, ha, ha," he clowned, spinning around and sitting down on the edge of the sidewalk. The others watched, waiting for him to stop, their faces too assuming an amused look. "If you make twenty-six lire, you can cut off my head," Caciotta finally said. Seeing this was the put-down Caciotta had been working up to, the boy Riccetto had called cousin clicked his tongue, gave Caciotta a shove, and without further comment took the handles of the barrow and made to leave. The other, the vaguely redheaded boy, called Begalone, started to follow, keeping the corner of an eye on Caciotta, still on the ground amid the feet of passersby and still laughing away. "Hey, twenty-six lire," he said, "we'll see this evening who has more cash in his pocket." "Yeah, yeah, yeah," Caciotta burst out laughing again. Begalone stopped, his big washed-out Arab's head turning back over his shoulder, and said solemnly, weighing his words, "Listen loser, you want to come along and let us buy you a drink?" "You're on," Riccetto accepted at once, having watched the scene from the vantage point of his armchair without making any comment. He jumped down and, with Caciotta's help, started pushing the cart with the armchairs into the traffic behind the barrow of the two ragpickers, who, without further ado, were shooting at top speed down the other side of the bridge toward Via Tiburtina. They stopped at a bar with a pergola, wedged between two or three hovels beneath a tower block. All four went in and downed a liter of white; they were thirsty from pushing their carts all morning, and Alduccio and Begalone had dry, burning throats after four or five hours in the heat sorting through a mountain of trash under a railway bridge. After the first swigs they were all already tipsy. "Let's go and sell the armchairs, Riccè," said Caciotta, propping up the bar, legs crossed, "and the hell with everything..." "So where are we going to sell them?" asked Riccetto with a professional air. "Fucking dummies," said Begalone, "go to Porta Portese!"

Riccetto yawned, then looked at Caciotta through sleepy eyes: "We off then, Caciò?" he said. The other drained his wine at a gulp, which left him drunk, and rushing out of the bar, waved a hand and shouted, "So long, bad boys." Riccetto drained his glass too, spluttering and splashing wine all over his T-shirt before following Caciotta out of the door.

Going to Porta Portese meant a walk of at least three miles. It was a Saturday morning and the August sun made their heads spin. Worse, Riccetto and Caciotta had to make quite a detour to avoid going through San Lorenzo, where their boss's workshop was, since he had sent them off early to deliver the chairs to Casal Bertone. "What if we can't find anyone to buy the stuff?" said Caciotta with fake pessimism, when in reality he was walking fast and full of confidence. "We'll find someone, right enough," chuckled Riccetto, pulling half a cigarette from his pocket. "How much you think we'll get, Riccè?" asked Caciotta naively. "Reckon about thirty thousand," said the other. "Then the hell we're going home," he added, cheerfully sucking the last drags from the stub. Home, after all, was pretty notional in his case: going back or not amounted to much the same thing. It was not like they gave him anything to eat, and you could sleep just as well on a park bench. What kind of a home was that? Not to mention that Riccetto loathed his aunt, but then, so did Alduccio, who was her son. The uncle was a drunk who got on everyone's case all day, every day. Then how can two whole families, one with four kids and the other with six, all live in just two small, tight rooms, without even a toilet, since that was down in the yard. This was how Riccetto had been living for more than a year, after the disaster at the school that forced him to go and stay at his aunt's in Tiburtino.

They took the chairs to Antonio, the ragman in Vicolo dei Cinque, where three or four years ago Riccetto, Marcello, and Agnolo had sold the manhole covers. They got fifteen thousand and went to buy some new clothes. Half embarrassed and half defiant, they headed for Campo dei Fiori, where skinny pants were going for a thousand or fifteen hundred, and smart, sharp T-shirts for less than two thousand; they even bought themselves pairs of pointed black-and-white shoes, and Caciotta picked up the sunglasses he'd been dreaming of for ages. Then, limping from the swollen feet they'd got walking all the way from Portonaccio, they set off to find somewhere to leave the bundle of their old clothes. It wasn't easy in that part of town. They left them in the toilet of a little café near Ponte Garibaldi, striding in like they didn't give a damn and thinking, as they walked by the counter under the gaze of the barmen, "If the stuff's there when we come back, so much the better, and if not, too bad."

They went to grab a pizza and some munchies at Silvio's in Via del Corso. It was already late, and high time to decide how they were going to spend the afternoon, damn it! Dressed up as they were, they were spoiled for choice: the Metropolitan or the Europa, the Barberini or the Capranichetta, the Adriano or the Sistina. In any event, they set off right away since, as they say, out and about you always get a bite, stuck at home your mouth tastes shite. They were pretty happy, kidding around, completely oblivious to the idea that the joys of this world are short-lived and that luck can turn any moment...They bought an evening paper to see what was happening in town, then fought over it and ripped it up because both wanted to read it first; in the end, pissed off, they settled on the Sistina.

"God, I like having fun!" said Caciotta, coming out of the cinema four hours later, feeling chipper after seeing the movie twice. He straightened his sunglasses on his nose and, staggering around on the sidewalk of Via Due Macelli, began banging into passersby on purpose.

"Old hag!" he shouted at any woman who put on a pained face when she saw him coming at her. If by chance she turned round after he'd passed, that was it: tottering on the edge of the sidewalk, hands cupped round their mouths, they yelled all the louder, "Hag, crone, hoity-toity."

There were some folks they couldn't stand, just truly couldn't stand. "Get a load of these two!" shouted Caciotta, staring down a tall woman with a huge ass coming along the street with a short guy in glasses; brushing against them as they went by, Riccetto and Caciotta smirked and stooped till their nostrils were almost scraping the ground, and began hissing and spitting like two pots on the boil.

Four-eyes turned pretty well right round to look, and now there was
no stopping them; looking each other in the eyes, they bowed down
like marionettes and burst into fits of wild laughter. "What a guy,"
yelled Caciotta. But a police car was headed right their way and so,
skedaddle, they hared off, boisterous as ever, toward Villa Borghese,
which, of all the places with benches to sleep on, was the one where
you could have the best time. Entering the park through Porta Pinciana, they went down the avenue beside the riding track that was
always busy with people and traffic till late. At the end of the avenue
beyond Piazzale delle Canestre, another road led down to the parapets
of the Pincio and the Casina Valadier. Two rows of meager oleanders
in rectangular flowerbeds between the avenue and the sidewalk offered some shade for the benches lined up against the fence, with the
slope of the riding track behind. People were sitting there enjoying
the cool. "Think I'll take it easy a while," said a carefree Riccetto, and
they went to stretch out on their backs on the dry grass of the slope,
humming away, full of gratitude for life, waiting for it to get a bit
later. When they went back to the avenue, feeling good, the benches
were already a little freer and there were fewer people about; but this
was when real life began. You could see some older men, here and
there, in shirtsleeves, or a knot of youngsters, some with jackets over
sloping shoulders, some with brightly colored T-shirts. Most were
sitting, chatting, knees tight together like women, or legs crossed,
one arm pressed to their laps, leaning slightly forward and smoking
in quick nervous drags, holding their cigarettes with four tense fingers.
Ahead, on another bench, under the shade of an oleander, you could
see a man talking to a dark youngster who was wearing one of those
blue open-neck T-shirts you can buy for five hundred lire at Porta
Portese; and even farther along, other figures among the trees under
the lamps. "Someone's flashing a load of thigh," said Caciotta suddenly, staring across the avenue, where in the glow from a lamp that
cut through the shadows a woman was sitting on a bench with a
blood-colored underskirt pulled up above her knees. "Will you look
at that!" Riccetto felt horny at once. "Hey, son of a bitch," voices
shouted at Caciotta from a bench nearby. "What's up?" asked a young

man with skin black as a frying pan and hair blacker still, filthy, greasy curls. He was sitting in the middle of a bench, legs wide apart, two friends to one side.

"Chat her up?" said Caciotta, getting excited, going to sit with them.

"Yeah, chat her up, for sure," said Negro* ironically, and loudly enough to be heard by two big men walking by with two of Villa Borghese's floozies in tow, all in high spirits. "Well, fuck you all," Riccetto muttered after them. "Meet my friend," said Caciotta, introducing Riccetto to the others. They shook hands. Down the avenue the two fatties and their whores were still whooping it up, lighting cigarettes now; Negro and the others watched out of the corners of their eyes. The younger of Negro's two friends was speaking in a low voice to the other, a solid guy with a big head and merry eyes. "Get off my back, Calabré," he answered calmly. "Tonight's looking good, hey, Cappello?" Caciotta asked him, testing the water. "Why not?" said Cappellone, mouth wide as a plank, and he sprawled on the bench, stretching his legs almost to the flowerbed.

Calabrese was all taken up with the seriousness of their business and didn't look at the new arrivals. "Let me touch it," he said, voice hoarse from the cold he'd had ever since he'd been sleeping out in Villa Borghese; he was twenty, but his dark, chubby cheeks made him look like a lout of fifteen. He reached a hand to touch Cappellone's bulging pockets. "Fuck off," said Cappellone with a start. "Here it is, OK?" and he pulled a gun from his pocket. "Whoa, crazy," said Negro. Laughing, Cappellone slipped it back into pants stiff with filth. "Shit," said Caciotta. "A Beretta, right?" asked Riccetto, coming close. But they didn't answer. Still probing, with a flat voice and a shrewd, glazed look, Calabrese said, "And the pen?" "You think I have the pen, asshole?" said Cappellone. "Picchio's got it!" snapped Negro, pissed off, holding Calabrese by an arm. "He's drunk, he'll let the whores clean him out," said Calabrese sullenly. "So go get him,"

*The nickname given to the book's only black character, following the original Italian.

said Cappellone. "We're off, then," said Calabrese. Cappellone got up from the bench and stretched his legs, laughing. Riccetto and Caciotta followed Calabrese and Cappellone, who were dragging their heels along the avenue; but Negro, watching them get to their feet, said, "Damned if I can be bothered, it's so comfortable here!" He lay back on the bench, pulling up one leg after the other and stretching out.

The avenue heading to Porta Pinciana was still leaping with women, guys in smart shirts, foreigners strolling about to the beat of the jazz coming from the Casina delle Rose. But where you left Villa Borghese, beyond the arches of the gate, the avenue that went down by the Muro Torto to one side and the riding track on the other was all dark and quiet; a couple of soldiers had pushed on down there, shambling loutishly, looking for trouble, then a kid on a scooter; they disappeared into the shadow of the trees. To the right there was still a fence separating the avenue from the slope, and farther down, in the dark before you got to the big open space lit up now by a low moon, were two fences each side of the sandy riding track. The grassy areas were all yellow, trampled by the kids who played football during the day, then the babysitters out walking, and now whole army divisions were headed down there, moving in gangs toward the riding school with its square-cut hedges, burned by the smell of horse piss. Emerging from the shadow of a clump of plane trees in the middle of the space, or from the tangle of the riding school's fences and bushes, came gaunt, dark sailors from Taranto or Salerno, then northern men, armored-car drivers, climbing back up the track with arms swinging loose and trousers sagging, or kids from the Prati or Flaminio districts, all wiped out and leaving behind, at the bottom of the slope, a deep, deep silence. When Riccetto and Caciotta turned up with the two other Villa Borghese regulars it was already late and the quiet moments between someone going down and someone coming back up were getting longer. "It's Picchio," said Calabrese, as if he had seen him. "Where?" asked Cappellone. "You deaf as well?" said Calabrese. "Well, fuck you," said Cappellone, and he sat down on the rail of the fence as if he were planning to be there an hour or more. From behind the track in fact, down at the bottom near the chestnut trees between the wire fences and darkest thickets of the riding school, came a voice shrieking for all it was worth. Approaching, it gradually grew louder.

"Cheats! Cheats!" it shrieked. For a few moments it faded, then picked up again: "Cheats!"

Each time the word seemed to be yelled more angrily. And whoever was shouting, from what you could sense without seeing him, must have been stopping every few paces to turn toward the riding track and shout in that direction. Or maybe he was walking slowly, head turned back, stumbling from time to time. And he must have been cupping his hands to his mouth, shouting so loud you could hear the catarrh bubbling in his throat:

"Cheeeeeeats. Cheeeeeeeats!"

Then he stopped again to walk a bit, or to spit. At first, since he was dragging out the *ee*'s, you thought he might be hamming it up, to be a jerk. But gradually the tones made it clear that whoever was shouting really was furious, beside himself, spraying saliva. You could have heard that shout from the middle of the riding track down to the avenue and as far as the Casina delle Rose. It fell silent, took a rest, then started up again, as if so angry as to be unable to find any other word but "Cheeeeeats!"

He was almost up to the fence now and you could see his tottering shape, trembling from head to foot as if an icy north wind were blowing. His hands never stopped moving: they kept tucking and untucking his shirt from his pants, tightening his belt, pulling the chewing gum from his mouth, pushing back hair that fell over his eyes.

"Cheating bitches," he yelled even louder at the women, who meanwhile had been wisely crouching down in the bushes, in holy silence; all of a sudden he sat down, then got up again and started climbing, but always turning to look back. After a few steps, he stopped again, wobbling inside his shirt that hung loose from his pants, and began a long tirade, full of complications, chewing up the words with his gum, spitting gobs of saliva.

"Hey Picchio," Cappellone interrupted him from above, "they've got you talking to yourself, if I'm not mistaken, hey, Pì?" Picchio looked up the hill without replying, then turned back toward the clearing at the bottom where the women were quiet as sphinxes and again yelled, "Cheats!" Then he came up the path between the fences and across the track. He reached the avenue and sat down with the others on the low trunks fixed there. He was chewing, stretching his whole mouth wide so his jaws squeaked and lips dribbled saliva. "What you been up to, Pì?" said Calabrese, his eyes finally smiling, like an animal with something to eat.

"Just fuck 'em all," Picchio suddenly yelled at the top of his voice. Shouting and chewing together, all the skin of his small dry face wrinkled up.

"They don't wanna give me a fuck," he yelled.

"And you let them fool around with you like that, hey, Picchio?" said Cappellone. Calabrese sniggered from his swollen face. Picchio got to his feet again, swaying, cupped his hands to his mouth, and turning toward the open space below them yelled, "Cheats!"

"The pen?" asked Calabrese, trying to launch an investigation. Picchio gave him a sideways glance, but as if not actually seeing him. "So dumb I've got earrings in my nose, have I?" he started shouting at the whores again, "like I'm not going to give you your five hundred? Cheats!" He raised an arm and pointed: "Tomorrow night I'll show you what's what, I will." "What'll you do, Picchio?" said Cappellone. "What'll I do?" asked Picchio, chewing and sucking snot through his nose, "that's their fucking problem. Here," he said, speaking to Calabrese, glancing at him out of the corner of his eye and stretching his eyebrows in resignation.

Calabrese took the pen and studied it in the light. "Who'd you rip it off from?" asked Riccetto, looking on.

"Kid on the tram," chewed Picchio.

"What do you mean, a kid?" said Cappellone, "didn't you say it was an American?"

Picchio ignored him.

"And what'll you do with it?" said Riccetto with a shrug.

"Shit," said Calabrese, "don't you think it's worth five hundred?"

"Tell me another!" said Riccetto.

"So," said Calabrese, "wanna bet?"

"Don't make me laugh," answered Riccetto. "Give me a break."

"Let's go drink," yelled Picchio all of a sudden, waking up and jumping to his feet, so light a gust of wind would have blown him away.

"He's loaded," said Calabrese.

"What do you mean, loaded," said Picchi, chewing and puffing, "I've got three hundred!"

Riccetto and Caciotta were sitting waiting to see how things panned out.

"Let's go," said Picchio hoarsely, tottering a step in the direction of Porta Pinciana. "OK, let's go," said Cappellone, following along with Calabrese. Riccetto and Caciotta stayed put. "Let's go, kids," Cappellone called to them.

When they got to Porta Pinciana, they found Negro with a small curly-haired guy the others already knew, a guy with a bloated delinquent's face and two hard, bright eyes; he was from Acqua Bullicante, name of Lenzetta. "Wow," said Cappellone, "two from Tiburtino, one from Acqua Bullicante, two from Primavalle, one drifter, and Picchio from the Valley of Hell: we could be the Bad Boys League of Greater Rome!"

All seven of them went to a pizzeria near Stazione Termini to down a liter with Picchio's cash; then they headed back up Via Veneto, shirts hanging out of their pants, or in just their vests, T-shirts around their necks, yelling and singing and banging into the rich folks, still out and all dressed up with their expensive cars waiting for them. Villa Borghese was almost empty now. You could barely hear the violins from Casina delle Rose. When they were across from the riding track, Picchio woke up and started bursting his lungs again, yelling, "Cheats!" He climbed the fence, walked down the slope, and as soon as he reached the clearing went down face-first in the dirt and fell asleep.

"God, I'm feeling horny," said Riccetto, "with all those big dolled-up babes on Via Veneto."

"Let's go down and see if the whores are still around," said Caciotta.

"Oh right," said Calabrese, "they want money, serious dough!"

"And don't we have money?" said Caciotta triumphantly. The others pricked up their ears.

"So let's go," said Negro, sniggering under the woolly curls that spilled over his ears, "what are we waiting for?"

They crossed the clearing in the moonlight, reached the riding school, and looked around, but the whores had already left.

"Patrol'll have been by," said Calabrese knowingly.

"That's that then," said Caciotta, "tonight…" and he pointed thumb and first finger and shook his hand. Nothing.

Lenzetta gave him a jokey slap on the butt.

"Wow," he said, "what a nice ass!"

"What a nice dick!" Caciotta corrected.

"Reaches right back there, does it?" asked the boy from Acqua Bullicante, Lenzetta.

"Why not," said Caciotta, allusively, "and with some left over for yours."

"He's got you there," said Negro, as if he were saying "amen." They climbed out of the clearing on the other side and emerged on the avenue where they'd met. But there were too many people hanging around for them to sleep here. They headed into the gardens toward Casina Valadier, stretched out on the benches, and dozed off.

The night was soon gone; the trams hadn't started trundling under the Muro Torto, Rome was still fast asleep but already the sun was beating down on the lawns and woods of Villa Borghese, a bright white light that glared on the walls and the little busts beside the flowerbeds.

Riccetto was woken by a kind of strange coolness in his feet. He turned a bit on the bench, tried to get back to sleep, but then lifted his head to see what the hell was going on with his feet. A ray of sunshine, fresh and dazzling, was streaming slantwise through the foliage, lighting up the holes in his socks.

"Did I really take my shoes off last night?" Riccetto wondered, sitting up sharply.

"No, I did not," he answered himself, looking under the bench, on the grass, in the bushes. "Caciotta, hey, Caciotta," he yelled, shaking the still-sleeping Caciotta, "they've ripped off my shoes!"

"What've you done?" asked Caciotta, half-asleep.

"They've ripped off my shoes," Riccetto shouted again. "And my money!" he said, thrusting his hands in his pockets. Sleepy as he was, Caciotta felt in his pockets too; nothing, not a single lira, and his glasses gone as well. "Fucking shit!" Riccetto was desperate. The others had woken up now and were watching from their benches.

"I didn't have a lira," said the boy from Acqua Bullicante, Lenzetta, sitting up on his bench. But Calabrese watched silently with his puffy face, shaking his head, eyes alive with the look of someone who knows the score but isn't going to say. Riccetto and Caciotta went off without a word or even a glance at the others, who were playing dumb, fake looks of concern and innocence on their shifty faces, knowing no one was going to risk complaining about them. In the whole of Villa Borghese, bright under the already warm sun, not a soul was to be seen. They went down to the field with the riding track and crossed it. On the other side, at the bottom of the slope, Picchio was still asleep, face down. He had a pair of blue-and-white canvas shoes, frayed on top and with holes in the soles. Riccetto carefully slipped them off and put them on his own feet, though they felt a bit tight; then they went off down Porta Pinciana.

That day they ate at the monks' kitchen. Had to, because despite hustling the whole morning in Piazza Vittorio they hadn't managed to scrape up a single lira.

Pale with hunger, they slouched under the station scaffolding and arrived at Via Marsala, where at No. 210 there was a small door with the word "Refectory" written over it, and then, of the Sacred Heart, or the Blessed Virgin, or some such. First they poked their noses in, then their whole heads, one step forward and half a step back, dressed up as they were, Caciotta barefoot and Riccetto in his canvas shoes; then they were in a short corridor that led to a clay courtyard, packed with penitents like themselves, shooting hoops, and it was pretty obvious they were only doing it to keep the monks happy. Riccetto and Caciotta exchanged glances, to get an idea of how they looked, and pretty nearly slunk off, given how pathetic they seemed. But they started joking around, shoving each other about, cheerful and cheeky, and took the plunge.

A big belly of a monk came toward them, all rumpled and sweaty, and they almost split, thinking, "What's this guy want?" But in a loud voice the monk called, "Want to eat, boys?" Riccetto turned away so as not to show he was dying to laugh, while Caciotta, who had been here once before, said, "Yes, Father." At the word "Father," Riccetto finally lost it and began to splutter; he had to pretend to be tying the laces of one those filthy shoes to hide his face. "This way," the monk said, and led them to a doorway on the other side of the courtyard where there was a small table with a register and a block of tickets. Pulling up his robes so that you could pretty well see his belly, the monk asked them for their "particulars." "Our what?" asked Riccetto, surprised, but obliging now, ready to help any way he could. When they realized what "particulars" meant for God's sake they just lied but were most respectful taking their tickets from the monk's hand.

Riccetto was feeling pretty positive now, seeing how smoothly things were going, and almost, in his unexpected embarrassment, a little moved. "So when do we eat?" he asked, hopefully. "Dunno, soon," said Caciotta. Meantime the other vagabonds were still tiring themselves out playing that dumb game. "So, let's play too," said Riccetto, determinedly, with every intention of asserting his rights. They went into the middle of the yard, had a bit of a tussle with the others, being in worse shape, and started to play, knowing nothing of basketball, they'd never heard of the game. The whole half hour they played, all Riccetto did was be careful not to shout "Fuck off."

Then the monks called them with a clap of the hands and had them crowd into a big room down the corridor from the entrance where there were tables thirty feet long with benches around them. They gave them each two dry bread rolls and two bowls of pasta and beans, made them say, "In the name of the Father, the Son, and the Holy Spirit," and let them eat.

For ten days or so Riccetto and Caciotta kept coming. Only for lunch, though, because in the evening the monks shut up shop. So more often than not the two were eating only once a day. Evenings they grabbed what they could. Either with the money they wangled in the mornings at the station or the market in Piazza Vittorio, or stealing from food stands. But one evening fortune smiled on them at last and the monks could just fuck off. It happened on a tram, when a woman got on with a purse inside her bag. This purse, spied through the window of the delicatessen on Via Merulana where the woman had been shopping shortly before, looked promisingly plump, and coming out of the shop the woman had slipped it into a bag that was already stuffed and didn't close properly. As luck would have it, Ricetto and Caciotta had exactly thirty lire in their pockets. They split it on the move, fifteen each, ran after the tram, and leapt aboard after it had already left the stop. They entered the car separately and went to stand close to the woman. She was holding on to the handrail, looking daggers at the people around her. Ricetto got right up close, because he was the one who was going to do the job; Caciotta stood behind him to hide his movements. Very slowly Ricetto opened the bag, lifted the purse with his right hand, and slid it across his chest, then beneath his left arm, till he had it gripped under his armpit. Then, with Caciotta still covering his back, he pushed through the passengers and they got off at the first stop, cutting down through the Piazza Vittorio gardens and

> you couldn't have said "Amen"
> as fast as they vanished.*

They vanished, in fact, toward San Lorenzo, through the Santa Bibiana arch. And since they were in this part of town they thought they might as well pay a little visit to Tiburtino to see how things were going since they'd ripped off the armchairs from the upholsterer in Via dei Volsci . . .

It was early evening and a pleasantly cool breeze was cheering up that time of day when workers come home from work and the trams

*Dante, *Inferno*, Canto XVI, lines 88–89.

are packed as sardine cans, so that you have to wait three hours just for the privilege of clinging to a running board. From San Lorenzo to Verano and as far as Portonaccio was one long party, a din, a song-fest. Riccetto crooned,

> *Quanto sei bella Roma,*
> *quanto sei bella Roma a prima sera,*[*]

at the top of his voice, entirely reconciled to life, full of wonderful projects for the coming days, fingering the cash in his pocket, cash that is the source of all pleasure and all happiness in this filthy world. Caciotta was right behind him, beside him, calm and sunny. They reached Portonaccio and waited for the Tiburtino bus in the big plaza beneath the overpass, singing with their hands in their pockets. They had just missed one and of course the next was a long time coming; when it arrived there were already so many people waiting it really seemed too much of a hassle to get on. They waited for a third, but it was the same again. Carried on a wind at once fresh and warm, three or four clouds drifted over from Saint Peter's; there was a crack of thunder, a shower of rain. Riccetto and Caciotta gave up on the buses, which were always a nightmare that time of day, and went off for a little walk, following groups of soldiers behind Tiburtina station, to the end of the road, amid warehouses, excavations, and building sites, across fields already soaked with rain, to see if there were any whores about. When they got back to the terminus under the overpass, the grave lights had come on in the Verano cemetery, pulsing red above the big walls in lines and circles. The bus was waiting: but so was the inevitable crowd, determined to storm aboard. "What time do you reckon it is, Caciò?" asked Riccetto. "Dunno, maybe eight, or quarter past," said Caciotta; instead, it must have been at least ten. "It's late," said Riccetto, but it didn't sour his mood: "Let's climb on."

They almost floored two or three old women, likewise two or three

[*]Riccetto's lines are from one of the many popular songs written to celebrate Rome at the height of Fascism in the mid-1930s.

old men, were rude to the conductor, trod on a few corns, did a little shoving left and right, and finally ended up in the corner behind the driver. Leaning against each other, they passed ironic remarks on the little dramas going on in the bus, then eventually turned their attention to a few friends who'd climbed aboard and whom they greeted cheerfully as soon as they saw them.

"So?" said Caciotta with a protective, confident air, shaking hands all around, "what are we all up to, then?"

"Can't you see," said one, with a glum look, his clothes stinking of the factory floor, "we're coming home from the grind?"

"No, I can see, I can see," said Caciotta.

The other went on bitterly, "So, we get home, eat, go to bed, and in the morning, back to the grind!"

Caciotta said, "Right, right!" giving them all a sunny smile.

"And how's things with you, hey, Caciò?" asked a blond boy, Ernestino, seeing the special look Caciotta had about him.

Caciotta turned to him a moment with glazed eyes; then without a word, hampered a little by the press of people in the bus, he slipped a hand in his pocket and rummaged around a bit, calm as you like, looking Ernestino and the other two or three youngsters in the eyes with an amused, detached expression that they returned, equally amused.

Then, very slowly, he pulled out his wallet, opened it with meticulous care, and produced, with delicacy, from one of its compartments, a wad of hundred-lire notes. This done, in a move that was quite unexpected, he slapped Ernestino, *wham, wham*, two or three times across both cheeks with the wad of bills. After which, he put them all back in his wallet and his wallet back in his pocket, with a tired, wholly satisfied smile.

Ernestino's eyes lit up with laughter, amused to have been chosen as the sucker for Caciotta's show: "So what's the big deal," he said cheerfully, "it's just a few hundred!"

"Right, and all the ones we've stashed away," said Caciotta, mouth twisting in a sneer and eyes glazing over even more than before.

Riccetto kept quiet, seemed a little sleepy, though not without a bit of swagger about him, since he didn't know Ernestino and the others too well. They were old friends of Caciotta's, who was born and bred in Tiburtino.

He'd known Ernesto and a certain Franco, nicknamed White Feather, who was also there, since they'd been in swaddling clothes and Tiburtino and Pietralata were still out in the fields with the fort and the new lots barely finished. Before they were eight years old they'd run off from home together and stayed away a week or two, eating next to nothing, just a few onions or persimmons ripped off from the markets, or a bit of pork rind sneaked from a housewife's bag. They had no particular reason for running away aside from the fact that it was fun. They'd scrounge a few smokes from the soldiers' barracks. When it came time to sleep, they might hide away under the awning of the guy selling watermelons, stretched out on top of the melons.

Caciotta's cheerfulness and general attitude of thankfulness toward life, due to the cash in his pocket, put him in a mood for sentimental recollections.

"Hey Ernestì," he said, almost tenderly, "you remember that time with the watermelon man?"

"Sure, I remember," said Ernestino, who, not having any cash in his pockets, was hardly enthusiastic.

"Hey Riccetto," said Caciotta, tugging his sleeve, "Listen up a bit . . . You remember, Ernestì," he said, laughing, "being so shit-scared that night around Bagni di Tivoli that we slept with big sticks under our heads?" Ernestino laughed. "This watermelon guy," Caciotta explained to Riccetto, "kept a pig in a coop in the fields in Bagni di Tivoli . . . Well, since we'd kept watch OK over his watermelons, he decides to send us to keep watch on his pig. There was a rabbit he had too, in the same place. One night the watermelon man's mother turns up and tells us, 'Go to Bagni and get me a loaf of bread.' You can imagine, more than a mile there and another back . . . with it being dark already and all . . . Then watermelon man's mother, while we were away, takes this rabbit, kills it, cooks it, and eats it. She gathers the bones, digs a hole, and buries them. The bitch! When we get back, first thing we do is check on the rabbit and the rabbit is gone. Then the watermelon man comes back, the boss, and it's, 'So where's the rabbit?' And me and Ernestino here tell him, 'Dunno, we went to get some bread and when we got back the rabbit was gone.' And the boss is like, 'Couldn't just one of you have gone?' We tell him: 'We were afraid of going alone, so we went together.' So the boss is all pissed off and he takes five hundred lire from his pockets and says, 'You're fired then, the both of you, and don't ever show your face around here again or I'll kick the shit out of you!'

"Still, what the fuck did we care," Caciotta went on, all pleased with himself, "we just went back to Pietralata to get into scraps with the other kids around the place, then got taken on working at the circus ... remember, Ernestì? With the lions ... and tigers ... And that time Rondella, the Maremma horse, escaped, and we ran after it all night on the fields behind Pietralata and caught it when it took a swim in the Aniene!" Riccetto listened happily enough, entirely sharing the point of view of Caciotta and his old friends. The others were nodding and laughing too, feeling all their old rascally instincts reviving deep in their souls. Alongside the boys from Tiburtino there was also a guy from Pietralata listening with a bored look, his face and hair black as an adder, a huge kid, head and shoulders taller than the others. He was standing beside them, holding the handrail, tired, concentrated, a soft expression on his shifty face. He was called Amerigo and Caciotta hardly knew him except by sight. The bus was bumping over the cobbles of Via Tiburtina, throwing around the passengers packed so tight you couldn't have slipped a needle between them, and the Tiburtino gang were getting more and more boisterous. "Just take a look at these fabulous curls he's got," said Ernestino in a gap in the conversation, looking at Riccetto. "Didn't you know," Caciotta offered with panache, "that to get his curls like that he has people fart in his face?" While the others were laughing, Amerigo, hardly moving from where he was, brushed an elbow against Caciotta: "Hey, you, what's your name," he said softly in a throaty voice, "I've got something to say to you!"

4. RAGAZZI DI VITA

> The people are a great savage
> In the bosom of society.
>   —LEO TOLSTOY

AMERIGO was drunk. "What about we get off at the fort here," he said. Caciotta listened politely and, for want of anything else to say, offered, "Let me introduce you to a friend of mine." Amerigo raised what seemed a leaden hand in Riccetto's direction; he wore the collar of his jacket turned up, and his face looked green under curly hair plastered with dust, big brown eyes staring glassily. He squeezed Riccetto's hand hard, without a word, as if there could be no doubt between them that both were rogues. Then he forgot Riccetto and turned to Caciotta: "Understand?" he asked. He was acting serious, but what Caciotta understood was that this was not a guy you could fool around with; once at Farfarelli's he'd seen Amerigo lift a row of six linked chairs with one hand, and in Pietralata he'd beaten the hell out of quite a few kids who'd ended up in the hospital. "What's going on?" said Caciotta, as if between two delinquents on equal terms. "Let's talk," Amerigo said, pulling his jacket collar up even higher.

The bus stopped at Forte di Pietralata; from the still open café a ray of light fell obliquely across the asphalt of the Tiburtina. Amerigo jumped down from the running board, bouncing on his knees with an athlete's stride, hands still in his pockets. "Let's go," said Caciotta to Riccetto, who didn't want to believe the turn things had taken, and the two followed close behind. "We can do this bit on foot," said Amerigo, walking past the barracks toward Tiburtino. When they were a bit farther down the road he gripped Caciotta's elbow; setting one foot very deliberately in front of the other, he had such a mean look on his face it seemed if you just touched him, anywhere, you'd get hurt. He dragged his feet like a boxer beginning to fade, but behind that flagging walk you could see he was alert and swift as a beast. With Caciotta and Riccetto he went on acting the serious kid, like he wasn't remotely aware of the strength he had or his reputation for being the toughest punk in Pietralata. Meantime, he carried about him the complicitous air of someone about to swing a deal with a person like himself, and no fooling. "If you come along with me," he said to Caciotta, "you'll be glad you did." "Where?" asked Caciotta. Amerigo nodded ahead, toward Tiburtino. "This way," he said, "Fileni's." Caciotta had never heard of the place. He didn't reply. Amerigo went on, acting like he thought the other had understood: "It's Saturday, let's go for it," he said in a dull, almost feminine voice, maybe the way his mother spoke, face more jaundiced by the minute. "OK, let's do it," said Caciotta, sounding tough; after all, there was nothing else going on and he was beginning to enjoy himself.

But Riccetto hung back, squinting at the others. When they reached Tiburtino III he said, "So long, kids, I'm off." "Off where?" asked Caciotta, stopping. Amerigo had stopped too and was looking sideways, hands half in his pockets. "To fucking bed. I'm so sleepy if I walk another step I'll drop down dead!"

Amerigo went toward him, weighing him with seemingly bloodshot, laughing eyes; laughing because it was unthinkable that anyone should oppose his will.

"Listen," he said, in a quiet voice that was still calm and persuasive, "I already told you that if you come with me, you'll be having to thank me...You don't know me." Caciotta, who did know him, was watching from a distance, amused. He knew Riccetto would come with them to this Fileni's.

"I'm telling you, I'm half-asleep," said Riccetto.

"Asleep, my ass," said Amerigo, laughing under tensely wrinkled brows, still tickled by the absurdity of someone not doing what he said. "Come on!" He put his hand on his heart: "Caciotta here can tell you, right, Caciò? I'm a guy no one can say nothing against, and if I make a promise, kid, be sure, everything will turn out like I say...

Why? We're all friends here, right? I'm doing you a favor, as they say, and another day you'll do one for me; we should be looking after each other, right?" He had turned solemn; not to go along with him would be dumb, was the message, but Riccetto was eaten up about what was going on between Amerigo and Caciotta, which seemed fake and dangerous. Caciotta was watching him with a strange expression: Do what you like, he seemed to be saying, I'm staying out of it. Riccetto shrugged. "Who's complaining?" he said to Amerigo. "Sure, you're right, go ahead with Caciotta to this place of yours, you don't need me along, do you?" But Amerigo didn't know which of them had the cash. He looked at Riccetto with a patient, very serious expression and came up so close as to mix his breath, which smelled of wine, with Riccetto's. But right then, two familiar shadows began to form in the yellowish murk of the first Tiburtino estates; they were coming down to the water fountain, where they stopped.

"Cops," said Caciotta. "They know me, the ones that wanted to put me inside, the other night at the Tiburtino cinema!"

Out of his sick eyes Amerigo watched them coming nearer. He put a hand over his face and squeezed his forehead between his fingers. He was white as a cloth, twisting up his mouth as if he were about to cry. When the two shadows with the gun belts across their chests had moved a little farther on, toward the center, he passed his hand across his forehead one last time. "My God, it really hurts," he said, "like a nail going right through my head." But the pain was quickly gone.

He went back to Riccetto and put a friendly hand on his shoulder. "Riccè," he said, "what's your name, don't play dumbass now; we'll have a better time if you come along too." He resumed his expansive, rhetorical style: "Word of honor," he said, "I'm the worst son of a bitch if after tonight you don't come and say, Amerigo, my friend, I gotta thank you and even beg your pardon." His hand on Riccetto's shoulder felt like a ton of bricks.

They went down the main street in Tiburtino, where the only lights still on came from the two bars, and high up in the middle of the filthy, decaying developments, amid bits of laundry hung at the windows, you could still hear the twang of a guitar. They turned down by the covered market, green and greasy with fish, cut across two or three of the streets going through the apartment blocks, all exactly the same, and arrived at one of those houses that have a fascist-style veranda, now battered and broken. They went up some steps, then along an outside stone gallery that looked down on the street beside, and finally knocked on a little door, already ajar, a faint light filtering out. The door opened from inside and they found themselves in a kitchen full of people gathered around a table in silence. Six or seven were playing cards; the others, standing against the walls or beside a sink full of dirty dishes, were watching.

Amerigo and the other two slipped quietly in among the little crowd, people moving aside a bit to make space, giving them no more than a glance; then they all concentrated on the cards from behind the players' backs. Amerigo stood watching the game, as if he'd forgotten about Caciotta and Riccetto, one hand following hard on another with constant wins and losses, then a few louder whispers and maybe a raised voice making a comment. Caciotta couldn't give a damn about the game but despite being desperately sleepy went on looking around with a big smile on his face; Riccetto, though, was remembering when he used to gamble with the money from the pipes as a kid in Donna Olimpia, and his cheeks flushed and his eyes burned. When each hand was over, Amerigo turned a bit, not toward his companions, but to one or another of the older men, shaking his head or whispering in a hoarse voice, "Fuck him." Sitting in front of him with hunched shoulders was a guy called Zinzello, hair slicked back Valentino-style, a carter who lost game after game, face growing grimmer and darker all the while; at last, he got up and someone else took his place. That was when Amerigo, behind him, made up his mind. He turned to Caciotta and, quite sure of himself, as if they'd already agreed, a bitter look in his eyes, said, "Lend me that grand you've got in your pocket." "I'm not the one with the cash," said Caciotta.

Amerigo's yellow eyes turned to Riccetto, who was standing a bit behind: "Out with the cash," he said in a quiet voice, so as not to be heard above the buzz in the room. Riccetto kept mum. "Oh, come on," said Amerigo brusquely, exasperated even, "I'll give it you back, what do you think, I'm not going to rob you, am I, you know that, right."

"Ah, get it out, who cares," said Caciotta.

Riccetto said, "Fifty-fifty on any winnings, OK?" and he pulled out a grand, holding it tight in one hand. "If you lose you give me half back..." he added. "I'm not going to rob you, am I," Amerigo repeated, "we can do like you say, come on," and in his impatience he grabbed the money from his hand. He put three or four hundred on the table and laid his bet; the cards slid from hand to hand like oil, one stack this side, one the other; a glance and you could see whether you'd won or lost.

Amerigo won the first hand, and flicked his eyes toward Riccetto who was keeping track, his face dark. Cacciotta's big mouth split wide in a laugh. "I'm dying for a smoke," he said, rummaged in his pockets for a stub, found one, and lit it. Amerigo won the second hand too; he turned, taking the cash, to make some remark to the guy with the Valentino hair, who was close by and hadn't said a word. To keep them happy, he sent the other two a satisfied look, putting all his winnings in his pocket. Then suddenly everything went wrong, and in five or six hands he'd blown it all. He looked at the others with a face like a corpse. Riccetto's eyes were hard, pained, as if he were about to cry; neither of them spoke. Amerigo went back to watching the game, trying to understand it, figure out how it worked; every now and then he exchanged a couple of words with the carter, explaining why he'd lost as well. After a while he turned to Riccetto. "Pull out some more cash," he said. "Are you crazy," said Riccetto, "who's going to give it back to me tomorrow if we lose again?" Amerigo bided his time; he stayed quiet a moment, then said, "Come on, give me the money." "But I don't want to play any more, understand," Riccetto said in a low voice. But he didn't seem sure of himself; Amerigo stared into his eyes. "We need to have a word," he said; he gripped his arm between two steel fingers like it was a twig and pushed him between a huddle of people through the door onto the gallery outside. It had started to drizzle again, but through a tear in the clouds the white of the moon lit up the tenements. "You're like a brother to me," he began.

"You have to believe me, what I say I really mean. Go ask anyone you like in Pietralata or Tiburtino about me, about Amerigo, because there's no one, no one, who doesn't know me, and I'm the most respected kid in the entire town, and if I can help someone I help them, it's not like I need to think it over, and if another time I need help, so what, that person helps me, fair enough?" Riccetto was about to say something. "But why?" Amerigo interrupted, grabbing him by his jacket collar. "Why?" he asked, shaking his head, so convinced was he of what he was about to say, "wouldn't you do a favor for someone that asks? Because another time, like, to offer a comparison, you might be the one in need, am I right?" "Sure, you're right," said Riccetto, "but if I lose these two hundred, what am I going to eat tomorrow." Amerigo eased his grip on the other's collar; he put a hand on his forehead and shook his head hard, as if he couldn't find words to explain something so simple. "You haven't gotten what I'm trying to tell you," he said, and he started laughing. "Tomorrow," he went on, "fix a time to see me; what time can you make it?" "Dunno, at three," said Riccetto. "Three it is," said Amerigo, "outside Farfarelli's, OK?" "OK," said Riccetto. "Tomorrow at three, outside Farfarelli's," said Amerigo, raising his arms, "we meet and I give you back your money. How much have you got?" "Maybe four hundred," said Riccetto. "Let me see," said Amerigo, sinking his fierce grip into the other's shoulder again. Riccetto pulled out the few hundred-lire bills in his pants pocket; Amerigo took them and counted. Then he went back in the room without waiting to see if Riccetto was following. Caciotta was talking to the carter who was following the game. Amerigo reached between the backs of the seated players and put the money on the table, and lost again. He played another hand and lost again. And again no one said anything. After a minute or two Amerigo explained what had gone wrong to Caciotta and the carter. They stayed there for another half hour, then left, without anyone noticing.

In one direction the sky had cleared and a few dewy stars were twinkling, lost in the vastness, as in a boundless metal wall, from which the occasional weak puff of breeze slid down to earth. In another direction, turning around toward Rome, the weather was still bad, the clouds dense with rain and lightning, though on the horizon they were breaking up to reveal a scatter of lights. But right above the three boys, the sky stretched over Tiburtino as if over the top of a courtyard, with the moon leaning timidly on the gleaming edges of some wayward patch of vapor. In the Tiburtino streets, all rigorously alike, no one was to be seen, with just occasional traffic noise coming from the main thoroughfare. The three walked limply toward Via Tiburtina, through developments where sparse grass clung to beaten earth, and Caciotta hummed to himself while the other two dragged their pointed black-and-white, still soaking shoes, without saying a word. "Let's say so long," said Riccetto. Amerigo looked at him from his broad face, and as he leaned forward a little his jaw seemed pale and enormous in the light of the moon. He showed no expression, but the sullen eyes and the swollen mouth that split his features like a wound, more blue than red, left no doubt as to what he was thinking. "What's the point us coming to Via Tiburtina," said Riccetto, for the sake of saying something, "we're almost there, it's a couple of minutes, you can go alone." More than any real anger at being crossed, what screwed up Amerigo's eyes was the thought that anyone could be so reckless as to cross him. But Riccetto was the kind of guy who needed all this explained, which was going to take a lot of patience; Amerigo could handle it, though with such dark sullenness in his eyes it sent a shiver up your spine. He began all over with the best will in the world. "If we go back now," he said, "I'm sure of winning, I've understood the game, get what I mean?" Riccetto didn't answer; he looked at Caciotta, whose face in the cold air was white and purple as an onion. "Sure, but we'd need money," he said hoarsely. Amerigo looked at him impatiently and it seemed he was about to shake his head and click his tongue as if to say that no one in his place, let alone Amerigo himself, could ever be so dumb as to accept a remark like that. He leaned on the decrepit doorpost beside a silent door. "Give me another half a grand," he said, as if Riccetto had always admitted he had more money, "we'll win back everything we've lost and double it." His voice was still dull, in contrast with his body, which looked, in the doorway, like those enormous pigs they hang full-length from butcher's hooks. His eyes too had gone small and glazed like the eyes of a pig on a hook, and the grimace that crossed his handsome face showed his patience was running out. Eyebrows raised like a child, Riccetto murmured, "But I don't have anything left, not a lira."

Amerigo sat on the battered doorstep. "Maybe I'll do ten years' time for it, but tonight I've got to play," he said quietly. Riccetto thought to himself, "We're in the shit here," and said nothing, so as not to get him going. But after a short silence that was no doubt supposed to give force to his words, in a voice hoarser now, but louder, as if one quality were canceling the other, Amerigo started up again, from square one, with his more friendly approach: "I guess I've already done a few years inside!" "Where?" aside Caciotta, "Porta Portese?" "Right," said Amerigo. His face had darkened and his thick, wrinkled lips were trembling. "They jailed me for carnal violence," he said. "Damn, who was the lucky girl?" asked Caciotta. "A sheep," said Amerigo, despairing. "Shepherd saw me giving it one up the ass, fuck him, and reported me." Mouth hanging open, eyebrows drawn up, forehead knitted with youthful wrinkles under curls worthy of a statue, he seemed on the brink of tears. "Damn," he said painfully, "the beatings I got!" His voice had grown shrill, like a woman whining over some old injustice that still rankled. "The beatings," he repeated. "Here, look," he said, pulling up the shirt from the waist of his pants and showing his back, "you can still see the marks." "What did they do?" asked Caciotta. "The whippings they gave me, whippings, fuck them, and fuck them," said Amerigo grinding his teeth. "And look, the marks are still there," he repeated, pulling his shirt right up to his neck. His back was left bare, broad as a steel girder, shining pale blue under the moon. There were no marks at all to be seen on that smooth, sunburned expanse of flesh. Caciotta bent over him and searched diligently along the big, curved bridge of vertebrae suspended between the beltline of his pants and his neck, hidden under his shirt; after looking carefully he stood up and said, "Uh-huh." "See," said Amerigo with his mother's-tired voice. "Can't see a fucking thing," said Caciotta. "What do you mean?" said Amerigo, "Look closer." Caciotta bent over the big back a second time, and like it or not, he had to see something, given the grim look Amerigo had sent him, his face pained. "Christ," he said in a loud voice. Amerigo pulled down his shirt and, standing up, pushed it into his pants. The tearful mistiness about his eyes had evaporated and they were once again dry and naked in their dark brown hue. The wheedling and whining about having been whipped had brought up issues that now made it inevitable, as if by common accord, that Riccetto give way without further ado. "Let's go," said Amerigo, as if matters had been cleared up and he had finally been understood. Then, since Riccetto still kept mum, he went up to him and took his jacket lapels carefully between his fingers: "What's up, kid," he said, "let's go. You don't want me to lose my patience, do you?" he added with a look of despair, as if these were words he would have preferred not to say, hence the only person to blame was Riccetto. So they went back to the cardplayers and when they were outside on the steps, at a look from Amerigo, Riccetto pulled out another five hundred without a word. Inside everything was going on as before. No one had noticed they'd left and no one noticed when they came back. But before Amerigo could lose everything again, while he was intent on playing, Riccetto quietly stepped back through the watching crowd by the sink and slipped out the door.

And he did well, because he had barely turned out of the gate of Block IX, behind the porch, when the cops arrived. He had just enough time to hide around the corner. "Well, fuck him," he said aloud, almost singing, he was so glad not to have got himself caught; and he started running through the deserted streets between the tenements, down toward Via Boccaleone, and then onward, still running, along the road to Tor Sapienza. There wasn't a cloud in the sky now; to his left, lights were shining, pylons full of spotlights, the lights of the power station, while behind him, already far away, the new blocks of Tiburtino stood out against the black sky. Beyond, in the vast warmth of the night, gleamed the lights of the other suburbs, as far as Centocelle, Borgata Gordiani, Tor dei Schiavi, and Quarticciolo. Slowing down, half-dead from exhaustion, Riccetto reached Via Prenestina and waited for the bus to Quarticciolo. He pulled out the five hundred-lire bills he'd managed to save and chose the most crumpled one to give to the conductor.

"Now what?" he said when the empty bus set him down in Prenestino. He looked around, pulled up his pants, and because there was absolutely nothing for him to do, burst, philosophically, into song. An occasional tram came down Via Prenestina, stopped with a faint glimmer under a gnarled tree, circled around behind three or four decrepit houses and filthy patches of grass before stopping again on the other side. Meanwhile, the people who'd got off either rushed, breathing hard, toward the buses to outlying districts, parked in a row outside the lighted window of a miserable café, or walked slowly home to their beds in Borghetto Prenestino nearby, where the hundreds of small houses looked like little boxes or chicken coops, white like Arab houses, or black like country shacks, full of hicks from Puglia or Le Marche, Sardinians and Calabrians. They were youngsters and oldsters, coming home late, clad in rags and drunk, or walking out to the shanty-towns piled up in the building sites around the sloping side roads that overlooked Via Prenestina. Riccetto decided to buy himself three Nazionali, since he'd been dying for a smoke for quite a while: with a light step he crossed the small square and went into the café, counting out the cash. He came out with a cigarette glued to his lower lip and shrewd eyes looking about for someone with a light. "Got a light, kid?" he asked a youngster leaning limply against a post, smoking. Without a word the boy handed him his lighted cigarette. Riccetto thanked him with a cocky nod of the head, thrust his hands in his pockets, and went off singing up the leaden side street to where the tram passed.

All around there was scaffolding, apartment blocks under construction, then open fields, junkyards, land set aside for new buildings; from somewhere in the distance, maybe Marranella, beyond Pigneto, came the sound of a gramophone, amplified through a loudspeaker. On the grass beside Via Casilina, before you got to Marranella, there used to be a funfair, and Riccetto headed that way, hands in his pockets, and head thrown back from the passion he put into singing out loud to himself.

For a while along Via Acqua Bullicante the only people he saw were old folks hurrying home; but when he came to the lane that turns up between the low walls of two factories toward Borgata Gordiani, a line of kids appeared, coming toward him, taking up the whole street, at an easy pace, shouting and fooling around like a swarm of flies on a dirty table. One cuffing another on the head, pissing him off, another shadowboxing, punching the air left and right, then throwing a hook that had his eyes curdling with pleasure, another showing how tough he was, playing cool, hands idle in his pockets and face full of an irony that said, "Why make the effort when you're so puny"; some arguing, sneering, twisting their lips in disgust, stretching out their arms with a click of the tongue, or, in the heat of the argument, cupping chins in hands braced against their chests, staying that way for ages, throwing challenging looks at their opponents. The whole of Via dell'Acqua Bullicante stood still to admire them. Riccetto's hackles went up at once. Not that their fooling around was aimed at him: they wanted, if anything, to defy the world in general, that whole race of people who didn't know how to enjoy themselves the way they did. But Riccetto was riled that they were all strutting their stuff together while he was on his own, excluded for the moment from such a rascally bunch of friends, forced to stand there listening tamely while they raised hell. He started whistling as loud as he could, paying them no attention, going his own way; but he had hardly moved twenty paces more when he heard a voice whining from the ditch that gave on grimy vegetable plots below; hurrying over, he saw a boy, bare-chested, crouched in the grass.

"What's up," he said. But the boy just went on crying. "Hey, what's this about?" asked Riccetto. Getting closer he saw the boy was completely naked; thin and soaked in dew, he was down on his knees and whimpering like a little kid: "They took my clothes off me and hid them, fucking bastards." "Who did?" asked Riccetto. The boy got to his feet, face wet with tears and little dick poking out: "That lot," he whined. Riccetto ran back toward the group he had passed a few moments before.

"Whoa, guys," he shouted. They stopped and all turned round together. "Hey, was it you that hid that kid's clothes?" Riccetto asked, voice firm but still polite. "They're right nearby!" said one of the boys cheerfully, "he'll find them soon enough." Riccetto took a couple of steps back; he wasn't looking for a fight and neither were they; there was even a certain complicity: they were smart and sharp compared to that dumb crybaby. "Forget it, he's a slimeball," said another boy, tapping a finger against his nose. Riccetto shrugged, "OK, poor asshole," he said. But at this point his white-knight duties were done, and in fact he saw the slimeball climbing out of the ditch, pulling on his pants, a torn up T-shirt in his hand. Still, the other boys didn't move along; on the contrary, one of them was staring at Riccetto and laughing. "You looking at me?" Riccetto said. The boy had big chapped fleshy lips, a small hoodlum's face, thick curls crinkly as cabbage, on a slim neck. "You know me, or what?" asked Riccetto, who couldn't see him well against the light of a streetlamp. "Sure, I know you," the other laughed. "Lenzetta," he said, "in Villa Borghese, remember!" "Oh, sorry!" said Riccetto generously, recognizing the other and holding out his hand. "Where you going?" he asked. "Where do you think, we're hungry," said Lenzetta. The others laughed. "And you?" asked Lenzetta. Riccetto smiled a philosophical smile, pulled up his shirt collar, and pushed his hands deeper in his pockets. "What do I know," he said. "I'm still away from home, and the fuck if I'm going back." "Why's that?" asked Lenzetta, amused. "You want them to put me inside?" said Riccetto. "I was gambling in a place in Tiburtino when the cops came, and it'll be tough shit for the guys they picked up. Bastards. Caciotta was there too." "Who's Caciotta?" asked Lenzetta. "The guy who was with me in Villa Borghese . . . the redhead. Guess he'll be in a cell right now, poor fucker." "I've left home too," said Lenzetta. "Not going back. If my brother sees me he'll kill me . . ." "Kill you, my ass," said another, "we told you they picked him up Saturday night." "I know, I know," said Lenzetta, "well, there's always my mother at home, right, a plague on her, I can't stand her." "That's your fucking problem," said one of the group, laughing and raising a threatening hand, "mother at home and brother in the clink, a no-win situation, if you go home, you're fucked; if they put you inside, you're fucked; take care, my friend!" Everyone laughed. "Who gives a shit!"

said Lenzetta. Laughing and jostling each other, the ragged band climbed back up the hill toward Marranella. "Anyhow," one said, "Elina's not up for it tonight." "Who said?" asked another, scandalized, "She's always up for it, always." "Oh, come on," the first said, "she's got a belly big as a bathtub, she'll be at the hospital having the kid." "What do you mean, big," the other challenged, "she can't be more than four months gone." "Four months, my ass," said the other, "she already had a big belly on her when I fucked her in spring!" "Right, ten years ago," said Lenzetta, "but who cares anyway, you can cut my throat if we have a hundred between the five of us." "It'd hardly be the first time we went to her broke," one said. "Right, we say, Give us a fuck and we'll give you a hundred, we fuck, then we don't give her a lira." "Son of a bitch," yelled Lenzetta.

Gabbing away, they were almost in Marranella and had long since stopped thinking of Elina. You could hear the tinkling of the merry-go-rounds, but also a buzz of voices, the sound of heavy feet, further on, right at the main crossroad, where the tram stopped. Everyone was headed that way, like something had happened or there was a party to go to, despite how late it was. "Must be the circus, fucking hell," shouted one and started to run. "Yeah, really, the circus," said Lenzetta coolly, but he did speed up, lazily, in step with the others. You could see a bunch of people coming down Via Casilina, a dark crowd on the poorly lit potholes and cobblestones. When they reached the Due Allori cinema they stopped, a stippling of lights from the candles in their hands. "It's a fucking procession," said Lenzetta, disappointed.

Having arrived at a run, the boys stopped at the crossroads, not sure whether to go on to Prato, where the fairground was, and maybe the blond woman's shooting gallery would still be open, or to stay put and watch this lousy show at Marranella. Mockingly, they sat on the edge of the sidewalk between the legs of people crowding up to watch the procession; one boy sang out loud, one was giving little thumps to another who insisted on watching, others rolled around wrestling in the dust.

Meanwhile the procession was coming closer. "Shit," said Riccetto, "we'd have been better off staying in Prenestino." "And what would you have done there?" asked Lenzetta. "There was Elina, right?" said Riccetto slyly. The people in the procession were mostly stale old women with here and there a few old men or little boys; they were all holding small cardboard cones to protect their candles from the night breeze. Every now and then they would start singing, each as he or she felt. When they reached the crossroads they stopped and gathered on the sidewalk outside a pizzeria. Two youngsters dragged a small table against a flaking wall and an elderly man climbed on it and began to give a speech condemning the Communists and extolling the spirit of Christ.

Where Lenzetta, Riccetto and the others were sitting there was such a din you could barely hear the guy, who was speaking with a northern accent. "Will you listen to that!" one of them shouted. "You want to be an altar boy, hey, Mozzò," said Lenzetta. Mozzone said nothing, straining to hear. "What a way to speak!" he eventually said, voice soft with amazement. Riccetto nudged Lenzetta. "Hey," he said, "Me, I'm fed up already." "What did you expect?" said Lenzetta. "Let's go back down," said Riccetto, nodding in the direction of Prenestino. "You mad?" said Lenzetta. "I've got cash, what do you think," Riccetto explained, "but only for us two." Lenzetta shot him a glance, then looked around. "Wait," he said. The others were looking elsewhere. "Get up," he said, "and head down Acqua Bullicante, I'll catch up."

Riccetto got up and quietly slipped away from the crowd, who were watching the old guy and making comments; but after barely five minutes the man wound up his speech and the procession moved off again, singing, and turned down toward the main street. Lenzetta caught up with Riccetto, at a run. "The others?" asked Riccetto.

"We've ditched them," said Lenzetta, "they'll have gone to the fairground."

Talking away, they walked the whole of Via Acqua Bullicante again, as the amplified sambas from the fairground and the procession's hymn-singing faded behind. The only people around now were a straggler or two returning from Preneste or Impero to Borgata Gordiani, or Pigneto, or maybe a drunk rolling home singing the Red Flag one moment, the Royal Anthem the next.

They found Elina in the shadows, where she was queen, behind the dirty grass and garbage dumps where the trams turned; there were potholed side streets, a plaza dwarfed on one side by the immense shadows of two or three half-built tower blocks and on the other by a tower that was finished but still without its approach roads and courtyards, marooned amid weeds and crap. All its windows lit up, the huge box rose solitary into a sky where a few sad stars were faintly twinkling. Elina had holed herself up behind the block, near the fences and bushes that surrounded the lots, which were still little more than enormous garbage dumps, with a few shacks in or around and the occasional heap of rubble.

Lenzetta and Riccetto came up to the woman, who was short and plump as a salami, spent a while fixing a price, then, slipping through a wire fence, pushed in among heaps of soaking reeds.

They weren't long about it; as soon as they were out again, they wandered calmly down to the water fountain, in the middle of the plaza where the tram terminus was, and washed up a bit. Lenzetta knew where to sleep. In a field behind Gordiani, with a view of all the suburbs from Centocelle to Tiburtino, at the bottom of a vegetable patch soaked in dew, there were two huge rusty bins, dumped behind a fence along with other bits of scrap iron. They were big enough to kneel inside and as long a full-grown man. Lenzetta had put some straw in one of them and now he took out a bit and shifted it to the other. They lay down inside and slept till ten next morning.

Lenzetta hung around the area bordered by Via Tuscolana, Piazza Re di Roma, and Via Taranto, where there were a few local markets, a couple of barracks, and a couple of monks' soup kitchens. When he was living away from home he got by working a bit (as little as possible) maybe for a fishmonger or salesman, stealing occasionally from market stalls or in trams. When he was in the mood he would stay away from the center, ranging between the districts of Prenestina and Quadraro, carrying a tattered sack and looking for scrap iron or bits of lead in the garbage; but he didn't do this often, because bending down gave him a backache and his mouth would get so caked with dust he'd soon need a liter of wine to clean it up, which meant saying goodbye to half the money he'd grubbed together. Riccetto wasn't keen on the scrap-iron racket either, since aside from anything else it was kids' stuff; so they mainly only came out to the districts to sleep in the big bins and spent the day in Rome. Then, if one day they managed to get together enough cash for the next as well, the hell they were going to go on working and slaving away; they took the bus and went to Acqua Santa. They pushed behind a few scrawny bushes along the Appia Nuova, climbed up the slope, nearly knee-deep in dust, between quarries and caves, along ridges, across scorched fields, deep little gullies, along old cart tracks with stumps of towers, entering at last the boundless and rugged promised land that was Acqua Santa. The hope was that on some knoll, or where two rutted lanes met, they might come across a hooker, waiting for the fresh-faced kids of the shantytowns or the first public-housing projects that loomed behind; or maybe, lurking outside a cave, or among the blackberry bushes beside a stream, newspaper spread on the ground and gold-framed spectacles on his nose, there might be some fat German guy they could fleece. They'd look him over, acting like nothing was up, or maybe they'd start to take a pee, and he would follow them, up and down over the mounds and gullies till they reached the filthiest of streams, pretty much as Rome's great poet described:

> I felt that Kraut say right at my back
> Panting hard: "The devil, pretty boy,
> Don't run so fast, I'm whacked."*

One day the two pretty boys—all on their own, though—arriving at the stream by the red gate, found a young thing from Tiburtino,

---

*A satirical poem by Gioachino Belli (1791–1863), who wrote in the Roman dialect and is considered one of the finest Italian dialect poets. Pasolini frequently mentions him and draws on his work. In Belli's original, *frocio* was a pejorative word for a German, hence is translated here with "Kraut," though later *frocio* came to be used as a pejorative term for a gay man, its common sense in contemporary Italian. There was a tradition of gay German men coming to Rome to look for adventure.

who was none other than Alduccio. In good spirits, Riccetto quick-ened his step to go and shake hands. "Hey, cuz, what's up?" he said warmly, slipping off his clothes. Alduccio was lying in his underpants on the dirty grass in the thin shade of a stand of reeds. He spoke playfully: "Same old stuff," he said. "The more it goes on, the more you feel like saying fuck it all, and turning gangster."

"Damn," said Riccetto, peeling his vest over his glistening hair.

"Don't work and you don't eat, right, and where can you find work?" He was chewing gum with a resigned, disgusted look.

"Well," said Riccetto, picking up Alduccio's comic tone, "if we get hold of a Beretta we can start a gang." Alduccio gave him a look that said he wasn't joking at all. "Exactly," he said. Lenzetta, who couldn't bear not being involved in any conversation for more than a minute and had pricked up his ears on hearing the word "Beretta," said mock-ingly, "Forget the Beretta, a Cappella's what you want!"*

Riccetto and Lenzetta laid down with the other beside the stream. "Well," went on Riccetto, "news from Tiburtino?"

"What's to tell," said Alduccio, "I already said, same old stuff."

"Do you know that Caciotta, that lives in Block IX?" said Riccetto.

"Sure, I know him," Alduccio answered, "pretty well."

"What's he up to these days?" probed Riccetto. Alduccio's hand-some face broke into a smile and without a word he pushed thumb and index finger under his eyes and pulled down his cheeks. Which meant Caciotta was inside, in Porta Portese.

"Damn," muttered Riccetto, smiling to himself.

"They caught him gambling at Fileni's," Alduccio explained.

"I know, I know," said Riccetto slyly, "I was there." Alduccio shot him an interested look. "Amerigo is dead," he said. Riccetto pushed himself up on his elbows and looked the other in the eyes. The corners of his mouth were trembling as though in a faint smile of amusement;

---

*Cappella is, or was, slang for "foreskin," but the word is also very close to cappello, Italian for "hat." Lenzetta is at once suggesting that a hat is as important as a gun for a gangster, and that perhaps money could be come by more easily by soliciting sex than by engaging in armed robbery.

it was dramatic news, and he felt extremely curious. "What happened?" he asked. "He's dead, dead," Alduccio repeated, happy to be bringing unexpected news. "He died yesterday at the hospital," he added. That shitty evening Riccetto had sneaked out of Fileni's, Caciotta and the others had been caught but hadn't offered any resistance. Amerigo, though, first let two cops grab his arms and pull him outside, then as soon as he was on the balcony he smashed them against the wall and jumped the ten feet or so down into the yard. He twisted a knee, but managed to drag himself along the wall of the block; the cops fired and got him in a shoulder, and he kept going just the same and got as far as the riverbank, the Aniene. They just about had him, but despite all the bleeding and everything he jumped in the water to get across the river, maybe hide in the gardens on the other side then head toward Ponte Mammolo or Tor Sapienza. But right in the middle, where the water was fastest, he passed out and the cops got him and took him to the station, soaked in blood and slime, like a sponge; so then they had to take him to the hospital and keep him under guard. After a week his fever passed and he tried to kill himself, cutting his wrists with broken glass, only they saved him again; then about ten days before Alduccio and Riccetto met at Acqua Santa, he'd jumped from the window, on the second floor: he was at death's door for a week, until finally he made it to the boneyard.

"Funeral's tomorrow," said Alduccio.

"Fucking hell!" breathed Riccetto, shocked. To show that nothing surprised him and that his watchword was "Always mind your own fucking business," Lenzetta crooned,

Little clogs, little clogs...*

*Another sad love song, written by Giorgio Consolini (1920–2012) and performed by Claudio Villa, among others. The singer's girlfriend, Nina, is remembered for the sound of her *zoccoletti*, literally, "little clogs"; however, in Italian *zoccola* is slang for a slut or whore, and *zoccoletta*, the diminutive, would be "little whore"; so there's a certain ambiguity here that perhaps explains Lenzetta's enthusiasm for this song lyric, which is also sung by other boys later in the book.

and he sprawled out more comfortably on the grass with his big fresh turnip of a head cradled in his hands.

But Riccetto thought about it all for a while and decided it was his duty to go to Amerigo's funeral; it was true he'd barely known him, but Amerigo was Caciotta's friend, and then, in the end, he felt like going. "I'll come along to Pietralata tomorrow," he told Alduccio, "but don't tell anyone, I wouldn't like my father to find out."

Amerigo was laid out on the bed in his new blue suit, white shirt, and black shoes. They'd crossed his arms on his breast, or rather on the double-breasted jacket he'd been wearing with such pride the last couple of Sundays, parading his mean walk up and down Pietralata. He'd got the money from a robbery in Via dei Prati Fiscali, relieving an idiot of thirty thousand lire, more or less, with the added satisfaction of beating the hell out of him; then he bought his blue suit and wore it around in an even more ferocious mood than usual. You had to be pretty careful how you looked at Amerigo, and his local friends, who were cowardly and hypocritical with regard to him, had learned how to brownnose him without making it too obvious, but other kids who didn't know him, boys he met in Communist Party dance halls or maybe in a billiard room, had gone home with black eyes and bleeding gums and could count themselves lucky that Amerigo had been officially banned from carrying a knife. It was a suit with drainpipe pants and a short jacket with wide, round shoulders; he would wear it with a white shirt open at the top and hair greased back. Now, here on the bed, he'd let them cross his arms over the jacket like some sacrificial victim, but his collar was still roguishly unbuttoned, framing a face that had looked like death even when he was alive. The result was it looked like he had just fallen asleep, hence was still a bit frightening. When his nap was done, his patience would run out, and he'd bust the snout of whoever had taken the liberty of dressing him like that. He lay there grim and silent on a bed too small for him, basket of curly hair gleaming with grease on the grubby pillow.

Riccetto went into the small room on the ground floor of the block with some of his Tiburtino friends to see him. Outside the entrance to the building, which had lost its door and had stairways to the left and right, was a small crowd dressed in black: all the Lucchetti family had come to do their duty as relatives and principal players on this occasion, wearing their Sunday best, the tiny children and younger boys and girls in bright colors, the teenagers in outfits more suitable for the dance floor than a funeral. The neighbors, meaning those who lived in the same block, ten or a dozen to a room, so that there was a whole neighborhood's worth, stood to one side, and Amerigo's friends, all dressed to the nines, were even farther away: Arduino, who had lost his nose and an eye to a grenade when he was a child; the consumptive boy who lived in Block XII; then Carogna, Napoletano, Capece, and Signora Anita's boy, who played guitar and sang, especially those nights when they came back from a heist and stayed up late splitting the cash and quarreling or taking a walk in the mud beneath the fiery moon that shone over the shacks for the homeless. There were some younger boys too, leaning lazily against the wall, talking quietly to their friends, or watching the kiddies playing football a little way off in a clearing in the middle of Pietralata.

Riccetto and the others had hardly got inside the room where the corpse was before they wanted out; it was damp and dark as winter in there, and Amerigo's aunts and sisters were all so fat there was barely room to move. They took a quick look at the corpse and, a bit embarrassed because they hadn't done this since their First Communion, crossed themselves, then went back out into the street, where the men were talking. At the heart of the group, but withdrawn somehow, as if minding his own business, was Alfio Lucchetti, the youngest of the uncles, dark as Amerigo, with the same cheekbones and the same curly hair, but taller and leaner; this was the uncle who three years before had stuck a bayonet in the belly of the owner of the café at the tram stop, and now people said he was ruining himself over a prostitute he kept in Testaccio. Really, rather than actually talking to the others, he just said a couple of words now and then, with a brooding, meaningful expression, shaking his head, then letting things drop at once, as if not wanting to expose his life to all these people standing around. He looked away beyond the circle of heads around him, hands thrust in the pockets of his gray pin-striped pants under his black jacket, grinding his molars so hard his jaws blew out and sucked in, just like Amerigo used to, and he was so tall that if he reached up he could have touched the power line.

He stood there, calm and resentful, brooding, despite the others, over the secret that more or less everyone in the block had sensed: that behind Amerigo's death was a whole bunch of things whose grim light was reflected on every face here. Certainly it lit up Alfio's face, gray with stubble, and black under the roots of the hair that fell low on his forehead, his boyish neck emerging from the folded-down collar of his white shirt, and likewise the faces of the other uncles and cousins, absorbed in their sense of duty and the silent rancor that made them the most important people in Pietralata, determined not to speak out, to keep any comments on the state of affairs resulting from Amerigo's death to themselves, in the family, or, at most, to drop a half-truth, a vague word or two, full of menace. Among the many cagey faces, there was Arduino's, a black patch covering the scarred hollow of his missing eye, though not what was left of his nose, then the faces of Signora Anita's son, and Carogna and Capece, a hawkish greed in all their narrowed eyes, and, behind the solemnity, a flash of healthy beatitude, the contentment of a soldier taking a shower. Alduccio picked up the vague insinuations that Alfio and the other men were dropping. His face flooded with the wisdom of one who has understood and, twisting his mouth and hunching his head down between his shoulders, he muttered, "That's his fucking problem."

"Whose?" Riccetto asked, showing a rather naive curiosity at last. Alduccio didn't answer.

"Whose, Ardù? Hey, Ardù!" Riccetto insisted.

"The person who spoke," Alduccio conceded with distracted generosity. Riccetto immediately thought of Block IX and its gambling den and said no more. He looked at Alfio Lucchetti with supreme respect. The man had now taken a couple of steps away from the group and was standing there, silent and sure of himself, his hands deep in his pockets.

Inside, you could hear the women weeping. But the men gave no sign of being moved; if anything, stamped on the faces of the fresh-faced youngsters and the shrewder seniors, was a vague expression of amusement. No one in Pietralata felt pity for the living, it wasn't done; so how the hell could you expect them to feel anything for the dead?

The priest was in a hurry and didn't stop to speak to anyone. Behind him trotted two creatures, scrawny as kittens, culled from one of the houses standing here and there among the scorched fields and the dump at the far end of Pietralata, where some elderly peasants still hung on. They trotted in their surplices, fiddling with their censers, past the people scattered here and there among the blocks and the smaller houses under the fierce midday sun, walking, playing, yelling. A group of boys kicked a ball around as they followed the procession like a swarm of wasps, in their beggars' rags, and went on whooping long after they'd fallen behind, in the violet light; and at the café by the tram stop there was the usual mill of deadbeats you find this time of day. They were talking and yapping like dogs in the half-empty bar, or standing around outside, leaning against the doorposts or the wilting trees, faces charged with irony, thumbs thrust into their belt-less pants, pushing the crotch down to their knees; others hung around the courtyards, under filthy windows beside what was left of the shitholes sold brick by brick to the peasants during the war; and right now everyone was busy watching the funeral, from a distance. The priest went into the building, did what had to be done, then came out again pretty quickly, his two puppy dogs at his heels, followed by a crowd of women, and the coffin on the men's shoulders. They loaded it into a black car and the procession set off, shuffling slowly along Via Pietralata; they went by the café, delaying a bus caught at the stop; then by the open ground where two or three merry-go-rounds had been set up on the knolls; past the clinic, bare as a prison; the charred fields; the pink cottages; the hovels; a couple of factories that were in such a shambles they might have just been bombed; and arrived at the foot of Monte Pecoraro, near Via Tiburtina, where the abandoned quarries have left the hillside broken and jagged.

"What now?" said Riccetto to Alduccio, speaking softly amid

people slouching along in no particular order, some falling behind, others ahead, keeping pace with the car and the priest. "What do I know," said Alduccio, dawdling with his hands in his pockets under the flutter of his shirttails. They were taking it easy at the back of the procession, which was going slowly down the slope, but they were going even more slowly and had to hurry a bit from time to time to catch up; they walked hunched forward, troubled, as if their feet were hurting. "I had no idea," Riccetto said mournfully, "that funerals were so boring, but really, really boring." "No, right!" said Alduccio, throwing him a glance. As their eyes met and they looked at each other in all that somber silence, they suddenly wanted to laugh and had to turn away, tensing all the tendons in their necks to keep it inside and not make a spectacle of themselves. What with the butter-soft air and the sharp shapes of things and the warm breeze with its April languor, it felt like it should be a holiday, one of those first spring Sundays after Easter when people head for the beach. Even the traffic on Via Tiburtina seemed strangely silent, muffled somehow, like in a bell jar, under a sun that paled over the low walls and a gray waste of filth, but burned golden on the lower slopes of Monte Pecoraro. From the fort, a cheerful trumpet sounded the mess call.

Outside the café on the corner of Via Tiburtina, after a short delay and with the usual muddle, the procession dispersed. The hearse got into gear and, followed by a taxi carrying the most important Lucchettis, set off at speed to Verano.

5. HOT NIGHTS

A full belly does not believe in fasting.
—GIOACHINO BELLI

MEANTIME Lenzetta was hanging around waiting for Riccetto and Alduccio, sitting in the dust beside a low wall, all dressed up in his velvet pants and red-and-black American T-shirt that, as he saw it, amazed the fuck out of everyone in Marranella. He was soaked in sweat after kicking a ball around a bit with the boys who were still playing on the small field just below him between Via Acqua Bulli- cante and Pigneto. Above the wall, crouched on the corrugated iron roof of her home, which looked like a sheepfold, Elina was enjoying the view of the passersby and cradling a whining baby, her youngest, two rings of fake gold dangling from her ears. Lenzetta wasn't after her at all but likewise immersed in contemplation of life, just cursing Riccetto from time to time for being late. But he was fairly cheerful. Curly head resting on the flaking masonry, he was singing and sing- ing with such passion, head slowly swaying left to right and right to left, as to bring down occasional flecks of dust and stone. He kept his eyes half closed and, since he was singing softly, as if confessing him- self, or just wanting to offer a little example of what he could have done if he wanted, someone even just a few steps away would have seen only his mouth opening and closing and the tendons in his neck stretching to breaking point at his throat.

Again and again, he would break off, right in the middle of a long note, to shout something at the kids playing football, panting and embattled; one boy, barely thirteen, was playing with a cigarette stub in his mouth, while another, exhausted, was lying down taking the piss out the others still running around.

"Hey, weaklings!" called Lenzetta, not even bothering to raise his voice much. "If you can't even stand up, leave us alone," shouted back the goalkeeper, leaning forward between the posts with nothing to do, his tattered shorts half-unbuttoned, cupping his mouth in gloves found on some dump site. The kid who'd been lying in the middle of the field came up the road, cursing football and the others, who got so worked up over it; he yanked up his pants, pulled out his filthy vest so it flapped down on his butt cheeks, and went toward another boy who was walking toward him, happy as a lark, with a bottle of milk in his hand. They started fooling around with some marbles, not far from Lenzetta, beneath the spot where Elina sat on her metal roof etched against the white sky like a Madonna in a procession. "Fuck them," Lenzetta fumed for the nth time, meaning Riccetto and Alduccio; but for all his irritation, he couldn't shake off his good mood; he just didn't feel like giving a damn about anything. The new arrival, who chattered away cheerfully as he played, even when he got angry with his friend for trying to cheat, seemed like a nice kid, and Lenzetta started to take his side. The other boy immediately turned goody-goody and started playing fairly, without trying to trick the smaller kid. They crouched down, took aim, and wham, pressed down under the palm of a hand, the marble shot into the hole. Lenzetta watched with a paternal eye. When the smaller kid won, he did a sort of dance around his milk bottle left lying on its side on the ground; then he crouched down again, little legs spread wide, sitting on his heels, shooting at the hole.

"Winning, are we, my little pup?" said Lenzetta, with a patron's complacency. The other boy was resentful, and, playing meaner now, started to win. "Whoa, what's up? Why do you let yourself get beat, little pup?" said Lenzetta jokily. Right then an empty hearse drove by at top speed, racing beneath the big housing blocks, then along the muddy hedges of Acqua Bullicante.

"Farewell, my lovely, farewell!" yelled Lenzetta, after the corpse it was going to pick up; and it made him think of Riccetto, who had also gone to a funeral. "Asshole," he said, flushing with anger.

Lenzetta had left home for fear of his bigger brother, and he was damn right to be afraid, since he'd done something that, thinking about it, he could scarcely believe, something he could have kicked himself for. Not that he'd behaved badly, as he saw it, it wasn't something morally wrong... Yeah! Morality! What the fuck did he or his brother care about morality! No, it was a question of honor, and to be hand-on-heart honest, not a minor thing. What the fuck had got into Lenzetta's head that night... You can only suppose he must have been in a daze from the beatings he'd got in the detention room, and again when they put him inside... As they were taking him to the jail—to Regina Coeli, not Porta Portese, because though he still looked like a kid, he was past eighteen now—he'd scratched his curly mop and thought, "Now I'm really in the shit?" And so he was, because one of the first things he'd heard as soon as he was in there, from a guy who looked like Lazarus fresh from his coffin, was, "What a cute little ass you've got on you, kid." But as luck would have it, his brother, Lenzetta the first, was one of the most important thieves in Regina Coeli; and out of respect for his brother, Lenzetta the second was respected too, cute though he was. A few weeks later he was out with a suspended sentence and went back to Tor Pignattara, where the first thing his mother said was, "Don't work and you don't eat, OK!" "Give me a break for a bit at least!" he said, cupping his chin in his hands, "I'm barely out of the slammer!" And that evening, off he went to have a bit of fun with his friends at the Green Carpet Café, also known as the Back Stab Café, where the self-declared mean boys of Marranella hung out, a bunch of sixteen-year-olds who'd only just started going to bars and playing billiards. He fooled around a while with them, showing off because he'd been in Regina Coeli, something that obviously demanded a little respect; they all drank a little wine and set off, totally smashed, to hit the sack.

Lenzetta slept with his big brother in a small, windowless room, one in a bed as old as a gondola, the other on a camp bed. Toward midnight, unable to sleep and wired up from the wine, Lenzetta threw off the old patched-up sheets and very quietly approached big Lenzetta, fast asleep in the other bed. "Turn over and stick your ass up," he muttered, looking at him. Blind drunk, Lenzetta climbed on top of his brother and slowly tried to have him. Big Lenzetta woke with a start, realized what was going on, and gave his brother a shove that flattened him against the wall, then dozed off again.* The following morning, going down into the street, Lenzetta saw his brother waiting for him on his scooter. "Climb on," he told him. Reluctantly, Lenzetta obeyed, and his brother set off at speed, weaving through the early morning traffic across Marranella, then cutting through the alleys of Tor Pignattara, since you couldn't use the main streets at that hour because of the market; outside town, he accelerated to forty, heading for Mandrione, went straight through it, and racing along like a hoodlum, finally arrived at Acqua Santa. Not that he got off or even slowed down to tackle the tracks there, deep in dust; he pushed on in fourth and only when they were in an area of meadows and caves, under a crumbling tower, did he turn off the scooter, get down, and say to Lenzetta: "Get your fists up." They fought for a half hour until finally, utterly exhausted, Lenzetta managed to escape.

Riccetto and Alduccio were dragging their heels because they'd walked all the way from Pietralata; now they were shuffling along on feet that hardly seemed to belong to them, their backs stiff, on legs that felt like putty, though never forgetting to make a kind of boast of their wise-guy weariness. They must have walked at the very least three miles, from Via Boccaleone, along the Prenestina, to Via Acqua Bullicante, from a field full of shit to a collection of hovels, from an apartment block high as a mountain to a rusty little factory. And it

---

*In the final version of the text, after Pasolini's publisher had insisted he make changes to avoid censorship, Pasolini changed this scene to the following: "Toward midnight, unable to sleep and wired up from the wine, Lenzetta threw off the old patched-up sheets and began to sing. His brother was sleeping like a log, mouth half-open and sheets crumpled between his legs, but after a while he started to show signs of irritation, until suddenly he turned over, pulling all the sheets under his stomach. Completely drunk, Lenzetta went on singing at the top of his voice. His brother woke with a start and said, 'Hey?' 'Fuck off,' answered Lenzetta, getting to his feet. His brother realized what was going on, gave him a push that flattened him against the wall, and dozed off again." In this version, however, it is hard to understand why Lenzetta's brother would react as violently as he does the following morning; for this reason the translator has decided to return to Pasolini's original text.

still wasn't over, the longest stretch was just beginning; they had to walk the whole length of Via Casilina. Lenzetta, fresh as a daisy, after giving the two kiddies a piece of his mind and having to hear himself called a good-for-nothing and an asshole for his trouble, was walking ahead at a good pace with the others limping behind, pissed off with their sore feet and their tiredness.

It was Lenzetta had found the place in Via Amba Aradam, and it was really neat. A bit out of the way, right where the road met Viale di San Giovanni, along the green and brown city walls, amid gardens packed with sickly plants and posh old villas in need of repair. At the top of an embankment was a long line of low buildings, roofed with rusty metal sheeting that glittered in the last rays of the sun. Right at the end, at the corner, was the smallest of the workshops, but beside it was a big, fenced-off yard full of iron. There was a deep hush all around, but from inside the huts, or from among the heaps of scrap in the storage yards, you could hear maybe a worker calmly whistling away, or someone calling and another answering. The three delinquents walked past in single file, humming a little, whistling a little; only when they were a little farther down, beneath the ruins, did they risk a few muttered remarks: "Damn," said Riccetto, "what a haul of axle shafts!" "What did I tell you?" demanded Lenzetta triumphantly. "OK, but it's still daytime," said Riccetto, to stop him gloating. "Then, out here, without a three-wheeler, we can't do fuck all." "Yeah, a three-wheeler! Where you going to get a three-wheeler, dumbo?" grumbled Lenzetta, screwing up his mouth. "Let's go down to Marranella and ask Remo, the ragman," said Alduccio, then turned sour when the others weren't interested. Lenzetta stared at him, screwing up his forehead in a look of pity, then clicked his tongue and didn't even bother answering. "Dick!" he suddenly said, "you want us all in the hospital? Here to Marranella, on foot again . . . and back! What have you got for a brain?" "Who said anything about walking again, who ever suggested that!" said Alduccio, flushed with disgust." "Watch this!" "What?" asked Lenzetta, beginning to get interested. Riccetto listened, taking it in. "We get together a bit of cash, OK?" hissed Alduccio. "Oh, right!" said Lenzetta, disappointed. "Let's go!" said

Alduccio. And without looking back he set off for San Giovanni. "Where's this spastic going?" said Lenzetta, hurrying after him with Riccetto, "Is he crazy or what?" "He's not crazy," said Riccetto, "not crazy at all."

It didn't take much to figure out what Alduccio was planning. But when they arrived in the plaza outside Porta San Giovanni, there wasn't a soul in sight. Or rather, there were a couple of people on the benches along the parapet that looks out over the big drop beneath the city walls, but they were not the kind of people our three stooges were after. There was a fat woman with folds of flesh pushing from under her cream silk dress, lips sugary from the buns she'd been eating, and a boiled fish of a face, and beside her an ugly little thing, her husband maybe, who had a fried fish of a face, poor guy, struggling with a hangover. And here and there a few kiddies and a few babysitters. Beyond the low parapet that served as a sort of terrace offering a view of the Tuscolano district, beyond the tennis courts and the areas of bare earth, a warm red evening was falling, setting alight the windows on pale blue apartment blocks, transforming the scene into a Martian landscape; meanwhile, on this side of the wall, where Alduccio and the others had gone to lie down, the gardens of San Giovanni stretched away in an equally melancholy scene of little flowerbeds and low trees, just grazed by a last ray of sunshine that struck the high loggia and big rooftop statues of the cathedral full on and tinged the red granite of the obelisk with gold.

Disappointed, and flaunting the fact with grimaces and sneers, the delinquents lounged on the wall. Lenzetta was lying on it, face up, hands under his dirty neck, singing; Riccetto was sitting with his legs dangling over the other side; only Alduccio was on his feet, hip and elbow leaning against the wall, legs nervously crossed. He was the only one not hamming his boredom, still hoping something might turn up. He stood there, one hand thrust in his pocket looking like the sheriff's son, big lips dark with black down, bright, brooding eyes like two mussels dripping lemon.

And faith was rewarded. Lenzetta and Riccetto had suddenly decided to go and get a mouthful of water at the fountain, taking it slowly to kill some time, but as they came back toward the parapet, they found Alduccio looking chipper and ready to go. "We're off, let's go," he said. He slipped a hand in his pocket and brought out three crumpled hundred-lire notes. "Someone came by," he explained, "and just gave me them, you know, out of kindness, I guess. For a little feel," he added cheerfully. The others didn't wait around to hear more; stuff happened. There was no time to waste; talking loudly and shouting so that people would notice, they headed for the tram stop, just below them at Porta San Giovanni, and not half an hour later were back in Marranella.

Remo the ragman was hopeless. He'd taken his three-wheeler home, it was in a courtyard crawling with people, in Pigneto, and he'd gone to the bar. He was sitting at a worm-eaten table, red as a lobster under a thick growth of black-and-white beard, face bloated like he had gas not blood under his skin. He was talking to a little old man who was lean as a post and still had his yokel's accent a century after moving to Rome; there was a third man between them, but you couldn't see his face since he'd fallen asleep slumped over the table and looked pretty much like a heap of rags. Lenzetta stood at the door and cast a trained eye around the room; he spotted Remo at once and, soft and sly, said, "Hey, Remo, have you got a moment?" Remo broke off his intellectual discussion with the old guy. "Pardon me, maestro," he said, "let me hear what this little asshole is after." The other made the face of someone suddenly left all alone and with a bob of his Adam's apple downed a gulp of wine. Outside, on the broken strip of sidewalk by the tram tracks, the other two were waiting." "Meet my friends," said Lenzetta, growing shrewder by the minute, face flushed. "My pleasure," said all three, shaking hands. "Remo," said Lenzetta piously, getting straight to the point, "you're going to have to do us a favor." "Of course," said the other, ironic and affable at the same time. "You're going to have to lend us your three-wheeler, if you can, eh!" Remo didn't say yes or no; he'd seen it all at once and done his sums even faster: his price for lending the three-wheeler, as a favor, was that they would have to sell the loot to him, and he would fix the price. With a good-buddy smile he pulled out his papers and, licking and spitting, began to roll himself a cigarette, but slowly and taking care no one bumped into him, since with its back-and-forth of cars and people the intersection there, in Marranella, where Via Acqua Bullicante met the Casilina, was busier than Via Veneto.

It must have been eleven or eleven thirty when Riccetto and the others, taking turns pedaling the three-wheeler—one on his back in the box, legs dangling over the side panels, the other jogging along beside with one hand on the saddle—finally reached their destination, dead tired, having done the whole of the Casilina all over again.

Hard by the wall and the villas, their masonry fancy as a family tomb or a beach pagoda, stuff the rich had built themselves in Mussolini's time before Riccetto could have known anything about it— not that he knew much about it even now—rose a moon big as an oil drum, to throw some light. Alduccio waited outside at the bottom of the embankment with the three-wheeler; Riccetto and Lenzetta got into the yard through a hole in the fence near the workshop, worming their way on their stomachs over sticks and dry, flattened hogweed. As soon as they had slithered through and pulled themselves up, like flattened roaches, on the other side, taking a good look around, Lenzetta couldn't resist a rhetorical flourish: "This is an iron paradise we're in," he said. The faces of the two gangsters were tense with excitement and fear, though the latter emotion was no more than a sensible professional concern, particular in Lenzetta's case, since he considered himself the boss, at least for this job. Without wasting another moment, he whispered, "Off we go, then." And when Riccetto hung back a little, ears tensed like a dog's to check that there were no strange noises, Lenzetta got mad: "Hey, dreamer," he said, "come on." He went to what looked like the best of the piles, inspected it, picked something up, examined it in the moonlight, dropped it again, and started moving around like a ghost between the other piles. Riccetto followed, checking things himself, moving noiselessly. Ignoring the heaps of tires and wheels and other things that didn't interest them, they found the good stuff in the middle of the yard and began to shift it. First, one piece at a time, they heaped everything near the hole, then Riccetto went through the hole, and Lenzetta passed him everything from inside. When it was all out, Lenzetta followed, and together, fast as possible, they scurried down the embankment to the three-wheeler, then from the three-wheeler back up the embankment, again and again, necks sore and backs stiff with the effort, red as peppers. Alduccio could scarcely believe his eyes as the haul of car batteries, bronze cogwheels, iron piping, and axle shafts piled up before him. At the end there was even a hundredweight of lead; he helped load it up, placing the pieces in the bottom of the box as the others came and went. "There's room for more," he said when they came back from the last trip. "Put this in!" said Lenzetta, oozing complacency; but he had barely spoken before his eyes settled on Via Amba Aradam, and clouded over. Fooling around by the three-wheeler, the others fell silent. Coming toward them along the road was a figure in a white T-shirt. As he got closer they could see he was a tubby teenager, face smooth as a piggy bank and dumb eyes; Lenzetta, seeing he was a rich kid, a pampered student, got his mojo back and, staring hard at him with eyes that had been melting with fear, said, "What do you think you're looking at?" "Nothing," said the other, walking on briskly, as if this was the most natural of polite exchanges at this time of night in this situation.

But looking at the two small round shoulders hurrying away, Lenzetta wouldn't let it go: "Hey, Tubs, if you don't see anything, you don't say anything, because if you do, I'll make you see stars."

The other didn't reply. But when he was at a safe distance he half turned and yelled, "Thieves!"

"That guy's going to blab," said Alduccio in a frightened voice, all his confidence gone. "Get moving, Ardù," said Lenzetta, equally crestfallen, "wait for us outside the hospital." And he set off running after the fat boy while Alduccio started pedaling in the other direction and Riccetto didn't know which one to follow. The fat boy, who had no illusion that Lenzetta was coming to say sorry and make up, started running for all he was worth along the walls of Porta Metronia. At this point Lenzetta turned around again and went back to where Riccetto was waiting for him and together they set off after Alduccio, who was giving it all he had, covered in sweat, face drained of blood from the effort. They took turns, running and pedaling, until they reached Via Appia Nuova. "Goddamn," said Lenzetta, collapsing on his back in the middle of the road, right on the tram tracks.

He lay there, legs spread and hands on his chest like a corpse. "If I do five more yards I'll drop dead," he yelled.

The others laughed, left the three-wheeler, and did the same, rolling around on the flagstones of the Appia under the young trees planted in two interminable rows down the middle of the road.

"Did you wet yourself, or what, hey, Lenzé?" shouted Riccetto, with his big head between the wheels of the bike. There was hardly anyone around at that hour, just a few kids on scooters who'd taken their girlfriends out to Acqua Santa.

Lying in the middle of the road, watching the couples pass, they yelled, "Get out of here!" or, "Don't listen to him!"

A soldier with a bedraggled slut holding on to his pants on the pillion wanted to sound smart and in a vaguely Neapolitan accent yelled, "Ah, give us a break!"

The three reacted like someone had stuck a pin in their butts, propping themselves up on their elbows in the dirt: "Hey clodhopper, come to Rome to get civilized, did you?" yelled Alduccio.

"See that?" shouted Riccetto with a travel-guide intonation, hands cupped around his mouth, "that's the Basilica of San Giovanni!"

"Still sending smoke signals in your neck of the woods, are you?" yelled Lenzetta, laying it on, and getting to his knees.

"Let's go," said Alduccio when they'd calmed down a bit, "or are we planning to spend the night here?"

Lenzetta got to his feet and lit a cigarette.

"Give me a smoke," said Alduccio, setting off. After a few drags Lenzetta grumpily passed him the fag and Alduccio, puffing away, had barely turned the pedals a couple of times when, *k-rak*, *screeeech*, *thud*, the front wheel jammed in the tram track and buckled over.

What's it matter, nothing! A joke. After all, how far was it from here to Marranella? And then it wasn't like Riccetto and Lenzetta had done a lot of walking that day. While Aldo, now thoroughly pissed off and vicious, stood guard by the three-wheeler and the stuff they'd heaped on the sidewalk of a road that crossed the Appia a bit farther along, Riccetto and Lenzetta, one right behind the other, walked back to Marranella and went to the carter's. Which was closed. "Fuck the bastard!" said Lenzetta, grinding his teeth and cursing the carter who'd gone God knows where to do God knows what.

"Like that, is it? He's closed now, is he?" said Riccetto vindictively, "let's teach him a lesson." To tell the truth it was past midnight; but they didn't give a damn; they went into the carter's yard and took his best cart.

"It's not like we're not going to bring it back tomorrow, is it?" said Lenzetta, pleased, aside from anything else, to have a clear conscience about it.

On the Appia where they'd left Alduccio, there was no one to be seen. But just before they reached Via Camilla, a shadow came toward them, gradually taking the form of a lean old man with a rag of a hat on his head; in one hand he held an axle shaft, which, upon seeing the two boys, he tried to hide.

Lenzetta flushed turkey red and, skipping any pleasantries, went straight to the point: "Hey, maestro," he said, "where'd you find that axle?" Riccetto waited with his hands on the raised handles of the cart.

The old guy took on a shrewd, secretive attitude that sharpened his white face beneath the floppy folds of his hat. "I'm hiding it," he said with a wink, "because there's a security guard wanted to arrest your friend. I helped him, but maybe the guard has gone to call someone."

"Well, fuck you," thought Lenzetta. Still, you never know, and he set off running to the place where they had left Alduccio, Riccetto following and the old man tagging along behind.

But dummy Alduccio wasn't there. They looked inside the gates, beside the shop shutters: "Ardo, Ardo!" they called. Finally Alduccio came running out of a dark alley where he'd gone to hide.

"Did the cops show?" asked Riccetto.

"No idea," said Alduccio, "I went straight down the alley." The boys stopped the debrief and pretended they believed the old guy. He was lurking close by, legs set apart, brazen-faced, the axle still in his hand. Smiling, his lips drew back and were sucked into his cheeks between toothless gums.

"Let's load up, come on," said Riccetto, eager to be off. While Alduccio was dragging the three-wheeler into the alley to leave it somewhere safe, Riccetto and Lenzetta began to load the haul onto the cart with the old man's help. When it was all on, Riccetto winked at Lenzetta, who turned to Aldo and in a thoughtful voice said, "Hey Aldo, you go ahead with the cart; if they see us all together they'll catch on." With a bit of grumbling Aldo reluctantly obeyed; sullen and chary, he started pushing the cart, leading the way.

The others followed, at a distance, ready to shoot off down a side street and dump him in the event of trouble. Lenzetta looked at Riccetto from a flushed face, and with a complacent grin and a nod toward Alduccio said, "Go for it, slave." The joke had Riccetto grinning too and, imagining himself one hell of a guy in partnership with another hell of a guy, his whole face lit up. The old man hurried to keep pace with them, dragging his canvas shoes on the sidewalk. Under his left arm, held tight in his armpit, he carried a rolled-up sack, which gave him a jaunty, almost sporty look. "Where you going with that sack?" Lenzetta asked, if only to have something to say to the guy, while Riccetto sniggered quietly behind. "I'm going to steal cauliflowers to feed five hungry mouths," said the old man. "You've got five boys?" asked Lenzetta. "No, five girls," said the old man. Lenzetta and Riccetto pricked up their ears. "And how old would they be?" asked Riccetto casually, to stake out the territory. Lenzetta in the meantime was walking with more conviction, like a donkey that smells home. "One twenty, one eighteen, one sixteen, and two still small," said the old man looking dumb, but leading them on.

Riccetto and Lenzetta exchanged glances. They walked on a bit, then Lenzetta gave Riccetto a quiet nudge with his elbow and stopped to take a pee.

Riccetto stopped too, standing beside Lenzetta, while the old guy went on at the same pace for a few yards before slowing down.

"Let's dump Arduccio," whispered Lenzetta, speaking fast.

Riccetto was upset. "How you going to do that?"

"Damn, make an excuse, come on," said Lenzetta impatiently.

Riccetto said nothing for a moment, then, as if he'd had an idea, said, "I'll handle it," and, buttoning up fast, was about to run after Aldo, who was now only a shadow, way ahead. But Lenzetta held him back: "Get him to give you some money as well," he whispered.

"OK, I'll handle it," Riccetto repeated, and ran off.

Lenzetta, sorting out his fly with worldly panache, caught up with the old guy while keeping an eye on what the other two were doing up ahead, under a big piece of scaffolding near the first open ground of Acqua Santa.

You could see that Riccetto was saying yes and Alduccio was saying no, then Riccetto yes again, Alduccio no again. But after a few moments Riccetto came running back, while Alduccio bent between the handles of the cart to resume his pushing.

"We told him to go on alone to Marranella," Riccetto felt he should explain to the old guy, "cause if they see all three of us together they might catch on."

"Good thinking," said the old man.

They'd reached Acqua Santa now; to the right was all deserted grassland and streams, to the left you turned into Via Arco di Travertino, heading straight to Porta Furba, and from there to Mandrione and Marranella.

Toward the end of Via Arco di Travertino two big huddles of ramshackle dwellings offered a magnificent sight to anyone walking by. A whole bunch of pink and white hovels, with shelters, huts, store sheds, and gypsy caravans deprived of their wheels, were all jumbled up together, some scattered across the fields, others clustered against the great walls of the aqueduct in the most picturesque disorder.

One of these dwellings, down the embankment from the road and slightly nicer than the others, had a leafy branch hung by the front door beside a sign where, in childish lettering, someone had written, "Wine." From a crack under the door you could see a light was still on. "It's open," said Lenzetta to Riccetto, and he gave a quick look around to check all was safe. Riccetto was ready with a wink, patting his pocket, almost on his prick. "You in a hurry to lift these veggies, maestro?" asked Lenzetta.

"No big hurry, no," said the old guy amenably.

"Then if you like we can come and give you a hand, if you don't mind, eh!" said Lenzetta.

"Not at all," said the old guy, "a pleasure."

"Yeah, right," thought Lenzetta. And out loud: "Would you be up for a drop of wine first, maestro? Oil the old joints a bit before the damp out there in the fields."

The old guy was only too pleased and his eyes shone with slyness, since for all he was playing the asshole, he hadn't entirely given up hinting that they were all on the same side. In any event, before accepting, he went through a few polite motions: "No need to trouble yourselves, though," he said, shifting his sack from one armpit to the other.

"No trouble at all," said the two of them, setting off at a run down the embankment, and since the old guy was coming down more slowly, Lenzetta muttered to the wall of the little tavern, "It's a tough life when you have delicate feet."

Five minutes later the two delinquents were already drunk. They started talking God and religion, the old guy their audience. Flushing with pleasure at the thought of his own originality, Riccetto asked Lenzetta a question, and Lenzetta, for the sake of the performance, listened carefully. "Hey," Riccetto said, "tell me something, do you believe in Maria, the one they call the Madonna, you know?"

"How should I know," Lenzetta said promptly, "I never saw her!" And he looked cheerfully toward the old guy.

"Well now, there are the facts," said the oldster, "that prove the Madonna exists."

But there was only one detail of the story that interested Riccetto. Spreading his fingers over his lips, he confided, "You do know she was a virgin and had a kid."

"Christ," said Lenzetta, turning redder than he already was and stretching his hands toward his friend, "you think I don't?"

"Do you believe in her, maestro?" Riccetto turned to the old man to pursue his inquiry. The old guy put on a long face, head hunched between his shoulders: "Do you, kid?" he asked, avoiding the question. Altogether pleased with himself, Riccetto launched into the subject, "You have to look at it from different points of view... as a human woman she could have existed, yes... from the point of view of holiness and virginity it might well be she didn't... The holiness could turn out true, but the virginity, no! OK, they've invented the stuff of artificial kids in test tubes, but even when a woman has a kid with a test tube she doesn't stay a virgin, does she... Then there's faith in Christ, in God, in the whole lot of them... And if you start reasoning with faith then you believe it, the Madonna being a virgin, but scientifically, myself, I don't think you can prove it..." He looked at the others with supreme smugness, as he always did when he repeated this spiel that he'd picked up from a guy in Tiburtino, and he looked ready to thump anyone who tried to contradict him. But Lenzetta grabbed the edge of the table with both hands and began to go "Pah, pah, pah," like so many puffs of steam escaping from under a saucepan lid.

"You sound like a movie director," he said, struggling not to laugh out loud.

"Ignorant dickhead," said Riccetto, feeling offended, and rightly so.

"Ah, let's have ourselves another half liter," yelled Lenzetta, offering his hand, "are you on?"

But Riccetto gave the hand a small slap: "I'll spit in your eye, damn it!" he said.

Lenzetta opened his arms wide: "What do you want to be talking about Jesus Christ and the Madonna for when you're hungry," he said, his face like a pork chop. Then, looking Riccetto in the eyes, he burst into even louder laughter: "And what do you want to drink milk for, when you've always drunk the pure water of the streams! And the sewers!"

"Ah, shut up," said Riccetto, "Born flat-footed for a career in begging, that's you!"

But Lenzetta was still staring him in the eyes, until, struck by an idea that brought on another fit of laughing, he waved both hands in front of Riccetto, fingers tight together, and yelled, "Remember when you used to go hunting for empty cans and sell them for pennies, for Christ's sake!"

Now Riccetto couldn't help laughing either. Lenzetta was almost choking. He got to his feet to calm down. "Don't you remember," he went on, "when you'd go to Maternity, and they'd line up the hungry hobos, and you'd get two or three cans off them…" he imitated a woebegone Riccetto getting the hospital porters to give him a can of soup, "you'd eat one, and the others you'd hang on to and go sell them to other hungry hobos like yourself."

That had both of them absolutely cracked up laughing. Lenzetta slipped, and as he suddenly shifted his weight, choking with laughter, there was a sharp crack at his feet under the table. Riccetto looked down and saw Cappellone's Beretta on the brick floor; it had fallen from under Lenzetta's pants. "Fucking son of a bitch!" he thought. "It must have been Lenzetta who took my shoes at Villa Borghese." Lenzetta bent down fast and got the gun back in his belt.

The old guy had the look of someone who's just had his ass kicked and, turning round, sees that the guy who's kicked him has twisted his foot and is howling with pain.

"You don't have a couple of photos of your daughters?" Lenzetta asked him, cheerful as ever. If they're ugly, he thought, we'll make you pay for the wine and skedaddle. Face drawn and bloated with drink, under a light bulb smothered in fly shit that turned him white, the old guy pulled out his wallet and, after looking through it with filthy fingers, one compartment after another, showed them a snap of a little girl dressed for her First Communion.

"That's what's she like now?" asked Riccetto, still annoyed.

"No, no! Not exactly!" said the old man, and started rummaging in his wallet again. He couldn't resist making the mistake of showing them his identity card where he was all spick-and-span, with a black jacket, a collar, and a Valentino look on his face. Bifoni, Antonio, father: Virgilio, deceased; born Ferentino, 11/3/1896. Otherwise the wallet contained a few lira coins, a Communist Party card, two applications for benefits, and his jobless card. Finally he pulled out the other photos. Lenzetta and Riccetto dived on them.

"Wow, what pretty things!" breathed Riccetto in what was more mime than speech.

"This one's mine," said Lenzetta, also speaking in a low voice and turning his back to the old guy, "you take the other."

To get where they were going from the dive meant walking to Porta Furba, turning down toward Quadraro, cutting through a scattering of isolated houses, not much more than huts, which brought you to a field with a chalk track on one side and more fields and meadows on the other, then a stand of pine trees and a villa in the distance.

There was a stink of pulped straw and manure and a rich smell off the fennel plants that you could see stretching away in a green cloud, with lettuces on the other side of a sagging fence, seen between the breaks of a soaking hedge of bamboo that ran alongside it.

"This way," said the old guy, with a werewolf face, moving hunched and stealthy to where the wire fence ended in a tangle and another fence made of wet, uneven boards began. Finally they reached the gate where there was kind of passage, a gap, hidden by thorny twigs and a few canes, between this and the wooden fence. On his knees in a shallow ditch, in among ribwort and hogweed, mallow and chard, all soaked with dew, the old man began to fiddle about to widen the gap. Then they slipped through into the field.

All bathed in moonlight, it was so big you couldn't see the fences at the other end. The moon was now at its zenith and had shrunk somewhat, as if didn't want to have anything more to do with the world, absorbed at it was in contemplating what lay beyond. All it was willing to show the world now was its butt, and from that silvery behind poured down a splendid light that flooded everything. It gleamed at the bottom of the field, on the peach and cherry trees, the willows, the philadelphus and elderberry bushes, scattered here and there in hard clumps, at once contorted and airy in their silver dusting. It came down skimming across the ground, releasing showers of light, or coating the plants with brightness: the curved crinkly surfaces of chard and lettuce, half in the light, half in the shade, and the yellow patches of lamb's lettuce, and the golden green of leeks and salads. And here and there were heaps of straw, then the tools the yokels had left behind, all in the most picturesque of muddles, since the earth did it all on its own here, there was really no need to bust your balls working it.

But the old guy only had eyes for the cauliflowers. Wasting no time, followed by his two business partners, he crossed the grassy edge beyond the ditch and hurried along the irrigation channel, a kind of path that crossed the cauliflower patch, but with water a couple of inches deep feeding other smaller channels left and right, likewise slimy with water and dividing the field into so many squares where the cauliflowers were lined up, big as peacocks, in rows about four or five yards long. "Off we go," said the old guy, who already had his knife in his hand. And, pushing into the plot along a channel, he got down between the lines of cauliflowers, which came up to his waist and began to take them down with a couple of thrusts of his knife. He cut them and shoved them in his sack, pushing them down with his hands and feet. His two accomplices, standing behind watching, looked at each other and burst out laughing, louder and louder, until their howls could no doubt be heard as far away as Quadraro. "Hey, shut up," said the old guy, looking anxiously from the blue tops of the cauliflowers. Their first amusement subsiding, the two gradually piped down; then, taking their time about it, they decided to get involved and started pulling a few plants themselves, but without moving from the path, choosing the first that came to hand. They pushed their loot, pulled from the muddy earth with the head, stalk, and everything, into the old guy's sack, squashing it down, half spilling the load and then kicking it back in. "Take it easy," said the old guy. But they were having fun seeing how many cauliflowers they could get into the sack, for a laugh. Finally the old guy grabbed the sack, swung it over his shoulder, and set off staggering this way and that back toward the hole. But Lenzetta said very coolly, "Hey, guys, hang on a minute, there's something I have to do," and, without waiting for an answer, he unbuckled his belt, lowered his pants, and calmly set about dropping his business on the wet grass. Since that was how things stood, both Riccetto and old Antonio did the same, so now all three were crouched under a big cherry tree, on the grassy edge of the field, their butts pale in the moonlight.

Doing his stuff, Lenzetta started to sing. Crouched beside his full sack, the old guy turned to look at him and, with a worried voice, said, "Hey, what's your name, you know my nephew did six months inside for a cauliflower, just one cauliflower? You want to put us all in jail?"

Hearing these wise words, Lenzetta shut up. "Hey, maestro," Riccetto said then, taking advantage of this intimate moment while Lenzetta was pulling up his pants, "does your daughter have a boyfriend?"

Lenzetta couldn't help laughing and came out with his trademark "Pah, pah, pah," pretending he was laughing at the smell and holding his nose; the old guy, shrewdly accepting the sucker's role that circumstances obliged him to play, said in a friendly way, "No, no boyfriend." They pulled up their pants, buckled their belts, and cautiously followed Lenzetta, who was pushing his way through the hole in the fence.

As soon as they were out on the road, the two delinquents were worried about the old guy wearing himself out—you can just imagine—and insisted on taking the heavy sack. They took turns at carrying it a bit, on their backs, playing all cheerful and nonchalant, fooling about as much as they could, while actually exhausted with the effort and cursing under their breaths, walking behind the old Antonio, who, though obliged to play the sucker, now had a couple of suckers of his own to carry the loot. When, taking it pretty slowly, they had got beyond Porta Furba and were deep inside a little Shanghai of lanes and vegetable gardens, wire fences, entire villages of shacks, empty open spaces, building sites, streams, and apartment blocks, and had almost arrived at Borgata degli Angeli, between Tor Pignattara and Quadraro, the old guy suddenly put on a polite man-of-the-world air: "Why don't you boys come up and visit?" he said. "Why, thank you," answered the two flunkies, sweating profusely, and thinking to themselves, "I'd like to see what would have happened if he hadn't invited us up, the jerk."

Borgata degli Angeli was quite deserted at this hour, and down between the big boxes of the public-housing units, built in so many parallel rows, you could see several dirt tracks full of garbage and, above them, a small moon slowly sinking in a cloudless sky.

The main door of the block where old Antonio lived was open. They went in and began to climb, one flight, two, three, among a muddle of landings, doors, and windows that gave onto inner courtyards, and anywhere the paint wasn't peeling off the local kids had drawn all over with filthy bits of coal. The old guy rang the bell of No. 74 with his two lackeys hanging around behind him, and after a couple of minutes who should come to open up but the eldest daughter.

She was a pretty piece of ass, not twenty years old, wearing a skimpy nightgown draped over her shoulders, hair all mussed, eyes puffy, and flesh still warm from her bed. Having taken one look at the two guests, she disappeared behind a tattered screen.

Old Antonio went in, put his sack down by the screen, and said in a loud voice, "Hey, Nadia!" No one appeared, but from the other side you could hear that swishing sound women make when three or four of them get together.

"Damn," thought Riccetto, "is there a whole tribe of them or what?"

"Nadia!" the old guy called again.

There were some louder rummaging noises, then the eldest girl came out again, in shoes, her nightgown belted tight, hair combed.

"Meet these friends of mine," said old Antonio. All bashful, Nadia sidled up with a smile, one hand clutching the neck of her gown and the other reaching out toward the two friends with slim, white, butter-soft fingers that immediately had them fired up.

"Claudio Mastracca," said Riccetto, shaking that pretty hand.

"Alfredo De Marsi," said Lenzetta, doing the same, with the ruddy, melting expression he got when things turned emotional; she was so shy and embarrassed you could see she was on the point of crying, all the more so with the four of them standing stock-still, looking straight at each other.

"Come in," said old Antonio, and led them through a curtained doorway into the kitchen. There, between stove and sideboard, surrounded by four or five chairs, was a low bed where two rosy, sweaty girls were sleeping side by side, each with her head by the other's feet, in tangled sheets that were more gray than white. The table was covered with dirty pans and dishes, and a cloud of flies, wakened by the light, buzzed and circled about as if it was high noon.

Nadia, who had come in last, stood back a bit, near the door.

"Don't pay it any mind," said old Antonio, "it's a workers' home."

"If you saw my place!" said Lenzetta, chuckling, to put him at his ease, but the way a little kid might, used to talking to other kids as grubby as himself. Riccetto chuckled too at his friend's little joke. Carried away, and without a shred of compunction, Lenzetta motored on as if he were in the Bar della Pugnalata, eyes simply pissing irony: "In our place the kitchen is pretty much a toilet and in the bedrooms it's a back-and-forth of mice on vacation!"

But now old Antonio suddenly made up his mind; he rushed back to the front door, dragged the sack of cauliflowers into the kitchen, and, looking extremely pleased with himself, shoved it under the sink.

"These two nice boys gave me a hand," he told his daughter, "otherwise when could I have got all these here! Christmas!"

Nadia had been doing all she could to keep smiling, but at this announcement from her father, her chin began to tremble like she was about to burst out crying, and she turned her face away.

"Hey!" said Lenzetta, all warmth and generosity, pushing out his belly and lifting up his arms, "you're not going to cry over nothing, I hope!"

As though she'd been waiting to hear those very words, the girl did indeed burst out crying and ran off behind the screen.

"Are you mad, are you crazy!" they heard someone yell from back there a moment later.

"My wife," said the old guy.

Sure enough, barely a minute later Signora Adriana appeared in her nightgown, like her daughter, but with her hair all done up, bun full of pins, and, up front, two shock absorbers easily as impressive as the sack of cauliflowers. "Better the mother than the daughters," thought Riccetto. She came flying into the kitchen bristling with disdain as she carried on the conversation she had begun behind the screen: "A plague on the dumb hussy! Bursting into tears just because a body's got to put food in his mouth, whoever heard of such a thing! These days as well! Who she got it from I've no idea, being she's my daughter and all ..."

She stopped, calmed down a little and, glancing quickly around, took in the guests, who offered themselves all bedraggled and roguish to her gaze.

"Meet my friends," repeated the old man.

"A pleasure," she said, frowning as she hurried through the pleasantries. "Claudio Mastracca," repeated Riccetto, "Alfredo Di Marsi," repeated Lenzetta. With this parenthesis of the how-do-you-do's behind her, she went back to the stuff that mattered, albeit in a friendlier tone: "So what am I supposed to do with a daughter already twenty years old who cries like a little girl, and God knows what over! Over a few soaking wet cauliflowers! Is that anything to be ashamed of?" And she lifted her chin, eyes flashing, hands on her hips, as if to defy some invisible audience, of men most likely. "Hey, Nadia!" she called, poking her head out of the door. "Nadiaaaa!"

Meanwhile the two little girls sleeping head to foot had woken up and were lying there wide-eyed, enjoying the mayhem. A few minutes later, drying the corners of her eyes with her hand, still bashful, but smiling over the silliness of her behavior of a few moments ago, Nadia came back wearing a not-to-worry look on her face. "Crazy!" her mother repeated, again defying her invisible audience: "So what's there to be ashamed of, hey?"

"It's not like we don't do our own stealing, is it?" said Lenzetta, trying to cheer her up again with his trademark tact. "We're unemployed, you know."

"Nothing to get excited about," added Riccetto, with what was almost a teatime chattiness, "everyone steals, some more, some less!"

Regaled with such fine consolations, the girl was on the point of bursting into tears again when as luck would have it her sister, the eighteen-year-old, came into the room dressed to kill. She had taken so long to show because she'd been putting on her best dress, the black silk one, and even a dab of lipstick. Counting on the element of surprise, she stepped forward with exemplary coyness. "Meet my two kind friends," said the old guy politely, for the third time. "This is my other daughter."

"Lucian-na," the girl said in a drawl, making eyes at them like the girls in the comic strips.

"Claudio Mastracca," "Alfredo Di Marsi," repeated the two nice boys.

"A pleasure," she said, sweeping her hair back with one hand.

"Very pleased to meet you," mumbled Riccetto and Lenzetta, smug and flushed as two young cocks. A moment later the third daughter put in an appearance, a redhead, cheeks sprinkled with freckles and a ribbon in her hair; she didn't actually come into the kitchen but stood at the doorway, half in half out, looking at the two nice boys, without a word, like her two younger sisters in the bed.

In fact she was hardly more than a child herself, with a flowery dress that fell straight as a monk's habit and two thin, bony legs beneath. Meanwhile, the mother had resumed her offstage rant, driven to speak from some firm, deep-seated conviction and knowing perfectly well whom she was accusing and why.

"You're right, Signora," Lenzetta concluded when she'd finished, "it's only normal!" But the real reason for his warmth was that he was hopelessly horny at finding himself surrounded by all that tit.

"What can we offer you?" said old Antonio. "Would you appreciate a coffee?"

"Oh, no need, Signor Antò!" said Riccetto, though Lenzetta had pricked up his ears at the offer. "You don't want to be troubling yourselves for the likes of us," Riccetto went on with an unexpected, rather cheerful disdain for those two guttersnipes, his friend and himself. But Antonio hadn't realized that upon his pronouncing the word *coffee* the four women and even the two little girls in the bed had exchanged glances. So he kept at it. "No trouble at all, on the contrary a pleasure," he went on, carried away by his own politeness.

The glances flying around him became increasingly dismayed. Signora Adriana half opened her mouth as if she meant to say something, but then closed it again and kept quiet, while the daughters watched her with a mixture of apprehension and feigned indifference.

"So make the boys their coffee," cried Antonio, entirely possessed by his duties as head of the household.

The wife didn't move, standing between her daughters who kept looking one moment at her, the next at each other, with Nadia on the verge of tears again and Luciana flashing an embarrassed little smile and jerking her head to toss her hair back on her shoulders. Suddenly shaking her head and putting a hand to her breast, Signora Adriana said, "I'd love to make a coffee, it's just that...how can I put it...we forgot to buy the sugar." Signor Antonio was shaken. "Oh, Antonio, what can I say," said his wife, "but with so much stuff to think about I lose track, you know..."

"Who cares?" said Riccetto, cheerfully plowing on with this determinedly low opinion of himself and his friend, "we're perfectly happy to have it without sugar!"

Lenzetta grinned his approval, face flushing in red blotches. At this the entire Bifoni family took heart. "So I'll make it then!" Signora Adriana announced and, with her daughters coming to help, picked up the pan and lit the burner, the sudden action sparking off so much general enthusiasm that while the two nice boys and Signor Antonio chatted affably away, even the two little girls came out from under their sheets in their nightdresses and started whooping around the room.

In no time at all the coffee was ready and served up to Lenzetta and Riccetto in little cups that didn't match while Signor Antonio and his wife drank from two larger, seriously chipped milky coffee bowls. Blowing on his to cool it down, Riccetto said, "OK, we'll drink up and be off. We don't want to disturb." "But you're not disturbing," said Signor Antonio, the soul of magnanimity. Drinking her coffee, Signora Adriana didn't attempt to hide her disgust, if only to preempt any criticism. "Yuck, pisswater!" thought the two nice boys, hiding a shiver of revulsion beneath polite, friendly expressions; they sipped the coffee cheerfully enough and finally set their cups down on the table among the flies.

"Time we hit the road!" said Riccetto again.

"Already?" said Signor Antonio, amazed, as if they'd barely finished dinner and it wasn't two or three in the morning.

"Damn," said Lenzetta, "pretty soon it'll be noon!"

"Come on, stay a while," insisted the old man, spreading his arms.

"We'll say goodbye, Signor Antonio," said Riccetto brusquely, stretching out a virile hand to the old man, with a sly look on his face.

"OK, I'll see you out then," said the old man. Long and white as a fillet of dried cod, he showed them to the door and waited outside on the landing while they said their goodbyes, methodically shaking hands, one by one, with Signora Adriana, Nadia, Luciana, and the late arrival, who stepped up, quiet as a mouse, for the babble of farewells. She shook hands without batting an eye or saying a word, while the two older sisters had already disappeared behind the screen with the faces they wore when they were alone.

Signor Antonio went wimpishly down the stairs, looking back at the others, making no noise in his canvas shoes. Riccetto took advantage of the old guy's being ahead to give Lenzetta a nudge. Lenzetta looked at him. "Give me the money," Riccetto said in a whisper that was positively fierce, for fear Lenzetta wouldn't play ball. Sure enough, Lenzetta grimaced and pretended he hadn't heard. "Don't play dumb," said Riccetto, speaking very softly, more with his eyes than any words. He clenched his teeth and threw Lenzetta a furious look, "Give me the money, come on." Lenzetta now felt he had to hand it over and pulled the cash from his pocket, looking daggers. They were already at the bottom of the stairs in the dilapidated hallway and the old man was opening the door. Outside dawn was coming; behind the forty apartment blocks lined up along Borgata degli Angeli, beyond Quadraro and the countryside and the misty outlines of the Alban Hills, a ruddy light was spreading across the sky, as if through a stained-glass window, so that it seemed that way off, in some part of the heavens, there was another Rome in silent flames.

"OK then, so long, kids," said Signor Antonio, "I'm off to bed."

"Good for you," said Lenzetta, "you've gone to enough trouble."

The old man smiled, head down, stretching his jaws as if he were chewing a handful of dry chestnuts.

"Take it, maestro!" said Riccetto brusquely, producing a hundred and fifty in crumpled notes. Signor Antonio looked at the cash, examining it very carefully. "Oh no, no, I couldn't . . ." he said.

"Come on, take it," urged Lenzetta.

The old man went on protesting a while but in the end he took the hundred and fifty.

"Well, I'll be damned, what a sunrise!" said Lenzetta when the old guy had gone and the two were alone in the street. In fact a barely purple light was hovering in the spaces between one apartment block and another, a translucent reflection of that invisible conflagration far away behind the hills; meanwhile two or three owls fluttered between the rooftops, letting out the occasional screech.

Listening to them and gathering his thoughts of the nice-boy act they'd performed that evening, thoughts of the Bifoni family and of death, and feeling a little weak at the knees, an anxious Lenzetta stood still for a moment, brooding, as if in meditation, then lifted a knee to his belly and let out a fart. But it sounded strained, because his heart wasn't in it.

Among the many topics Marranella's fledgling hoodlums felt called upon to express an opinion about, as they shot a little pool, perhaps at the Back Stab or Green Carpet Café, or watched others do the shooting, leaning with affected weariness against the walls of the dive where there was scarcely room for the two tables and you could hardly lift your arm before you were touching the ceiling, was the question of Riccetto's girlfriend.

In one mood they might approach it in a brotherly way, with delicacy, taking the thing quite seriously, in another they went for it head-on, not giving a damn. For his part, Riccetto felt he was the most interesting member of the group, and as such had seen the need to buy himself at least one new pair of pants. Always friendly and playful, but preserving an air of mystery as far as his private life was concerned, he would come slouching along, new pants sheathing his narrow young-tough's hips. They were gray, skinny-fitting pants, with side pockets, and he would walk leaning forward a little, thumbs in his belt, dragging his feet a bit, putting on the weary, awkward look of the country hick. It was like he had two narrow pipes on either side of his crotch that would swing back and forth as he walked, pipe this way, pipe that, pipe rising, pipe falling; and when he stopped, crossing his legs as he leaned against the billiard table, they would form a single, tightly stretched bulge, at once relaxed and threatening. As for the rest of his life, he was still sleeping in the bins in the fields of Borgata Gordiani, along with Lenzetta; but that arrangement couldn't last long now, being hardly suitable for someone of Riccetto's new status.

Lenzetta knew a place in Via Taranto, on the top floor of a build-ing six or seven floors high, between a landing with a broken door on one side, always open to a kind of barn with water tanks, and on the other a door to an empty apartment that had been closed for months. They would take a bunch of newspapers up there—during the day they hid them between the water tanks—together with their stuff, and use the landing as a bedroom.

Having a girlfriend meant living more seriously, and in fact Ric-cetto, who was more than happy to play the part of the serious kid, an attitude that prompted the more sensible of the comments at the Back Stab Café, the ones he liked best, had got himself a job. He was working as a fishmonger's assistant at a market stall in Marranella, and on Sunday, mystically faithful to his new role, he would forgo his outings with Lenzetta and the others, to Centocelle or downtown, to take his girlfriend to the cinema. His girlfriend was not the twenty-year-old, nor the eighteen-year-old, but rather the plain, freckly red-head, the daughter who hadn't said a word that evening when the two nice boys had had coffee at old Antonio's, just made eyes at them from the dirty curtain covering the door. When Riccetto was alone with her and they weren't necking—a rare combination if only because they were never entirely alone, something neither of them much minded—Riccetto would get so bored he'd be plunged into the deepest gloom. Then the slightest excuse was good for starting an argument and he'd end up slapping her about a bit. He couldn't wait to be away from her, at the Back Stab Café, getting together with Lenzetta and their hoodlum band; then he'd turn up looking pleased with himself, of course, like a man who has settled down, outgrown all the restlessness of youth, and has nothing more to expect from life.

At the same time, though, playing the serious kid didn't mean he intended to give up the temptations and pursuits of those streetwise hoodlums who were his friends. Not at all. If there was a bit of hell to raise, he raised it, and he never missed out on the petty thieving they occasionally organized at the expense of the owner of the Back Stab Café, a real sweetheart of a man, who, cleaning up the place the following morning, would vent his anger by complaining to, of all people, them. Since Lenzetta and one or two of the others had already been in the Porta Portese Youth Detention Center, they knew what "modern" educational methods were appropriate to the kind of delinquents they were pleased and proud to think of themselves as being; so, since the owner's sister was hard on them, to justify themselves and soothe their consciences—not that they really cared, but because the opportunity presented itself—they'd say they organized these little robberies because she didn't know how to treat them right, that they did it to punish her . . . Then, as far as Riccetto was concerned, the peanuts he earned as fishmonger's assistant just weren't enough. And when that's the case, how can you play the good boy! So when there was stealing to be done, he stole, what do you expect, cash-starved as he'd always been! And now he'd have to buy his girl a ring as well . . . So, he and Lenzetta decided to organize a major job: to carry off a haul of axle shafts and other scrap iron that would put them in the money for at least a month.

There were four of them when they set off: Riccetto, Lenzetta, Alduccio, and a kid called Lello, a friend of Lenzetta's who hung out with the others at the Back Stab Café. They had a cart.

Just as they were turning into Via Casilina a wind blew up and spirals of white dust and litter began to move here and there across the big crossroads and open spaces, making the power lines for the Naples railroad hum like a guitar. In no time at all the sky behind all this whiteness turned black, so that the pink and white facades along the Via Casilina shone like candy wrappers against a dark wintry background. Then even that light faded and the whole world was dark, lifeless, and cold beneath fierce gusts of wind that filled your eyes with grit.

The four took shelter in a narrow doorway just in time to avoid the first heavy shower. The thunder boomed so loud it was as though six or seven Saint Peter's domes had been put in a drum big enough to hold them all and shaken violently together, up there in the middle of the sky, so that their banging together could be heard, albeit a little distorted, many miles away, behind the rows of houses and open fields of the outlying districts, off toward Quadraro or San Lorenzo, or God knows where, maybe even in the far, far distance where there was still a patch of blue sky and sparrows in flight.

After half an hour the rain eased off and the four of them, soaked through and shivering cold, made it to Porta Metronia, where they'd gone to steal that other time. It had stopped raining but the sky was still quite dark, as if someone had cloaked it with a veil to hide something frightening, though the veil itself was frightening enough; here and there, red bolts of lightning ripped through the sky. Darkness had fallen at least two hours early and Porta Metronia was dripping wet and deserted. They tossed a coin to decide who would do what: Riccetto got to wait outside with the cart. The others went in, and once inside the yard, they tossed the coin again to see who should go in first with the sack. Lello. Trembling like a leaf, Lello went into the shed and filled the sack so full of axles, drill bits, and other stuff he could barely lift it. He came out to ask Lenzetta and Alduccio to help with the carrying, given that the toughest part of the job was done. Only they weren't there. So he ran out of the yard to where Riccetto was waiting with the cart and asked him where the other two had got to. And Riccetto told him he'd seen them going in. So Lello went back in to try to bring out the sack on his own and get it to the cart. Riccetto saw him disappear inside the shed but just as he reappeared dragging the sack, the guard jumped out and grabbed him. In the meantime Lenzetta and Alduccio had gone into another shed that stood behind the scrap-iron yard and couldn't be seen from the road. They were now coming back with the other sack full of stuff that Riccetto couldn't make out, actually big wheels of cheese. But as soon as they were in the yard they saw Lello in the clutches of the guard, trying to wriggle free and run for it. In vain. So, to help him, they dumped the sack with the cheese and jumped the guard, poor guy, who started to yell for help, at which point a baker came running out of his bakery together with his helpers. Only Alduccio managed to get away, but before he could reach the street where Riccetto was waiting right by the gate, acting like he had nothing to do with anything, some other people came running and barred his way. So Alduccio ran off along the wire fence toward another, smaller gate some distance away. He started climbing over it, but hurrying his foot slipped on the wet metal and a sharply pointed bar speared his thigh and sank right in. For a moment he was stuck, then managed to jump down to the other side anyway and Riccetto ran to help him. When the others who'd been chasing saw the boy was hurt, they let him be, not wanting to get involved. Riccetto put an arm around Alduccio and helped him down the slope toward the Passeggiata Archeologica, and when they reached a place that was particularly dark he bound his wound tightly with a piece of his vest. Then they kept going, took the tram, standing on the platform at the back, and got off at Ponte Rotto. Riccetto left Alduccio at the door of the Fatebenefratelli Hospital. The weather was slowly worsening, it had started to rain again and thunder rolled across the districts and streets where Riccetto, reflecting that someone was bound to blab, either Alduccio in the hospital, or the other two, maybe beaten and blackjacked with a sandbag in a police cell, prepared himself to spend the whole night wandering.

The light was coming up. Above the roofs of the houses you could see banners of cloud, torn and scoured by a wind blowing freely up there, the way it had blown when the world began. Down below it merely tugged at the loose strips of posters hanging from the walls or lifted the litter in the street so that it skittered across the broken sidewalk or along the tram tracks.

Where the houses stood farther apart, in a square maybe, or above an overpass, quiet as a cemetery, or in some open lot that was just a building site with scaffolding up to the fifth floor and rancid patches of grass, you could still see the whole sky: it was covered with thousands of clouds, tiny as pimples, or soda bubbles of every shape and color floating down toward the decayed and broken tops of the tower blocks in the distance. Little black rabbits, yellowish mussels, deep blue moustaches, egg-yolk gobs of spittle; and behind them, beyond a strip of blue, clear and glassy as a polar stream, drifted a great white cloud, frizzy, fresh, and so enormous it might have been Mount Purgatory.

And Riccetto was coming back, face white as a sheet, toward Via Taranto, taking it slowly, waiting for the market stalls to set up and the shoppers to arrive. He was hungry, poor kid, fainting almost, putting one foot in front of the other hardly knowing where he was going. Via Taranto was close now; how long before he got there? He turned onto the street at last, to find it empty as a minefield, the thousands of windows on the blocks huddled in the dark on the slope, all shuttered, blind to the sky with its saccharine fireworks. From time to time a gust of the same chill wind that was turning faces white and blue as fennel bulbs shook the sleepy, sickly saplings on either side of the road, climbing beside the apartment blocks toward the sky over San Giovanni. But when he got to the crossroads with Via Monza, or maybe it was Via Orvieto, where the market used to be, there wasn't a stall to be seen. No litter even, not an apple core, nor an orange peel, nor a crushed clove of garlic; nothing, as if there had never been a market here nor ever would be. "OK then," thought Riccetto, hands thrust so deep in his pockets that the crotch of his pants was down at his knees; he huddled into his shirt and pulled up the collar. Then he turned onto the first street he came to, moving slowly. "Shit and shit," he said, suddenly angry, loudly, through gritted teeth. "Who's going to hear me anyway?" he thought, turning an exploratory eye right and left, "and even if they did, who gives a fuck." He was shaking like a leaf. The streetlights that had been on suddenly went out; the light falling from above was harsher and sadder, clinging to the walls. Janitors and office workers, cleaning ladies and big shots, everyone was still asleep behind the painted shutters of Via Pinerolo. But all at once, from the bottom of the street, came a screech of brakes you could have heard up at San Giovanni; then right afterward a clanging sound boomed through the whole district, which was now flooded with daylight. Riccetto went toward it, without hurrying, and came out in Piazza Re di Roma, where the racket was coming from. Behind the young trees on the wet, black flowerbeds with their empty benches, a garbage truck had stopped, and lined up along the sidewalk were a dozen trash cans, with a couple of garbagemen hanging around cursing, their sleeves rolled up. The driver had gotten out and was leaning on the filthy fender of his truck, curls falling over his eyes, hands in his pockets, talking to the men. A kid with his mouth twisted in a grin was enjoying the situation. Not giving a damn about what they were saying, just happy to be taking time out, he stood silently a few paces off from the others, holding a plank. "Didn't you go and call the son of a bitch?" the driver suddenly turned to the kid to ask. The youngster flushed a little, then said quietly. "Sure I did." "Well, my fine friends, what can I say!" said the driver, turning to the two garbagemen. "Sort yourselves out!" And he climbed back into the cab, stretched out on the seat, and stuck his feet out the window. In the end it was hardly a disaster for the garbagemen: they'd just have to empty the trash cans into the truck themselves instead of leaving one of the kids to do it. The boy watching, dirty as a gypsy, with a cheeky smirk on his face, was up for it. After all, damn it, if there hadn't been so many kids in Borgata Gordiani and Quadraro ready to get up at three in the morning and work their butts off for four or five hours just for the right to sort through the garbage, the men would have had to do it themselves every day, wouldn't they? But the poor guys had been pampered for too long and it rankled to find themselves having to work like this.

Riccetto stood by, hands already half out of his pockets, and eyes that said it all.

A toothless guy with a coal-black beard on cheeks white in the chilly air, and a doggy glint in his sad shit's eyes, like he was drunk at four in the morning, said, "Go on, then." Riccetto didn't wait to be told twice, and while the garbagemen were chuckling, leaning over the frozen trash cans, saying, "Go on, there's rich pickings to be had," and, "Take advantage, buddy, it's an easy life," he paid them no attention but grabbed the other plank sticking out of the truck and got busy together with the other kid rolling the cans up into the truck and emptying them.

In the meantime, a dirty gray vapor like watery ink was spreading across the strips of sky you could see above the apartment blocks from the open spaces of the piazza; the rout of tiny clouds had begun to lose their color before being absorbed into the filth. The big fluffy white cloud with its steely tones had broken up, torn to shreds, and was vanishing along with the others like snow in mud. Summer was almost over. For three hours Riccetto and the smart little hoodlum from Borgata Gordiani tipped the garbage cans into the truck onto a heap that got higher and higher, scouring your lungs with a stench like a burned-out orange orchard. Already the first maids were out and about with their empty shopping bags, and the trams screeched and squealed more and more frequently as they hit the bends; the truck left the salubrious streets where respectable people had cash, turned along Via Casilina to offer its fresh stink to the tenements of the poor, danced a samba through streets full of potholes and sidewalks like sewers, between the big shabby overpasses, the hoardings, the building sites and scaffolding, rows of grim little houses, clusters of hovels, passing the trams from Centocelle with their crowds of workers hanging on the footboards, until, by way of Strada Bianca, it finally arrived at the foot of the first blocks of Borgata Gordiani, stuck out there like a concentration camp in the middle of a small plateau between Via Casilina and Via Prenestina, flayed by the wind and sun.

Where the truck came to a stop, shortly before entering the development, open fields stretched away on both sides of the road, fields

meant for wheat, but full of brambles, reeds and open pits; farther
along there was a vegetable garden with trees even older than the
crumbling farmhouse beside, unpruned for at least twenty years. A
shallow ditch was full of black water and a few old stray ducks were
waddling about on grass and earth that was blacker still. Just beyond
the farmhouse the wheat fields came to a gradual end in an expanse
of abandoned quarries, themselves reverting to fields, but bleak and
bare, good only for flocks of passing sheep, from the Sabina maybe,
or Abruzzo, and broken up here and there by little gullies and bluffs.
"Let's go, jump to it," said the driver, when he had turned his truck
around with its front toward the Strada Bianca and its back on the
edge of the embankment, right above the drop. The two workers
opened the tailgate and the heap of garbage slithered off down the
slope. When there wasn't enough weight to keep the pile rolling down,
the two got to work on what was left stinking in the wagon, tomato
reds and Prussian blues, pushing it wearily with their brooms. Then
the driver started up his truck and drove off.

Riccetto and the other kid were left alone in the stench, with the
quarry floor beneath them and scraggy little fields all around. They
sat themselves down, one above the heap and one below, and began
to search through the garbage.

The other kid was used to it, concentrating, bent forward, his face
serious, as if he were doing a job that required precision. Riccetto
copied him but felt so disgusted trawling the filth with his fingers
that he went to a fence to break off a branch from a fig tree on the
other side that looked like it had been around since the last century.
Armed with that, he crouched down and started moving the grungy
packaging, broken plates and pots, boxes of medicines, food leftovers
and all the other stinking stuff around him. The hours passed miserably slowly, and before turning definitively gray as the sirocco began
to blow, the sky had just enough time to clear up for a while, above
Borgata Gordiani, so that the small, burning nine-o'clock sun could
beat down on the bent backs of the two workers. Riccetto was soaked
in sweat, and now and then his eyes dimmed and in the dark all
around him he saw green and red stripes; any moment now he was

going to faint with hunger. "Fuck this!" he suddenly said, foaming with rage. He got to his feet and walked off without a word to his companion, who for his part didn't even bother to look up. Stumbling with exhaustion he went down the Strada Bianca, which was indeed all white with dust and sun, though the sky was clouding over now, and reached Via Casilina in a totally befuddled state. He waited for a tram, hung on to the fender, and half an hour later was back in Via Taranto, wandering around the market stalls like a stray dog, sniffing at the smells that wafted about by the thousands on the haze of the sirocco, all mouthwatering in that narrow space shut in by apartment blocks on all sides.

He gazed at the fruit stalls and managed to snatch a couple of peaches and two or three apples, then went off down an alleyway to eat them. With that first taste of sugar in his belly he came back hungrier than ever, drawn to the smell of cheese that came from the row of white cheese stalls right opposite the alley, on the wet cobblestones behind the water fountain. Lines of mozzarellas and caciottas with provolones hanging above them, then slabs of Emmentaler, Parmesan, and pecorino ready-cut on the counter; there were even some small pieces, half a pound or even less, scattered among the whole cheeses. Wired up, Riccetto set his sights on a slice of yellowish Gruyère with a simply luscious smell. He sidled up, putting on a show, waiting until the stall owner was deep in conversation with a woman, fat as a bishop, who'd been spending a while sizing up the cheeses with venomous looks, then, quick as lightning, he snatched the Gruyère and thrust it in his pocket. The owner saw. The man planted his knife in a cheese, said, "One minute, lady," came out from behind the counter, grabbed Riccetto by the collar of his shirt as he was slipping away, playing dumb, and with a sly look on his face, as if perfectly within his rights, whacked him twice and sent him spinning. Riccetto was furious. Recovering from the blow, he went for the guy without a thought, throwing desperate hooks at his ribs; the owner wobbled a bit, but being twice the weight of Riccetto started hitting him so hard he'd have sent him straight to hospital if the other stall owners hadn't come running to pull the two apart. Tough hunk as he was, the cheese man could afford to calm down at once. "Let me go," he told the guys holding him back, "let me go, I won't touch him. You think I'm going to fight with a little kiddie like this, me?" But Riccetto, all bruised and beaten with blood trickling between his teeth, went on kicking while the others held him tight. "Give me my cheese and scram," said the cheese man, almost ready to make up. "Come on, give him his cheese," said a fishmonger standing by. Wiped out, face blank, Riccetto pulled the piece of Gruyère from his pocket and handed it over, nursing vague thoughts of revenge but swallowing his rancor with the blood from his gums. Then, as the knot of people who'd gathered began to break up, since what he'd done was really no big deal, he slid off into the crowd between the red, green, and yellow of the market stalls, the mountains of tomatoes and eggplants, with the fruit sellers hawking their wares loud enough to bust their bellies, all happy and cheerful as could be. He headed down to Via Taranto and slowly climbed the four hundred steps to the landing where he slept. He could barely keep on his feet at this point, he felt so weak; he did notice that the door of the empty apartment, usually closed, was open today, banging from time to time when the draft caught it, but he thought nothing of it. Lurching in slow motion, like he was swimming underwater, he found a piece of string in his pocket, passed it through the two keyholes, and tied a knot, to keep the two sides of the door closed. Then he stretched out on the floor and instantly fell asleep. Not half an hour could have passed—just enough time for the janitor to call them and for them to get there—and Riccetto was being woken by the kicks of two policemen's boots. In brief, the apartment had been burgled that night, which was why the door had been open. Poor Riccetto, waking up from God knows what dreams, of eating in a restaurant maybe, or sleeping in a bed, sat up rubbing his eyes, and, completely bewildered, stumbled down the stairs after the policemen. "Why've they arrested me?" he wondered, still not entirely awake. "Weird." They took him to Porta Portese and sentenced him to almost three years—so he would be stuck inside till the spring of 1950—to teach him right from wrong, obviously.

6. A SWIM IN THE ANIENE

Come forward, Alichino and Calcabrina,
He went on, and thou Cagnazzo,
And let Barbariccia direct the squad.

Let Libicocco come too, and Draghignazzo,
Ciriatto with the tusks, and Graffiacane.
And Farfarello and mad Rubicante.
            —DANTE, *Inferno*, Canto XXI, lines 118–123

"I'M SO hungry I'm shitting myself," yelled Begalone. He pulled off his vest, standing on the filthy trampled grass beside the Aniene,* among the burned-out brambles, unbuttoned his pants and pissed right where he stood. "What you pissing here for?" shouted Caciotta who was taking his socks off farther down the bank. "Oh, I'll go piss in Saint Peter's then," said Begalone, "dummy."

"What about a swim," said Caciotta, looking pleased with himself. He'd filled out these last three years. "Then we could go to the movies." "Where d'you keep your money?" asked Alduccio ironically. "My fucking business," answered Caciotta. "Last night he was picking up cigarette butts," yelled Alduccio, already naked, with his feet in the water. "Fuck off," was all Caciotta could be bothered to answer, tying up his clothes in his belt.

He put them with the other clothes by a dusty bush and climbed to the top of the embankment, to a field where two or three horses were grazing in the freshly cut stubble and the younger kids who'd

*Sixty or so miles long, the Aniene River rises in the Apennines and flows west through Tivoli to join the Tiber in the northern part of Rome.

come in the morning were chucking mud at each other. "Starkers, eh, filthy brats," shouted Caciotta. "Mind your fucking business," yelled Sgarone. "Son of a bitch!" Caciotta shouted, and made as if to go after him. But the boy ran for it, down the steep part of the embankment behind the diving place. In the end, Begalone, Tirillo, and the others were all naked too. Caciotta had only said that because that morning he'd stolen his nephew's underpants and made himself a pair of trunks, sewing them tight. "Someone's looking smart!" said Begalone, laughing. Kids were yelling at the top of their voices in the middle of the river that slid by, narrow and dark, under the sun between banks of reeds and brambles. The boys who'd gone upstream to dive near the dredger floated down, shouting and clutching onto rafts of reeds. "Let's cross the river," shouted Alduccio down by the water, and he dived in. Almost everyone followed and the kiddies stopped chucking mud and came to the bank. "Aren't you going in?" they asked Caciotta. "I'm a courageous guy," he said, "just that the fear gets to me!"

The others crossed with strong strokes, running into the boys coming down with the reeds, and reached the other bank, which rose sheer and filthy from the water. Halfway along, trickling out from under the bleach factory with its green tanks and brown windowless walls, a lime-white stream cut through the dry mud and old brambles. Begalone went to swim below the white bleach culvert.

"Just what you need!" yelled Caciotta. Begalone cupped his hand and barely turned to yell across the river, "Come here and wash your sister!"

"Shitbag!" shouted Caciotta.

"Fucking rat!" came back Begalone.

The kids who'd floated down with the reeds had stopped under the diving place and were rolling around in the black mud under the sheer bank, where the smaller kids came down to join them.

Only three or four little kids were left on the embankment above. They'd climbed down from Ponte Mammolo, and after stopping for a while to watch from the bridge they'd come to join the others on the edge of the embankment, where the river took a bend, only they couldn't decide whether or not to get undressed. They were all eyes, watching the others fooling around in the shallow water and the mud, and the boys splashing about in the stream trickling from the bleach factory on the other bank. The two youngest were happy enough with that, laughing and enjoying themselves, but the bigger boy watched in silence, then very slowly began to undress. The others copied him and put their clothes together in a pile. The smallest boy tucked them under his arm while the other two climbed down. He stood there sulking. "Hey, Genè," he shouted, "don't I get to swim?" "Later," called Genesio softly. Other gangs of kids were coming along from beyond the bend through the stubble that smoldered on the embankments of Via Tiburtina, beside the river; here and there small tongues of flame crackled and sputtered. The kids came on, two or three at a time, bickering and skipping against the backdrop of the empty countryside with the white walls of the Silver Cine and the hump of Monte Pecoraro in the distance.

They were almost naked, shorts held up with string, vests or T-shirts hanging loose, in shreds. They slipped off their pants as they walked, arriving at the end of the field with their clothes already in their hands. "I can swim better than you, wanna bet!" shouted Armandino angrily, spitting and holding his German shepherd by the collar. "Like hell you can," said the boy trotting behind, in a hurry to be free from his filthy gray vest; as soon as they reached the swimming place and the diving platform made of reeds and mud, Armandino threw a stick in the water and the dog bounded down the dusty embankment, sniffed the water, and jumped in. All the kiddies gathered around to watch. The dog got the stick, gripping it between bared teeth, and climbed happily up the bank, spraying mud all over. Armandino gave it a good stroking to show his satisfaction and threw the stick in the water again, farther away this time, making the dog go through the whole rigmarole once more. Again the animal climbed up the bank, immensely pleased with itself, dropped the stick, and began to jump on the kids. It pounced on them, putting its front paws on their chests, tail tucked between its back legs, soaking wet, whimpering with pleasure. The kids dodged to the side, laughing.

"Son of a bitch!" they shouted fondly. The dog went to jump at Sgarone's chest and almost threw him to the ground, squeezing the boy between its front paws as if it wanted to hug him, mouth open.

"He wants to screw you," said Tirillo.

"Fuck that," said Sgarone, pushing the dog away, not at all sure what it wanted.

"Let's get the dog to screw Piattoletta,"* shouted Roscietto, laughing.

"Yeah!" shouted the others.

"Hey Piattolè," they shouted down the side of the embankment, where Piattoletta was fooling around in the mud and garbage of the river on his own. "Come here and stick your ass in the air," the kids shouted from up top. He didn't answer, bent over with his shoulder blades sticking out, skinny arms and mousey face, his chin pressed down on his ribs. He wore a floppy beret to cover the scabs on his head, and his hairless neck seemed even smaller than the rest, covered in lumps. His cheeks were yellow with two big hollows under his eyes and lips that stuck out like a monkey's. Sgarone and Roscietto went down the bank and began to drag him by the arms. The boy started to cry, softly, and at once his whole face down to his neck was streaming with tears. "Come and give the dog a taste of your ass, come on," they yelled, "see what a dick he's got!" The boy clung to the weeds, the mud, crying without saying anything. Meanwhile, the dog, still prancing on one boy after the other and whimpering with contentment along the edge of the stubble field, suddenly started grabbing bundles of clothes in his mouth and carrying them back and forth. "Great big son of a bitch!" the kids yelled, running after it, laughing, afraid the dog would jump in the water with the clothes. Sgarone and Roscietto laughed and let go of Piattoletta who ran straight off into the bushes while they climbed back up the bank to rescue their clothes, which were tied together with string.

Mariuccio was clutching his own and his brother's things against

*A *piattola* is a louse or a roach, and the word can be used to refer to someone who irritatingly clings on to others. The nickname Piattoletta is the diminutive. Riccetto later makes a pun referring to the unfortunate Piattoletta as a roach.

his chest, backing off whenever the dog came near; but the dog wasn't interested, though it actually banged against him at one point, almost knocking him over and muddying him with its soaking fur. Then it did notice him and jumped up playfully, trying to grab the clothes. "Genè, hey Genè," pleaded Mariuccio, frightened. The dog got his brother's shorts between its teeth and pulled. The other boys laughed. "The rascal," they shouted at the dog. Genesio and the other brother came up the bank, dripping wet, and chased the dog off with a stick. They took the clothes from Mariuccio and, without saying a word, rolled them up again.

Things were quiet for a moment; all you could hear was an old drunk rolling around in the filth, singing, under the bridge. But the boys who had swum across to the other bank were coming back now, crossing the river together, yelling and singing. Caciotta, who still hadn't been in the water, shouted, "Hey, Bégalo, is it warm? Bégalo!"

"It's warm, it's warm," answered Begalone, splashing arms and legs in the oily water, "piss-warm!"

"Jump in, get on with it!" shouted Sgarone, mocking.

"Can't even swim," said another kiddie.

"OK, asshole, you learn me, come on," said Caciotta, clouding with anger.

"And cross the river," said Armandino, who had undressed now, but like Caciotta still wore a pair of underpants, found God knows where.

"Let me poke in just the point . . ." sang the old drunk under the bridge.

"Go for it, Caciò, go for it," Alduccio and Begalone shouted beneath the bank.

"Right, like now he'll jump!" said Armandino with a sneer.

Roscietto threw a clod of mud at Caciotta from the water below the bank. Caciotta lost it: "Who did that?" he yelled, going to the edge of the embankment and looking down. The boys laughed.

"If I find out," warned Caciotta, "I'll thump his face into a football."

"You can swim, right," said Armandino, "so how come you don't cross the river?"

"I would if I had to," Caciotta admitted, "but it gives me the fucking shivers!"

Genesio had found half a cigarette in the pocket of his shorts and was watching the mayhem, smoking; he and his two brothers were the only ones from Ponte Mammolo and they kept to themselves. All of a sudden, a dozen boys were crowding around him. "Will you give us a drag?" they said, "Come on, give us a smoke." "Going to smoke it all yourself, are you?" They hunkered down around Genesio like beggars, waiting for a drag, pushing and shoving each other. "Where d'you live," asked Garrone, trying to make friends. "Ponte Mammolo," said Genesio. "We're building our own house," Mariuccio announced. After a few puffs, without a word, Genesio passed the cigarette to Sgarone, and the others gathered around Sgarone waiting for a puff from him.

"First a swim," said Caciotta again, pleased with himself, "then the movies."

"What's on in Tiburtino?" asked Armandino.

"*The Lion of Amalfi*," said Caciotta, stretching out happily in the dust and the dirty twigs.

He was in a good mood because of the hundred and fifty lire in his pocket. From time to time buses from Casale di San Basilio and Settecamini passed by on Via Tiburtina, under a silent sun that veiled the distant hills of Tivoli, beyond the scorching countryside, in a thick haze. All around, the rotten-apple smell of bleach hung heavy in the air, as if a sticky pool of oil were spreading out from the factory buildings whose walls and tanks gave the whole place the look of a huge spider; the stench came spilling down the banks of the Aniene, across the asphalt of the road and the stubble that crackled with flames that were invisible in the brilliant sunshine.

"Hey, Borgo Antico!" yelled Riccetto, with a protective air, to the older of Genesio's brothers. He was coming along the path from the bridge, straight-backed, chest bulging in his white vest, walking his walk; seeing him, one of the Tiburtino boys yelled, "Look who's here!" "Hey, Borgo Antì!" Riccetto called again from the top of the embankment, cheerful and mocking, since Borgo Antico hadn't responded at all, as if he hadn't even heard, crouching down in the dirty soil near the river, scowling at the water. Still mocking, Riccetto began to undress. In no hurry, he arranged his clothes in a pile at his feet, tugged up a pair of bright red trunks, then pulled a cheap cigarette from his pocket and lit it. He crouched on the burning dust and once again looked down toward the bottom of the embankment and the kids fooling around. Mariuccio came to stand beside him, holding his brothers' clothes tight against his ribs. "Hey, Borgo Antì!" Riccetto yelled again. "Keep trying," said the little boy, who had already got his measure, twisting his mouth in a grin. But Riccetto barely noticed. "Hey, sing us a song, Borgo Antì," he yelled. Borgo Antico still wouldn't turn, but stayed put, face dark and shiny as chocolate. "So he can sing too, can he?" said Sgarone sarcastically. "You bet," said Riccetto, equally sarcastic. Borgo Antico still wouldn't say anything and even Genesio kept mum, as if he hadn't noticed what was up. Mariuccio, the smallest of the three brothers, said, "He doesn't feel like singing." "Hey, asshole," Riccetto called to Borgo Antico, "throat dry or something?" "What'll you give him?" asked Genesio, spitting the words out. "A cigarette, what about that," said Riccetto. "Sing," Genesio ordered his brother. "Now he'll sing," pronounced Mariuccio. Borgo Antico shrugged his thin dark shoulders and pushed his bird-like face even more sharply against his chest. "Sing, will you," ordered Genesio, getting angry. "So what am I supposed to sing?" said Borgo Antico in a hoarse voice. "Sing 'Luna Rossa,' go on," said Riccetto. Borgo Antico sat down, pulling his knees into his chest, and began to sing in Neapolitan, producing a voice ten times bigger than himself and so full of passion he sounded like a man of thirty. The other boys, who'd been quiet for a while in the mud behind the hillocks above the embankment, came to stand around him and listen. "Damn, he can really sing,"* said Roscietto, as the voice drowned out every other sound along the river. Right at the climax, with everyone standing still to listen, a fresh clod of mud hit Caciotta, who still hadn't been

*The boy's gift for singing suggests the origin of his nickname: "Borgo Antico" was the title of a song that was popular at the time (see p. 21).

in the water, right on the head. "Who was it?" he yelled again, losing his temper. "Show me what's in your hand," he said, seeing Armandino with his dog beside him and one hand hidden behind his back. Acting nonchalant, defiant, Armandino looked him in the eyes, his own at once mocking and a bit frightened. He kept mum a bit before showing his hand; then, in a flash, he pulled it from behind his back and showed it, palm open, to Caciotta, but Caciotta jumped behind him, grabbed him under the armpits, and forced him to stand up.

Armandino wasn't expecting this and nervously pushed his hair off his eyes, still looking at Caciotta with a mix of cheek and fear. "What do you want, loser?" he said. "What did you have down there?" demanded Caciotta, furious, and he bent and picked up a clump of mud that had been worked into a ball. "Get off my back," muttered Armandino. "It was you, right?" said Caciotta. Armandino jumped back and pointed his open hand at Caciotta, fingers spread: "See this, who gives a fuck about you, dickhead!" He took a good dozen steps back as he spoke. Choking with rage, Caciotta looked at him and, without a word, started to move threateningly toward him. If he meant to run for it, Armandino had all open fields and the banks of the Aniene as far as the dredger, the Fisherman Café, Tiburtino; instead he stood his ground, right where he was, hunched a little, face flushed, ready for anything, to score a victory maybe, or maybe to get himself thrashed. Just as Caciotta came up close he bent down fast, crying almost, picked up a piece of dry shit, and threw it in his face. But as he turned to run, the enraged Caciotta leapt forward and grabbed him by the back of his underpants. Armandino fled with his torn underpants dangling under his bare ass. He kept running, amid roars of laughter, as far as the bend in the river, and while Caciotta walked back to the others with ill-concealed satisfaction, the boy sat down and turned his underpants around: he didn't give a damn if people saw his dick, what mattered was that his ass was covered. Meanwhile, all the boys gathered at the top of the embankment were still sniggering. "See, even Piattoletta's laughing!" said Bégalo, who had come back across the river with the others and caught sight of Piattoletta with his mouth open wide. As soon as he heard these words, Piattoletta stopped laughing and turned to run back down the embankment. But Begalone reached out a hand and grabbed him. It would be impossible to give even an idea of the difference between Piattoletta and Begalone. With his mean eyes, red hair, and freckles, Begalone could definitely be thought of as the sharpest of the gang, and the kids did think of him that way, as, without even needing to look, a patient expression on his face, Begalone grabbed Piattoletta by the neck. You get the picture: he'd spent half the night dozing in Salario and half in Villa Borghese in the company of toughs and queers, or on the trams putting his hands in suckers' pockets. The other kid had come to the river after spending the morning with his granny sorting through filth in the stinking fields and hovels where the hospital sewer emptied into the Aniene. So now, with Bégalo's hand forcing him to the ground, the boy crouched mutely, like an animal playing dead, ready to burst out crying under the filthy white beret that flopped down his neck and onto his back; only his sticky-out ears stopped the thing from falling over his snout.

"Even he's laughing, the little rascal," repeated Begalone, affecting a cheerful protectiveness and giving him a few hard slaps on the little bones of his spine. Shaken by the blows, Piattoletta looked at him. "Oh, he'll break in two," said Riccetto. "Are you joking?" said Begalone, more mocking than ever, "a hunk like this isn't going to break, is he?" and he gave the boy another punch between the shoulder blades. Piattoletta's mouth twisted in a forced laugh.

"You know why he was laughing?" said Sgarone, "Do you? Because he saw Armandino's ass."

"Is that so?" said Begalone. "The son of a bitch! I never thought I'd have to lower the shutters when he was around! You like ass, do you? Well, fuck you and that Arab of a father of yours."

Piattoletta pressed his head down into his chest, squinting out of the corner of an eye while the others laughed.

"Ass? Are you crazy?" said Tirillo, spreading his legs wide and squirming and pushing his crotch in Piattoletta's nose, "this is what he likes, the little queer."

"Go stick it up your sister," whispered Piattoletta, who was crying now. But Tirillo banged his bare crotch two or three times in his face, then rolled around in the dust. "Ah, forget it," said Begalone, "now he's going to tell us a thing or two in German, right, Piattolè!"

"German, is he?" asked Riccetto.

"Fucking right," said Begalone, "he's German-English-Moroccan, go ask his mom!"

Piattoletta was drenched in tears, he let them roll down his cheeks and neck without trying to dry them.

"Let's see how much German he knows," said Sgarone. "Say something, Piattolè"

"Come on, spit it out," yelled Begalone, "you and your fucking granny."

"If you don't," said Tirillo, jumping up, "we'll put a hole in your ass the size of a house."

"Right, what'd he want it tight for?" said Roscietto.

"Leave him be, dumbos," said Begalone, putting his arms around Piattoletta, "cause if he doesn't give us a little talk in German, we're going to chuck his clothes in the river and leave him in Pietralata without a stitch."

Piattoletta went on crying. "Now, where has he hidden his clothes, the little snot-rag," said Begalone. "Down there on the mud," shouted Sgarone, and ran to get them. "And this cap and all," said Begalone, snatching Piattoletta's beret, leaving his shaved head bare, covered in white scars.

Making a bundle of the clothes and holding them high, he plunged in the river and crossed it. When he reached the other side, where the bleach drained into the water, he yelled to Piattoletta:

"If you don't want to talk German to us now, you can come and get these filthy rags tomorrow!"

"Just do it, come on," Riccetto said cheerfully.

"Well, fuck you," yelled Sgarone and landed a kick on his back. Piattoletta wept all the louder, his monkey face scummier and uglier by the moment. But now he made up his mind to speak. "Ach rich grau riche fram ghelenen fil ach ach," he said softly as he wept.

"I can't hear! Speak up!" yelled Begalone from the other bank. "Ir

zum ach gramen bur ach minen fil ach zum cramen firen," said Piattoletta more loudly, and burst into tears again. "Play Indian," yelled
Begalone. Tears still streaming from his screwed-up eyes, Piattoletta
obeyed at once, hopping up and down, waving his arms and shouting:
"Yoo-hoo, yoo-hoo." Begalone dropped the boy's clothes in the un-
dergrowth and plunged back in the water yelling, "The hell if I'm
going to bring them back."

The sun had sunk a little in the sky over Rome, and there was a
smell like coal dust in the air. "Let's go," said Genesio to his brothers.
He got Mariuccio to give him his clothes and, as he pulled on his
pants, saw that the dog had torn the hem with its teeth. "Fuck and
shit," he muttered. "What will Mamma say?" said Mariuccio. Genesio didn't answer but took another half cigarette from his pocket,
waited till they were a bit farther along the path that climbed the
embankment to the Tiburtina, then lit it. "Wait for me, guys," Riccetto shouted, seeing they were leaving. The three boys half turned
and stopped; they couldn't decide whether or not to wait. "Let's wait,"
said Genesio quietly, still scowling, and without even checking what
his brothers were up to, he sat cross-legged in the dust, smoking with
his eyes down.

Riccetto dressed slowly, first one sock, then the other, singing and
passing comments on the others doing belly flops and nosedives in
the water; finally, after putting things on back to front or inside out
a couple of times, he was ready; he got to his feet and set off slowly,
lazily wriggling his shoulders, eventually overtook the three smaller
boys from Ponte Mammolo, and with a mocking nod of the head
said, "Let's go." They walked single file along the path beside the
Aniene, then climbed the near-vertical embankment up to Via Tiburtina and crossed the bridge.

Riccetto was ahead, a little plump in his vest, skin shiny from his
swim, showing off his tough-guy walk. He was in a good mood, singing away, eyes alight with mockery, wet trunks dangling from his
hand. The three boys tagged along behind, Genesio with his licorice
skin and coal-black eyes keeping slyly to himself and the others trotting along like puppies, as if it were a procession with Riccetto up

front, leading. They turned off the Tiburtina, climbing up Via Casal dei Pazzi through farm fields plowed in a zigzag of furrows, small, whitewashed houses, building sites, ruins. Not a soul was about, and in the hot sunshine that had the fields and asphalt sizzling, the only sound to be heard was Riccetto's singing.

The workers digging holes for the sewers along Via Casal dei Pazzi—there was an election coming up—were asleep on their backs in the shade of a low wall. "Look!" shouted Mariuccio with his shrill birdy cheep, leaning over one of the holes where a winch rope was hanging loose. Borgo Antico ran up, both boys amazed to see how deep it was; Genesio gave it no more than a scornful glance. "Come on," said Riccetto, seeing the three had fallen behind, busy looking into the holes that stretched out in a line the whole length of the road, each with a trestle above.

"You'll be in the shit with your dad," shouted Riccetto cheerfully, moving one hand energetically up and down.

"Who cares about him," said Genesio, in a hoarse voice.

"Yeah, yeah, a breeze," jeered Riccetto, still waving his arm. He was hinting at the beatings the three brothers got more or less daily from their drunken, vicious peasant of a father. Riccetto had been working for the man since the spring, as a laborer at Ponte Mammolo, and knew him well. They turned off into Via Selmi, leaving the row of fenced-off holes that stretched away on and on, under the hot sun.

"He'll give you a black eye, he will," Riccetto went on, enjoying himself.

"Bullshit!" said Genesio; Riccetto's predictions had touched a nerve, and the boy didn't want to accept the truth of them; but there was nothing he could say to the contrary and Riccetto took advantage to poke fun.

"Especially if he's had a drink or two," he said with a sigh, "he'll grab a stick and show you what for!"

"Oh, give us a break," said Mariuccio, who was still too small to tell Riccetto to fuck off, and looked doubtfully up at him. "Sure, have a laugh about it," said Riccetto, "but you'll soon be howling, you will!"

"Give us a break," Mariuccio repeated, not sure whether to make a joke of it himself or be offended. Riccetto sang to himself for a bit, as if he'd forgotten about the three brothers, then: "I wouldn't like to be in your shoes," he said playfully, mouth twisting and head shrinking down between his shoulders as if to dodge the blows raining down.

"Give us a break," Mariuccio said again, bitterly. Genesio kept quiet, taking a last pull from his cigarette, now no more than a glowing coal, and aiming kicks at the cobblestones on Via Selmi, sunk between meagre vegetable plots, half-built houses, and armies of drying laundry.

"Here we are then," said Riccetto, jeering, when they got to the end of the street near the boys' house, just one floor of masonry with no stucco; but they had made a start on the second floor and there was scaffolding all around, a puddle of lime in the trampled earth of the garden and a few heaps of plum-colored sand. None of the two or three workers were at it yet. Riccetto had arrived first and sidled up in leisurely fashion. The boys' father, from Puglia, had just given his wife a beating and was sitting on the doorstep, face flushed and blotchy, eyes bright and wild as a dog's. The three boys, who had seen their father from a distance, hung back, among crumbling garden walls and heaps of dirt in the street, expecting the worst. But Riccetto walked calmly and cheerfully into the garden, took his comb from his back pocket, wetted it under the garden tap and began to comb his hair, handsome as Cleopatra.

"The dogs, the dogs!" shouted Roscietto, appearing from lower down the embankment of the Aniene with all the gang. Zinzello, the carter with the slick Valentino hairstyle, and Miccia, with two big German shepherds, a dog and a bitch, were coming along the Tiburtino path. At the bend in the river, while the dogs ran about in the stubble, they undressed, took bars of soap from their pockets and, chatting together, went to paddle around and wash in the shallow water.

They had no time for the others, the smaller boys or the bigger. Zinzello's face was hard as stone and Miccia was already big and solid, with a beard that darkened his well-fed cheeks; feeling the cold water running down their backs, they both began to sing, paying no mind to the kids playing with their dogs.

Armandino's dog had begun to growl, but keeping well away, tail tight between his legs, turning round and round, so as never to expose his wet flank to the other two animals, rolling himself up in a ball, then stretching right out. All the smaller kids, Piattoletta included, had gathered around.

"His dick's trembling," jeered Roscietto.

"He's just a puppy," said Sgarone, taking the dog's side.

"Just a puppy? Are you dumb?" said Roscietto, in a shrill voice. "He was around when I was born!"

Armandino clicked his tongue and raised his eyebrows with a look of pity. "He's not even a year old," he said.

"So?" said Roscietto. "What's he scared of another dog for?"

"He's not scared, you think he's scared? You're pissing me off," snapped Armandino.

He went to his dog, grabbed it violently by the collar and dragged it toward the other two dogs, which were already snarling and running back and forth in the stubble.

Armandino bent over the creature and in a voice so low you could hardly hear, speaking angrily, dribbling saliva, began to whip it up:

"Go for it, Lupo, go for it, Lupo, go, go, go!"

The dog quivered hearing this soft goading voice that barely reached his pricked-up ears. Chest pushed forward, he was trembling all over, like an engine revving in neutral. All at once Armandino let it go.

All the kids stood watching, hardly speaking. Of Zinzello's two dogs, the male was the smaller and lighter. Seeing Lupo coming at him, urged on by his master, his dander up, he slunk idly away, toward the middle of the field, coming back every now and then to bark and snarl.

But the bitch was a real beast. Lean and black with a sharp nose, ragged tail, and slanted eyes, she stood still as a statue waiting for Lupo. But having rushed close at top speed the dog suddenly stopped, barking at the bitch like a demon.

She stood still a while, listening, grim, and you could hear the cries of the kids too; then she turned away and wandered off to mind her own business, like she was thinking, "Leave me be, OK, or we'll have a massacre on our hands!"

But every now and then she turned her head, pointed nose pressed against her lean shoulder, dark dull eyes flecked with blood.

"Go for it, Lupo, go, go, go," whispered Armandino, bending down to the dog's ear again, and the little kids joined in, urging the dog on, yelling like monkeys, making an uproar you could have heard in Tiburtino. Naively, the dog raced after the bitch, who hadn't made a noise as yet, barking wildly, putting on a bit of a show.

"I reckon someone's a bit too full of himself," the bitch seemed to be thinking, mulling the situation over, "for the likes of me at least." And a second later: "Well, fuck you," the creature growled, suddenly losing all her patience. It was a snarl of such ferocity that Lupo stopped dead, and even the kids were a bit frightened. The bitch in the meantime had turned around on herself, grimly watching Lupo, who was slinking off.

"What did I say, hey, Sgarò?" said Roscietto.

Armandino bent to it more intensely. "Go for it, go for it, Lupo, go on," he said, almost trembling like the dog. Lupo got a bit of his mojo back, forgetting he'd nearly shit himself a moment ago, and started barking again, even more wildly and menacingly than before. "Here we go again," the bitch seemed to be thinking. "You filthy slut, you shitbag, there's no point looking at me like that, you know!" Lupo barked furiously, "You're not going to scare me!" The bitch stayed mum. "If you're not going to say anything," growled Lupo, "I'll zap you one that'll take your head off!"

"Oh my, what a sweetheart you are!" joined in the other dog, the male.

"Oh, yes?" growled Lupo, and lunged, but the dog skedaddled. "Wonder what that loser was after?" Now the bitch let out a snarl. "Come and snarl on my dick," yelled Lupo.

"That's it," the bitch pronounced, "I've had it, OK?" She turned sharply around to face him. "Let come what fucking may," she said quietly, then snarled with fury, "but I'd happily go down for thirty years for this pleasure."

"They're going to kill each other," said Sgarone, but he'd hardly spoken before the two German shepherds had clashed, hind legs braced in the dirt, front paws on each other's chests, mouths yawning, showing rows of teeth down to the gums. Both gasping, each tried to bite behind the other's ears, and between one bite and the next they snarled so loud you couldn't hear the kids shrieking. Lupo rolled in the stubble, raising a cloud of dust, and the bitch was on him, teeth at his throat. But now Lupo was up again and after prancing back a little, lunged at the bitch again, standing almost straight up and waving his paws like he was drowning. The dogs roared, writhed, choking with rage. But just as things were getting exciting, Zinzello came up the embankment seriously pissed off, and gave a whistle. At once, as though someone had waved a wand, the bitch shed all her anger and, with the dog following, ran toward him, leaping lightly, wagging her tail, submissive, almost cheerful. Zinzello sent a hail of curses in the direction of the kids and when he'd got it out of his system, went back down to soap himself in the river, taking his dogs with him. Lupo was in a sorry state. "Look at the bites!" cried Tirillo, voice loud with amazement. "So many!" Everyone bent down over Lupo, whose neck was stripped of fur, with swollen reddish wounds and black scabs amid a mess of sticky black hairs. "Fucking hell!" said Sgarone in the same voice of amazement Tirillo had used. "Let's chuck him in the water," said Roscietto, and they all went down the bank dragging the dog after them.

Meantime, Caciotta came up from the bank where the older kids were playing cards, glancing from time to time at a little window lost among the walls of the factory to see if the janitor's daughter would show, then they could play bad boys with her a bit, naked as they were. Caciotta looked around and said, "So where have my clothes got to?"

"Clothes, where are you?" he yelled with his usual good humor.

"Already off?" said Alduccio.

"What's to stay for?" said Caciotta, looking for his clothes among the brambles and bamboo.

"Let's take another swim, come on," yelled Alduccio.

"No-oh," shouted Caciotta.

"Ah, leave him be," said Begalone to Alduccio, nudging his elbow. Caciotta had found his clothes and was turning them over in his hands looking at them.

"Wonder who messed with these," he said to himself. "No idea."

"Hey, one of you guys like to go through pockets by any chance?" he asked out loud.

"Nope," called Sgarone mockingly.

"If I catch anyone going through my pockets, I'll gouge his eyes out," said Caciotta cheerfully.

"You're a hell of a guy," Begalone called from below, having heard what was going on. Caciotta began to pull his socks and shoes on, singing:

"Little clogs, little clogs..."

"Claudio Villa got nothing on you, Caciò," said Begalone.

"I know," said Caciotta, breaking off his singing and then starting again.

"Go on, cheer yourself up singing," said Alduccio.

"I do, I do," said Caciotta. *"Little clogs, little clogs...* Am I not supposed to be cheerful, or what? Do I have to ask someone's permission to sing a song? *Little clogs, little clogs...* If we get dressed, we can take a walk and then go and chill at the movies..." Singing and talking, he had put on his socks and shoes, and now he undid the belt that was holding his clothes.

"Great, go to the movies, but I don't hear you offering to take your friends with you, eh?"

"Idiot," said Caciotta, "I've only got a hundred and fifty..."

"OK, OK, do what you want," said Begalone.

Caciotta started singing again, "Little clogs, little..." He broke off. He stood there for a moment, without saying anything, then came toward the others, clothes in his hands, pale as death.

"Who stole the money I had in my pocket?"

"Hey," said Begalone, "what you looking at me for?"

"Who was it?" said Caciotta, white-faced.

"Whoever it was is sure going to tell you," said Zinzello, going off with his dogs, shaking his head.

"You all show me what's in your pockets!" said Caciotta.

Suddenly losing it, Begalone jumped to his feet. "You cretin," he said. "Here, look." He picked up his clothes and threw them in Caciotta's face; Caciotta took them and, without saying anything, went carefully through all the pockets. Then he looked in Begalone's socks and shoes as well.

"Found anything?" yelled Bégalo.

"Just your fucking shit," said Caciotta.

"You'll be getting your face kicked in soon," said Begalone. Caciotta went to check Alduccio's clothes, then all the little kiddies' stuff, one by one, but nothing. He dropped the things back in the dust, without looking at anyone now; God knows how many weeks it had been since he'd had a hundred lire in his pocket and felt as good as he'd felt after lunch today. He finished dressing in silence, deep in thought, then left. Along Via Tiburtina the traffic was already heavy, though the sinking sun was still scorching through the dark fumes amassed over Rome; the Silver Cine raised its shutters and here and there, in the outlying developments, distant noises and voices began to make themselves heard. Alduccio and Begalone took another swim, then they left too. The last to leave the river were the little kids.

Some went straight home down Via Boccaleone, others hung around for a while; they made their way slowly along the river to the first streets of Tiburtino, stopping for a half hour outside the Silver Cine to gaze at the posters and wind each other up. Then they went farther down, through the ragged oleanders along the Tiburtina, till they reached the bus stop, which was where the smaller kids and groups of teenagers swarmed, on the open ground facing Monte Pecoraro.

There were some little girls playing here too, in the yellowish ground that flattened out between the four or five crests of the hill and the Tiburtina, which was full of workers cycling home, some toward Ponte Mammolo or Settecamini, some turning here at the corner toward the developments of Tiburtino III and Madonna del Soccorso. Some had already been home and come out again, taking a walk with friends toward Pietralata, maybe, or going to one of the two nearby cinemas, their vests and T-shirts hanging out of their pants.

Coming along from the Aniene, still half-naked, the little kids climbed the dark brown path that skirted the hill with its multiple crests, following the edge of a limestone quarry, then plunging into the thorns and brambles of Monte Pecoraro.

The girls followed them, and they all met in the middle of the hillside, out of sight of the street, on an open stretch full of abandoned quarries that gaped like so many little gullies in the middle. Since a storm was brewing over Saint Peter's, it felt like it was almost evening; the setting sun had sunk into clouds already flickering with lightning, though the sky overhead was still clear, almost red with the glare and the heat. And now that the sun was gone the slopes of Monte Pecoraro were scoured by a sort of African wind, bringing with it all the noises of the developments. Piattoletta was tagging along with the gang of boys too, laughing under his floppy beret, keeping a little distance from the others, so he could be around them without their noticing. Anyway, they had calmed down a bit now, because of the girls. They gathered together under the electricity pylon, and Sgarone and Tirillo began to play rock, paper, scissors; for fun at first, then they got wound up and started yelling at each other, Sgarone kneeling, Tirillo crouching, in the sparse grass under the pylon.

Armandino had gone to sprawl out where the shade was losing its sharpness as the sun was lost behind the storm, though there was still a glow coming through; the others, headstrong as a bunch of monkeys, had gone to bait the girls, only from a distance, though, because however bad they liked to be, they were a bit shy, and they hung together, arm in arm, bragging, acting ironic and lazy. But the girls always came back sharp and shut them up.

"Talking to that lot," said Armandino with a gravelly voice, "you might as well be talking to yourselves," and he started to sing. But the others pretended not to hear and went on joking with the girls. Since he couldn't think of anything else to say, Roscietto got up and gave one of them a slap on the head that almost knocked her over. At which the other girls took offense and went off in a huff beyond the pylon, where you could look down on Pietralata, and the boys followed them, acting as rowdy as the girls were standoffish. On the other side of Monte Pecoraro, wedged in among more old limestone quarries, the Fiorentini factory made the air hum with its machines, and from time to time its glass doors and big shabby windows flashed white with the light of welding torches. Pietralata lay beyond, its rows of pink huts for the homeless under a hard crust of polluted dust, and farther still you could see the big yellow tenements, a row of tall narrow blocks reaching into a countryside so scorched by the sun as to seem bleak and wintry.

But the girls retreated to the far side of a small clearing between the lips of two big holes and wouldn't speak to the boys anymore, barely talking among themselves while they waited to be on their own. The boys had gathered a bit farther up the slope, on the ridge, fooling around; but the girls' behavior was working them up, even if they didn't want to show it. So their jokes got more spiteful and physical; unable to outsmart the girls with their talk, they started throwing sticks and stones at their tattered cardigans and the dirty hair they'd combed out like they were young debs.

The girls just moved off again, lower down the slope, but not before giving the boys a mouthful of what they deserved. "For Christ's sake," they yelled, "why don't you go piss off your sisters, idiots!" Their voices trembled with anger, growing shriller, dragging out the words. Hearing them, the boys started to snigger and mimic, the way their older brothers did, taking off the snobs they heard in Via Veneto, and the smallest boy yelled, "You lezzies!" Climbing to the top of the slope they began to put one hand on their hips, reaching the other out in front or slowly stroking the hair on the back of their heads and necks, swaying with long, slow steps.

Under the pylon Armandino went on singing as loudly and heartily as he could while the other two were standing up, playing rock, paper, scissors, using their left hands to keep the score. "Fuck all of you!" shouted the boys coming back up the slope. "So what are we going to do now?" They jumped on the three under the pylon, all wound up, some rolling around wrestling together while others lit a stub of cigarette, tossing the live match into the grass that flared angrily and shriveled black as the breeze came and went on the crests of the ridge.

The clouds were growing denser, the lightning at intervals tinging them red, and as the air darkened and you could see them more clearly, the flashes from the welding torches in the factory flickered faster and more often while the hum of the machines drowned out the voices of the poor folk of Pietralata and Tiburtino.

Piattoletta was sitting on the ground, cross-legged, beret pulled way down to cover his ears, laughing with his long, droopy lips.

"Hey, Piattolè," shouted the others, rolling around in the dry mud, "get a load of this," but they went on fighting among themselves, paying him no mind. Sgarone was lying on his back with Roscietto on top, belly to belly, to hold him still, hands gripping his wrists to keep him pinned to the ground.

Sgarone was trying to free himself. "Don't move!" yelled Roscietto, flushed with the effort. But Sgarone had had enough and was wriggling like an eel. "Fuck you," he yelled. "You're staying put, Sgarò," said Roscietto. "Get off my cock," said Sgarone, beginning to get seriously angry, his voice hoarse. Roscietto started to bounce on him, like he was on a girl.* "Watch out, Rosciè," said Sgarone, laughing, "something's standing guard here." All fired up, Roscietto jumped off him. "Let's play Indians," he shouted. "Oh, get lost," said the others scornfully. "Come on, it's fun," Roscietto insisted. "Yeah, wonderful," sniggered Armandino. "Woo, woo, yeehaw!" cried Roscietto, prancing about. "Come on, Piattolè!"

Piattoletta got to his feet and joined in the yelling, hopping on one foot, then the other. "Woo, woo." Roscietto stood beside him so they could hop together: "Woo, woo," they yelled, laughing.

The others started hopping about too, bending their bodies backward and forward, yelling, "Woo, woo." The girls came back to see what the fuss was all about and, standing around in a circle, sighed,

---

*Pasolini, to appease his publisher and to try to avoid censorship, changed this in the published Italian version to "as if he had Saint Vitus' dance."

"Out of their heads!" But the boys just hopped and yelled even more, to piss them off.

"Let's do the death dance, the death dance!" cried Roscietto. The others started shrieking even louder, "Woo, woo, woo!" and when their hopping took them close to the girls, they aimed a kick or a whack at their heads. But the girls were expecting it and ducked back fast. "God, what a bore you guys are," they said. "Give it a rest, dumbos," but they didn't go away this time, standing and watching the dance; and though they were worn out with hopping and yelling, the boys went for it harder, to show off.

"The torture stake," shouted Roscietto.

"Oh right, the torture stake and all," smirked the girls, "you're ridiculous, ridiculous!" and they affected an air of pity and boredom.

Roscietto jumped on Piattoletta, who was still yelling "Woo, woo" in the middle of the group but barely moving his feet, he was so tired. "To the death stake," cried Roscietto as soon as he'd grabbed him.

The others yelled too and gave him a hand, dragging Piattoletta toward the pylon.

"Tie him up," yelled Sgarone. Piattoletta flailed about, then went down on the ground playing dead. "Well, fuck you," yelled Roscietto, arms around him, pulling him up, "stay on your feet, scumbag."

But Piattoletta wouldn't play ball and threw himself on the ground, kicking out, while the others stood around him shrieking. "I'm fed up already," said Roscietto, and kicked him in the stomach.

Piattoletta began to wail so loudly you could hear him above the boys' yelling. "Now the little prick's blubbering," said Armandino. "If you don't get up ..." shouted Roscietto. But Piattoletta really wasn't up for it and went on writhing in the dust, howling at the top of his voice.

"Ten of them and they can't handle that little cripple," said the girls. But Roscietto had managed to drag him up by his collar, and when Piattoletta yelled, "Leave off, son of a bitch," he shouted, "Take that," and spat in his eye. Then he squeezed him hard, and with Sgarone and Tirillo helping, they dragged him to the pylon and tied his wrists to an iron hook sticking out of the cement.

Even strung up like that, Piattoletta went on writhing and kicking and screaming. The others started dancing around him, shrieking louder than ever, "Woo, woo, woo," keeping their distance, though, to stay clear of the kicks he was launching into the air. "Damn," cried Roscietto, "doesn't anyone have another bit of string?"

"Who's going to have any string?" said Tirillo.

"Piattoletta, Piattoletta's got some," yelled Sgarone. "To hold up his pants."

"They jumped on Piattoletta, who was moaning and begging, and with the girls all laughing and shouting "What a bunch of idiots!" they grabbed the string holding up his pants and tied his ankles together.

"Now let's burn the death stake," yelled Armandino, lighting a match.

But the wind blew it out. "Woo, woo, woo," shrieked the others, circling around, at the top of their voices.

"Your lighter!" Sgarone shouted to Tirillo.

"Here," said Tirillo, pulling it from the bottom of his pocket; he brought up a flame, and while the others, still shrieking and dancing, kicked bunches of twigs into a pile under the pylon, he began to light the dry grass here and there.

The wind was blowing hard up on Monte Pecoraro, and coming from all directions; it was almost dark and, amid the flickering of the factory and the lightning in the storm, you could already hear a rumble of thunder and smell the coming rain.

The dry grass flared at once, the blood-colored flames spread to the twigs, and puffs of smoke began to lift around Piattoletta, who was yelling his head off.

In the meantime, without a string to hold them up, his pants had slipped down, leaving his crotch bare, and fell in a heap at his bound feet. So the fire passed from the grass and twigs that the whooping boys kept kicking toward the flames and set the dry cotton alight, with a merry crackle.

7. IN ROME

BENEATH Monte Pecoraro there was a big open space and, near the sign that said "End of Zone—Beginning of Zone," just before you got to the wide open fields sloping down to the Aniene, there was the old bus shelter, for the 309, which turned here, leaving Via Tiburtina and heading through the neighborhood developments and on toward Madonna del Soccorso. Like Begalone, Alduccio lived in Block IV, at the end of the main street, just before the marketplace, where the rows of streetlamps lighting up in the dusk, along buildings that were only a couple of stories high, gave the impression you were in the poorer part of some seaside town, the road, after its brief dip down, stretching away under the darkening sky, and the noises of people eating or preparing for the night echoing around the walls and courtyards of the blocks. At that hour there were a lot of kids and young folks out and about; but the guys who really knew how to live were keeping to themselves, in the cafés, or just hanging out in groups, waiting for darkness to fall, not to go to the movies or to Villa Borghese, but to meet in a dive somewhere and gamble till dawn. And while here and there teenagers strummed their guitars in the courtyards, women were still washing the dishes or sweeping the kitchen while their kids whined, and buses were still spilling out crowds of people coming home from work. "See you, Bégalo," said Alduccio when they reached their block. "Bye," said Begalone, "catch you later." "I'll be waiting at nine," said Alduccio, "give me a shout, right!" "OK, but you be ready," said Begalone, climbing up the shabby stairway, teeming with little kids. Alduccio lived three or four doors down, on the ground floor. There was a kind of porch in front, as at all the blocks, with little columns and walls that were buckled and cracked. His sister was sitting on the doorstep. "Hey, what you up to?" said Alduccio. She didn't reply, watching the street. "Fuck off and die then," he said and went into the kitchen, where his mother was cooking over the stove. "What are you after?" his mother said, without turning around. "What do you mean, what am I after?" said Alduccio. She turned brusquely, hair all mussed up: "You don't work, so you don't eat, you know that, right?" She was a tall, solid woman, almost naked under her soiled cotton nightdress, sweaty hair glued to her forehead at the front and gathered in a bun that was falling apart behind, long strands dangling down her neck and the collar of her nightdress. "OK, OK!" said Alduccio, acting reasonable. "You don't want to feed me? Who gives a fuck!"

He left her and went to the bedroom, where the whole family slept, since Riccetto's family slept in the other room. Undressing, he whistled so his mother would realize he really didn't give a damn. "Keep right on whistling," she called from the kitchen, "lout that you are, the hell with you both, you and your dirty, drunken father!" "Right, and my slob of a mother," muttered Alduccio, naked on the bed, pulling on his moccasins. "Yeah, you're all wired up over that slut of a daughter you have, go hang yourself, what are you taking it out on me for? You don't want to feed me? So don't feed me! What do I care! Just shut the fuck up!" "Shut up?" yelled his mother. "Shut up? When I have to see a son almost twenty, old enough to be called up and doesn't bring home a lira, nothing, you're a disgrace!" "God, what a bore you are!" shouted Alduccio, getting dressed up for the evening. But now there was the sound of yelling out in the street, women's voices bickering. Alduccio's mother kept quiet a moment, listening, while the words came muffled to Alduccio's ears in the bedroom. "What a total moron!" shouted his mother, speaking to herself over the stove. She knocked something over in her hurry to be outside and went to the front door. She stopped there a while in silence, listening, then went out into the street, and you could hear her voice yelling along with the others. "Bedlam!" Alduccio muttered to himself. "Why don't they all just fuck off!" After almost ten minutes of squalling and shouting out in the street, or maybe on the stairs, he heard the door flung open, but not closed, because his mother had stopped there; maybe she still had something else to say. In fact she went back out on the landing: "You slut," she started yelling at someone outside, "you've been a whore your whole life, and you come calling my daughter a tramp!" A voice shouted back from somewhere above, but he couldn't make out the words. "Fucking swamp creatures," Alduccio thought, "they'll be the death of me." "Good job!" yelled his mother, hand on her hip, answering a din of words he couldn't make out. "Look who's talking! And you, getting your man to give you money to send the kids to the cinema so you could be alone with him!" The voice from the courtyard, or maybe out on the landing, got angrier and shriller, then went on, at the top of its register, pouring out whole catalogs of insults of every kind. When she was done it was Alduccio's mother's turn again: "Don't you remember, slag face," she yelled, with a voice so shrill and sharp not even Jesus Christ himself could have shut her up, "when your husband came home and caught you in bed with your lover boy, and the kiddies right there, watching?" She slammed the door and came back in the kitchen, talking to herself now, voice trembling in her throat, sharp as a knife: "Ah, shut the fuck up, bitch, when I get my hands on you in the street tomorrow, I'll tear out every hair from your fucking head, I swear to God!" A while later, the door opened again and Alduccio's father came back. As always in the evening, he was drunk. He went to his wife and made to hit her, but she put a hand on his chest and pushed him away; he turned right around on himself and collapsed on a seat. But he was on his feet again in a second, determined to give his wife a good hiding. From the bedroom farther down the corridor where Riccetto's family lived, Riccetto's sister appeared, wanting to see if anything serious was going on. She arrived in time to see her uncle collapse on the seat again. "What are you doing here?" Alduccio's mother turned to her, furious: "What the fuck do you want." The girl, who was carrying another little Riccetto in her arms, turned on her heels and went right back to her room. "Scrounger! You and your whole family, scroungers and spongers and losers," the mother called after her, "four years here, and has anyone ever said, here's a thousand lire, take it and pay the electricity, no, never once." After a minute or two in contemplation, the father managed to find his voice, and at the third or fourth attempt got out something like, "Always complaining, this pain in the ass!" He got to his feet, swaying back and forth, and put together a sort of reflection in mime; he moved a hand from chest to nose two or three times, then did a pirouette with his fingers as though to suggest some idea all his own that was going through his head. Finally, in a rush, before he could fall over, he made for the bedroom, where Alduccio was dressing, and threw himself fully clothed on the bed, lying on his back. The wine he'd been drinking all afternoon had left him white as a sheet and somehow hardened the rough, unshaved skin around his nostrils and the corners of his mouth into something dark, damp, and wrinkled as a dog's muzzle. He was all floppy; arms flopping outspread on the coverlet, mouth flopping half open, jaw flopping, eye sockets flopping, black hair flopping back on his head, soaked in sweat that looked like grease. The lamp over the bed lit up one by one the chocolate-colored stains of old filth ingrained in his face, together with more recent crustings of dust and sweat beneath his forehead, while a web of wrinkles shifted of its own accord up and down across skin that was drawn and flabby with drink, and yellow with God knows what ancient illnesses of that pickled liver, buried in those miserable bones covered with a few old rags. Here and there you could see brown blemishes circled with freckles, very likely blows he'd taken as a child, or in his youth, when he'd been a soldier, a laborer, centuries ago. And all of this was, as it were, fused together by the gray pallor of poor eating and drink, and the tufts of a four-day-old beard.

Alduccio was ready now, with his drainpipe pants and finely striped open-neck T-shirt worn loose over them. But he still had to comb his hair. He went to the little mirror in the kitchen and, after holding his comb under the tap, started to fix his hair, standing with his legs apart because the mirror was too low for him. "Good-for-nothing pimp," spat his mother, gray with rage, finding him in her way again. "Give me a break, Ma, come on," snapped Alduccio, "I've had it up to here, OK!" "And I've had it up to here with you," came back his mother, more fiercely. Alduccio started crooning, bent over the mirror. "Doesn't work, doesn't help around the house..." "Ma," Alduccio broke in, "didn't I tell you I'd had enough, are you going to stop it or what?" "No, I'm not, no way," she shouted, "if I feel like griping, I'll gripe as much as I want, understand, Mr. Asshole Dandy." "Leave me alone, Christ," said Alduccio in a rage and went out, hair carefully combed, slamming the battered door behind him. He didn't even glance at his sister, who was crouched on the step with her skirt pulled down to her heels. She was so pale as to seem green, and her rouged lips looked like an open wound. Her hair fell flat and dry on her neck, with a stray spiky lock or two over her eyes. "Shameless hussy!" was all Alduccio thought, heading out for the evening. Ever since she'd gotten herself knocked up by Signora Anita's boy—Anita lived on the corner and sold fruit—there hadn't been a moment's peace around the house. She was going to have to marry, only the fruit seller's boy couldn't stand her now. The night they'd kicked her out of the house, he'd kept her company, slept with her on the steps of Block III, where he lived, but only to show off. When she realized she was pregnant they had gotten engaged, despite neither his parents nor hers at first being in favor of it. Humiliated, she had slashed her wrists with a piece of glass and almost died; in fact she still had two fine, fresh scars.

Waiting for Begalone, Alduccio went for a stroll in the development. The storm had cleared and the air was warm, almost springlike. Begalone had spruced himself up too, a kerchief knotted jauntily around his neck, his flaxen hair combed smooth and flat with a side part, then falling long on the neck so it looked like crusty bread. "Hey Bégalo!" Alduccio called. "How much you got?" Begalone asked at once. "Thirty lire," said Alduccio. "Just enough for the bus," said Begalone, "me too!" "What, and the rest?" asked Alduccio, getting suspicious. "It's here, it's here!" said Begalone, slapping his hand on his back pocket where he'd folded away the hundred and fifty filched from Caciotta. "We're good for a couple of smokes then," said Alduccio as they passed the bar. "Hold on, Ardù!" answered Begalone, then said "Bye-bye!" to a bus that was roaring off. "There'll be another," said Alduccio, cheerfully stretching his arms and legs.

Begalone hadn't eaten either. And under his yellow hair his face was yellow too, a fine yellow tending toward green that provided the perfect backdrop for his reddish freckles. He was so spent not even the fever he had could bring his color up. Every evening since he'd been released from the Forlanini, his temperature had been at least one degree over normal. It was tuberculosis; he'd had it for two or three years now, and it had reached the point where there was nothing really that could be done; in a year or so he'd be dead...

Walking beside Aldo, he rubbed his hands over his empty stomach, leaning forward and cursing his brother and his father and most of all his wretch of a mother, who one night—the first in a series of miserable nights—had tumbled out of bed, shrieking like a moron that she'd seen the devil. She said a snake had come into the room and coiled itself around the foot of the bed, staring at her and forcing her to strip naked; and that was when she'd started screaming. The whole day long she'd suddenly start shrieking again, yelping like a dog, complaining of a splitting headache, clinging to her daughters or whoever was around, begging them to protect her from only she knew what. The next night she woke up screaming again, only this time it wasn't the devil. In fact she'd moved over on the rumpled bed to leave a little room for someone else, though she hardly took up much space, dry little sprat that she was. Sitting right next to her on the gray sheets—she later told them—had been a dead girl, dead, that is, if her clothes were anything to go by, her best dress, white woolen socks, and a coronet of orange blossoms, since she was supposed to be marrying in a few days' time. She'd started complaining to Begalone's mother, saying the petticoat they'd given her was too short, the flower coronet they'd put on her head was too tight, it was pinching her temples, and then they weren't saying Mass often enough for her, that Pisciasotto, her little cousin, never came to the cemetery to see her, and so on and so forth. Begalone's mother had never met this girl, but the following day, people in the neighborhood, talking about the shrieks heard in the dead of night from the broken windows of

Begalone's apartment and echoing around the courtyards of the various buildings, came to the conclusion that the dead girl was a relative of a family that lived a few doors down in the same block; all the details fitted perfectly, including the girl's young cousin, Piscia-sotto, who was alive and kicking in Prenestino. Then the devil turned up again, in various forms: a snake, a bear, a neighbor whose teeth had grown into fangs, all wandering in and out of Bégalo's flat as if they owned the place, to torment his mother. At this point the family had decided to take action, and they called on an elderly relative in Naples who was an expert in such matters. First thing this man did was to have everything belonging to Begalone's mother plunged in boiling water, which meant saying goodbye to twenty kilowatts of gas in just a few days, and no dinner for anyone. The three brothers, four sisters, and all the neighboring housewives were kept busy driving off the bewitchment. Having found feathers twisted into the shapes of doves, crosses, and crowns in Bégalo's mother's pillow, they had immediately boiled them; at the same time they plunged bits of iron in boiling oil, then tossed them into cold water to see what shapes they formed, and for days the only sound in the house was the stamping of feet on the floor to make circles around the haunted woman who did nothing but beg for help and whine.

"If they'd given me a bit of bread, OK, but no, nothing, the bastards," said Begalone, pressing a hand into his stomach. "Both of us starving to death," laughed Alduccio, handsome face twisted in a grin of irony and resignation. They put their hands in their pockets and walked as far as Monte Pecoraro.

It was hot, not a humid heat, not a dry heat, just hot. As if someone had put a coat of paint on the breeze, on the yellowish walls of Ti-burtino, the fields, the carts, the buses with people hanging onto the doors. A coat of paint that was all the fun and the wretchedness of summer nights, past and present. The air was taut and vibrant as a drumhead; piss streaking the sidewalk was dry almost before you could button your pants; heaps of scorched garbage simmered away

and didn't even smell anymore. What smelled were the stones and
the steel shutters still hot from the sun, with maybe lines of wet rags
hung out and shriveled by the heat. In the few gardens that clung on
here and there, laden with lush fruit and vegetables growing untended,
as in the Garden of Eden, there was not so much as a drop of dew.
And in the district centers, and at the crossroads, as here in Tiburtino,
people flocked together, rushing around shrieking so that you might
have thought you were in the slums of Shanghai; even the more
isolated places were hectic, with armies of men out in search of a
whore, maybe stopping to chat at one of the mechanics' workshops
that were still open, the man's Rumi* parked outside. And beyond
Tiburtino there was Tor dei Schiavi, Prenestino, Acqua Bullicante,
Marranella, Mandrione, Porta Furba, Quarticciolo, Quadraro...
Hundreds of other centers all like the one in Tiburtino, with oceans
of people waiting at traffic lights, slowly spreading out into the surrounding streets, noisy as tenement lobbies, their sidewalks all broken,
moving along huge, ruined walls with rows of hovels nestled beneath.
And droves of young men racing each other on their Lambrettas,
their Ducatis, their Mondials, half-drunk, oily overalls open on bare
chests, or maybe dressed to the nines, as if they'd just stepped out of
a fashion window in Piazza Vittorio. A vast multitude encircling
Rome, between the city and the surrounding countryside, with hundreds of thousands of human lives swarming around their housing
developments, the huts for the homeless, the tenements. And all that
life wasn't just out there in the suburban districts, but right inside
Rome too, in the center of town, beneath Saint Peter's dome even:
yep, right there by the old dome you only needed to stick your nose
beyond the colonnade of Piazza San Pietro in the direction of Porta
Cavalleggeri and there they were, yelling, getting ornery, jeering,
bands and gangs of them crowding around the little cinemas, the
pizzerias, strewn here and there in Via del Gelsomino, Via della Cava,

---

*The Rumi Sport was a light motorbike popular in Italy throughout the 1950s.
Lambrettas, Ducatis, and Mondials, mentioned subsequently, were other popular
motorbikes.

in the empty lots surrounded by heaps of garbage where kiddies play football in the daytime, couples in the bushes covering themselves in old newspapers that people chuck away between Via delle Fornaci and the Gianicolo...And down beneath, on the other side of the dripping underpass, more and more of the same, in Piazza della Rovere, where crowds of tourists strut about, arm in arm, in their plus fours and stout shoes, singing mountain songs together, watched by young men in drainpipe pants and pointed shoes, leaning against the parapet over the Tiber, beside a blocked urinal, passing remarks with bored, sarcastic expressions on their faces, remarks that would slay the tourists on the spot if only they understood. And down along the roads beside the river where the occasional clapped-out tram rattles over uneven flagstones under galleries of plane trees, and the Lambrettas fly around the bends carrying one or maybe two young guys out looking for trouble, toward Castel Sant'Angelo with the Ciriola barge all lit up beside the river, on toward Piazza del Popolo, elegant as a theater, to Pincio and Villa Borghese, with its whine of violins and muted cries of whores and queers, herds of them wandering along singing "Sentimental" with eyelids lowered, mouths drooping, keeping the corner of an eye half-open to check there wasn't a police van in the offing. Or, on the opposite bank, toward Ponte Sisto, beneath the filthy, sparkling Fontanone, where two teams of Trastevere boys are playing football, yelling wildly and running this way and that like a herd of sheep amid the wheels of the stylish sedans driven by swells taking their tramps to Cinecittà for dinner at the Antica Pesa; at the same time, behind, from every alley of Trastevere, comes the chomping sound of all the jaws, male and female, chewing on pizza or crostini at tables in Piazza Sant'Egidio or Via Mattonato, their children whining and the street urchins scampering over the cobblestones, quarreling, light as the litter that the breeze shifts back and forth.

"Let's get off here, Ardù," said Begalone, jumping from the buffer, limp and lithe as a witch.

Alduccio stood up on the platform so that the conductor could see him and, knocking on the window, yelled, "I'm off now, loser!"

He jumped down from the tram onto the cobblestones, while the conductor had the satisfaction of sticking his head out and, with his block of tickets in his fist and people waiting to pay, yelling, "Fops."

"Up yours," shouted Bégalo, bending his knees, belly pushed out, using his fingers to make the shape of two big swollen eyes that, bristling with energy and cunning, he held up tight against his chest.

Right ahead was the Colosseum, burning like a furnace, with puffs and columns of bloody smoke rising from its arched apertures, the color of grenadine and candy paper, drifting up into the sky all around, over the Caelian Hill and the Oppian Hill and Via Labicana, glittering with cars, between the fans of floodlights scissoring over Via dell'Impero.

"So what do we do now?" said Alduccio.

"Let's take a stroll, come on!" said Begalone.

"A stroll it is," said Alduccio. They went down beneath the Colosseum, skirted around it, went under the Arch of Constantine, straight along the Viale dei Trionfi, dark and hot, sunk between ancient ruins and the pines climbing the greenish hump of the Palatine Hill, then onward in a long bend toward the Circuses.

They did it on foot, hands in their pockets, all scruffy and sluggish, walking a little ways apart, each crooning whatever came into his head. "Little clogs, little clogs . . ." crooned Begalone, then broke off. "Did you see the look on Caciotta's face?" "Little clogs, little clogs . . ." he went on, raising his voice to fill a whole stretch of empty avenue under pines green as billiard tables among the broken stones of the ruins. But Alduccio paid no attention, busy as he was with his own singing, hands in his pockets, bent forward, head up, turning left and right, neck down between his shoulders.

A tiny, dusty moon hung over the Circuses, but it spread a boundless light over the whole grassy expanse, the dark brambles, the stones, the heaps of shards and trash. Everyone there kept half an eye on it, irked that the only place you could find any shadow was under the big walls that surrounded the immense oval of Circus Maximus. By the time Alduccio and Bégalo turned up there were already men and teenagers and even a few younger kids sitting on the low wall, with the Circus beyond in the dusty moonlight, while farther down, near where the tram stopped, but still inside the park, you could see shadows moving, coming together or splitting up.

"Police!" shouted Bégalo mockingly, hand open beside his mouth, and he began to shake with laughter.

The two went on laughing for a while, even after the whores were too far away to hear, bending their knees, leaning on the wall, slapping each other on the back; more than laughing, they were pulling faces and spitting. But they soon stopped, thinking maybe those fat little sluts might have given them a go, or at the very least offered a hand job. They were both so horny they could have done it with a seventy-year-old. That's why the wild laughter didn't last, and now they were trudging along super serious, pissed off almost, predatory eyes searching the dark beyond the wall, the broad oval expanse with its ruins and brambles forming dark thickets in the pale aura of dusty moonlight. There were crowds of soldiers, a few stray youngsters, and the usual sluts yelping like bitches and threatening each other with their handbags.

"We've lost out all round!" said Begalone gloomily as he walked. "We'd have done better to retire to a fucking nursing home! I was really up for a good feel tonight, and instead zilch . . . Fucking poverty, what shit! Take a look at him," he went on, pointing to a guy driving by in a sports car, "he's having a ball! You think it's fair, him all spiffed up with that sweet pussy, loaded with cash, and us: zilch? Big-shot bastards! But their time is up. The world's changing!" And for a while he walked in silence, mouth twisted in a grimace of disgust.

But when they turned into Via del Mare, crossing the little gardens below the Temple of Vesta, Begalone said, "Wow," and stopped to stare goggle-eyed into the gardens.

"What's up?" asked Alduccio, not sure whether to pay attention or tell him to fuck off.

Begalone bent down and whistled. "Rounding up the sheep?" asked Alduccio.

"Are they hot, or what!" yelled Bégalo. "They" were two girls sitting on the steps of the temple; two blond babes who checked every box, male-baiting split skirts, and necklines so low half their tits were showing.

The girls seemed dazed, sitting in silence, turned toward each other, but as though not really seeing, staring vaguely at the gardens and flowerbeds that followed the slope in a curve down to the Tiber, looking above and below, toward Piazza di Bocca della Verità, the Arch of Janus, the old church, with moonlight gleaming everywhere, and everything bright as day.

Coming down from the Circuses and heading toward Ponte Rotto, Bègalo and Alduccio passed roguishly by, singing away. But after climbing a little farther up the road, they thought better of it and sneaked slowly back.

The two beauties hadn't moved, hadn't even breathed, it seemed. Keeping close together, like two mangy dogs who've been chased off with sticks and then slow down on some grungy sidewalk, tails between their legs, the boys climbed back up Via del Mare, then turned around again. This time they went to stand in the middle of the gardens, keeping a constant eye on the two pretty peaches. But the girls didn't seem to have noticed them. They went back down toward the temple, on the other side this time, looking down over the slope, went into the shadows under the little colonnade and advanced, slowly, toward the part bright with moonlight in the direction of Bocca della Verità.

But once again the two darlings paid no attention, sitting quite still, just as before. Bedraggled and exhausted, the two mangy dogs sat down, half in the shadow, half in the moonlight, their backs against the pitted yellow wall of the temple.

"So which would you like to dip your dick in," asked Begalone, "the blond or the redhead?"

"Both," said Alduccio.

"Yeah, and then all the others!" said Begalone.

"Both or neither," explained Alduccio, joking, "otherwise one would get upset."

"Tell me about it, these two are waiting for the sucker who'll pay!" muttered Bégalo.

"So, what's the problem, couldn't we make good suckers?" said Alduccio optimistically.

"Shall we go for it?" asked Bégalo after a while.

"I'm game!" said Alduccio. But they sat still, speaking softly, chuckling away, their knees pulled up to their chests, asses in the dust, tops of their heads and toes of their shoes brushed by the light. Only when the two women finally exchanged a couple of words did they pluck up courage and raise their voices to cause a little stir.

"Give me a smoke, come on," shouted Bégalo.

"When we've smoked this, we're out," said Alduccio, lighting the cigarette.

"So why don't we go and get some more?"

"Oh, yeah, when we don't even have a lira for the blind!"

"Damn, it's hot," shouted Bégalo, blowing out air, "hot enough to crack a turtle's back!"

"Christ," he went on after a moment, "I'm going to die of this heat, you know..."

"And so?"

"Let's take a dip in the fountain," Begalone proposed.

"You mad?" Alduccio found it funny.

"I'm not joking, you know," said Begalone, disgusted.

"Oh, fuck off, go on!" laughed Alduccio.

The two girls chuckled to themselves.

"Come on, Ardù!" shouted Begalone.

They got to their feet in the shadows and, still joking, began to unbutton their shirts as fast as they could; they peeled them off and threw them down where the shadow was deeper. Standing in just their vests, thick hair greased back, they might have been Samson and Absalom, but then, to take off their drainpipe pants without losing their balance, they both sat down again.

"Let me get my shoes off first," said Alduccio more softly, feeling a sudden affection for his smart new shoes, and with the air of someone who likes making fun of himself. He took them off and tossed them away. Last of all, the boys peeled their vests over dark sweaty chests, and were left in just their underpants.

"God, what a hulk I am," said Begalone, puffing out his chest.

"Tough as a truck," said Alduccio.

"Little clogs, little clogs," Bégalo began to sing, picking up the clothes they'd scattered about to seem more rascally; they tied them together with their belts and tucked them under their arms. Then they stepped out of the shadow, stopped a moment on the steps in the moonlight, and began to run, yelling as they raced across the flowerbeds. They threw their clothes on the grass under the chains that sagged around the fountain, clambered up the basin, which was a good three feet off the ground, and stood on the edge.

"I'm already fucking shivering," said Bégalo, twisting his mouth and crouching down.

"Ah, come on, Bégalo, it's hot, remember," said Alduccio.

"Hot as hot broth," said Bégalo, balancing with his toes hooked over the edge like a monkey. Alduccio gave him a push, and he went into the water like a sack of potatoes.

"Damn, what a belly flop," said Bégalo, climbing out again, head dripping.

"Watch the master," shouted Alduccio and dived in arrow-straight, the water splashing out of the basin and slapping onto the marble base beneath the fountain. Bégalo was singing at the top of his voice, head and shoulders out of the water.

"Shut up, idiot," said Alduccio, "if a guard hears we're fucked."

"What about this for a floating corpse, eh!" said Begalone. He played dead, then his nose went under, and he came out spluttering, half-drowned, hair brittle as spinach and longer than the Maddalena's falling over his face, which he was desperately trying to dry. "You want to show off, but you're not up to it!" laughed Aldo. Just three minutes in the water and they'd soaked the pavement for yards around, exposed roots and flowerbeds included.

"I'm getting out," said Bégalo.

"Me too," shouted Alduccio, "I'm not planning to die of pneumonia."

They climbed back on the edge again, underpants transparent now, clinging to their skin, dived in again, headfirst, then jumped out of the fountain.

"Fucking hell," said Bégalo, teeth chattering.

Dripping wet, they gathered their clothes under their arms and started to run across the cut grass, dodging between the low hedges. They sprinted here and there, to warm themselves up, laughing, then leapt up the steps of the little temple, went under the colonnade, and, passing behind the two girls, sneaked back into the shadow. They started fooling around, slapping each other; the girls barely glanced at them, unimpressed, or smiling a superior little smile.

"Come here," said Begalone, "and let's wring out these knickers." Laughing, teeth chattering, they retreated a little farther, beyond the curve of the temple, took off their underpants, and started wringing them out, one twisting one way and one the other. As always when he got dressed after a swim, Bégalo was overcome by a wave of senti- mentality: "Never, oh never did I love you so much in all my life . . ." he sang, wet underpants slung around his neck, pulling on his socks. But while these slouches were taking their time dressing, the two young angels hit the road. They set off toward the river, one carrying a book, their ample pleated skirts swaying in the sharp moonlight. Still half-naked and holding up his pants with one hand, Begalone went to the steps where they had been sitting.

"You're so hot!" he yelled.

Likewise half-dressed, Alduccio cupped his hands to his mouth to have his say: "Fantastic tits!"

"Come on," he said, "let's dress and go get them!"

The girls were already at Monte Savello by the time Alduccio and Begalone, skin still damp under their clothes, caught up.

"OK, show me how you approach a woman," said Begalone as they hurried after the two girls, who were walking calmly and swiftly ahead.

"Jesus, they're so fast," said Alduccio, who always walked like his feet were killing him. "Why don't you start the talking?" he said, panting now.

"Oh right, me, Mr. Weakling," said Bégalo, more exhausted than ever.

"You're such a Casanova, just fucking say something."

"Kiss my butt," said Begalone, disgusted.

Meanwhile, turning onto the road by the river, the two girls stopped by a car ten yards long, climbed in, the engine roared, and bye-bye, little boys...

The two good-for-nothings leaned on the parapet, dead as two plucked turkeys. "You look like a bum," said Alduccio after a while, looking Bégalo up and down and bursting out laughing. "And you look like a detention room," said Begalone. "Fuck and shit and damn," he said, "but the night's not over, you know." "Right, with a hundred and fifty in our pockets, what were you planning?" He put a hand in his pocket and gloomily fingered the hundred and fifty he'd stolen from Caciotta. "Let's go and get a fuck at the Circuses," said Begalone, "we can flip for it." "You're cuckoo," said Alduccio, tapping two fingers on his forehead. "And then we walk all the way back to Tiburtino, right?" "No way," snorted Begalone, "can't we get hold of another hundred and fifty somehow? There must be an asshole around here who'll part with a little cash." "Good luck finding him before Christmas!" said Alduccio. "Damn," said Bégalo, "how much you want to bet we find someone?" They headed toward Ponte Garibaldi like two hungry wolves. By the urinal at the end of the bridge on the Via Arenula side, an old man was slumped against the wall. Begalone stood at the urinal to take a tinkle, then went to lean on the wall himself, beside Alduccio. They stood there in silence for a while. Then Bégalo dug half a cigarette from his pocket and, bending politely over the old guy, asked, "Got a light, please?" Five minutes later, they had persuaded him to cough up fifty lire.

They scrounged another fifty at Ponte Sisto from an old man with a bag under his arm who went into the kind of over-the-top whining and whimpering that would have made an old woman's milk flow. Begalone cut him short: "We're so hungry we're fainting, asshole, we haven't eaten all day!" The gentleman handed them a hundred lire to buy four doughnuts, and they set off at once along Via dei Giubbonari, moving fast toward the brothel in Campo dei Fiori, and talking seriously. "So you're a thug too, are you?" demanded Alduccio angrily. "Will you listen to this dick!" yelled Begalone, stopping in the middle of the road and raising his arm to point: "Who was it that got us the cash?" "What's that supposed to mean?" said Alduccio. "Oh, nothing at all," Begalone retorted, "I get the cash, and he gets laid. Idiot!" he yelled, tapping two fingers on his nose. But as they were speaking, they passed a diner; "Fuck this," Begalone said, and went in. They each wolfed down three stuffed rice balls and when they came out they were back to square one. But since they were nearly there they drifted on down Via dei Giubbonari anyway, until, just as they were reaching the end of the street and about to turn onto Campo dei Fiori, Alduccio nudged Begalone and, with a nod and a narrowing of sly, sleepy eyes, pointed out a guy walking ahead of them, occasionally throwing them a glance over his shoulder. "Got him," said Begalone. The guy kept slowing down then speeding up; he turned into Campo dei Fiori, then turned left, among a bunch of boys playing with a rag ball in the wet piazza, and stopped a moment beside the latticed shelter over a urinal, turning to look back. Begalone and Alduccio gave him the stare. The guy was short, but dressed up for the occasion, with a stylish little shirt and a nice pair of sandals. Hesitating, he went on toward Piazza Farnese, then back up toward Campo dei Fiori along a dark alley, a move he repeated two or three times, going round and round the same streets, like a rat drowning in a bucket.

"Well damn," said Begalone, moving ahead, "what are you doing here!"

"What are you doing?" said Riccetto, looking down on Begalone, then Alduccio, then at the guy they'd picked up.

"Give me a light and keep your voice down," said Begalone, approaching Riccetto with a cigarette between his lips. Riccetto handed over his lighter, without moving an inch, just lowering his lids a little, since, with respect to Begalone and the others, he was perched higher up, on the parapet above the river, one leg hanging down and the other pulled into his chest.

"Meeting someone?" pressed Begalone.

"Yeah, like who!" said Riccetto.

"Wise guy," said Bégalo.

Alduccio and the other man had moved away a bit.

"He's got the hots for Alduccio," chuckled Bégalo, with a touch of envy.

But the man was sizing up Riccetto too, deliberately sitting in there in that tempting position, legs wide apart.

"Looking at me?" Riccetto asked.

The man smiled: "Yes," he said, a bit coy, but laying it on.

"Oh, right," said Bégalo, as if he'd just remembered something that had slipped his mind, breezy and relaxed, "let me introduce you to a friend of mine."

Riccetto let the leg against his chest slither down and held out the right hand that had been holding it toward the new arrival. The man shook his hand with the prim smile of a convent girl: "My pleasure," he said, alluding to the pleasure he hoped to get from this acquaintance, if all went well, and letting his eyes slide over the body that would be dispensing that pleasure, sitting calm and content on the parapet, as if about to burst out singing.

"All over me," said Riccetto, following the man's eyes.

The queer pretended to have been caught out, then pretended to smile a bashful smile, but with a suggestion of challenge in his dark mouth, tongue flicking about inside like a snake's; and he lifted a hand to his chest, nervously pulling the open flaps of his shirt together over his throat, almost as if he wanted to protect himself from the damp of the night, or perhaps out of modesty to hide whatever the boys were looking at.

"You'd like him, would you?" said Begalone.

"Hmmmm, I would!" said the queer, but shrugging and playing bored.

Alduccio was getting impatient, and feeling a bit left out. "So, are we going to move on?" he asked.

"Move on where?" said the queer, voice drawling.

"Down by the river here, come on," said Alduccio. They were on the road by the Tiber between Ponte Sisto and Ponte Garibaldi.

"You're crazy, sweetheart," said the queer, offended.

"Oh, come on," Alduccio insisted, "we can climb down the steps, go under the bridge, and do a little stuff."

"No, no, no, no, no," said the queer, waving a hand and shaking his head, face absolutely set against it.

"Why not?" said Alduccio, getting worked up, "Where are you going to find a better place? Or are you planning to be there half an hour? A couple of minutes, and catch you later! We make out, we need a shit, nobody's going to bother us down there!" Even as he spoke, the queer's attention strayed back to Riccetto, smiling, teeth gleaming, searching out his eyes, then looking between his legs. Only when Alduccio stopped did the queer realize he was still there; in a sharp dry voice, as if to settle things once and for all, he said, "No, I'm not going down there."

Then he was smiling again, making soft eyes at Riccetto.

"Damn, you're ugly," Riccetto told him.

Alduccio went back on the offensive: "So what are we going to do?" Begalone backed him up: "Listen, don't take too long about it, hey, pretty boy!" The queer must have been pushing fifty but was trying to look at least twenty years younger; he kept tugging his collar closed over his chicken chest, like he was worried about his health. "OK, let's go," he said, more amenably.

"Yeah, right! You keep saying, 'Let's go, let's go,' and then you won't move your ass!" said Alduccio.

There was almost no one along the river road between Ponte Sisto and Ponte Garibaldi now, but Riccetto remembered, when he was a kid, right after the war, how busy it used to be here: along the parapet, sitting the way he was sitting now, there would have been at least twenty young men, ready to sell themselves to whoever would pay, and the queers came by in droves, singing and dancing, the baldies and the peroxide queens, some of them very young, some very old, but all acting crazy, not the slightest bit worried about passersby, or people watching from trams, calling each others' names out loud—"Wanda! Bolero! Ferroviera! Mistinguette!"—whenever they caught sight of someone they knew in the distance, running to meet him, kissing each other softly on the cheeks, the way women do so as not to ruin their makeup; and when they all got together, opposite the young men leaning against the parapet watching them grim-faced, they'd start dancing, maybe a ballet step or two, or the can-can, and while they pranced about, from time to time they'd cry out: "Liberated! We're liberated!"

Those were times when no one had any problem going down the steps, among the prickly bushes, thick with mud and scattered with litter, under Ponte Sisto or Ponte Garibaldi, and doing everything they felt like doing, without being afraid. Sometimes the police came by and a few guys would run for it, but soon enough everything was back to normal. Riccetto hadn't come here to hustle or meet anyone this evening, just to pass a little time, remembering how things used to be.

"Come on, I'll take you somewhere really nice," he said, with a sudden rush of generosity.

The queer hammed up the prim little smile he used as a mask, tiny wrinkles spreading all over his face, but feeling absolutely radiant, with his sidelong look, like some soubrette photographed bare-shouldered for an Altieri fashion poster. He even made the gesture women make when they toss their hair back, then he leaned forward, a little lopsided, ready to follow Riccetto.

Riccetto had them catch the 44 and took them up to the area where he'd lived as a boy. They got off at Piazza Ottavilla, which had been practically out in the country when Riccetto was growing up. Then they turned left down a road that hadn't been there then, or was only a path leading down between open fields with willow trees and clumps of bamboo ten feet high, like you find on the sides of a valley; but now there were apartment blocks with people already living in them, and new building sites as well. "Let's go farther down," Riccetto said. They went on, beyond the last building sites, and came to a path that led toward Donna Olimpia; but first it crossed the courtyard of an old tavern with a pergola, full of drunks. They kept going, but the path soon ended because at the far end of the fields, now entirely built up, there was a new road, with yet more blocks, either finished or under construction. Right behind them was the climb up to Monte di Casadio where Riccetto had spent whole days as a boy. They headed that way, and when they got to the top, with what was now almost a sheer drop below, they found themselves looking at the Ferrobedò. It stood at the bottom of the hollow below them, pale in the moonlight. Behind it, against the whitish clouds and forming a big semicircle, you could see the dark, jagged tangle of Monteverde Nuovo, and to the right, behind Monte di Casadio, the tops of the tower blocks in Donna Olimpia.

"This is it," said Riccetto, "now you guys climb down here to the right," and he showed them a path of sorts that wound through the weeds down the hump of the rise, and seemed a perfect place for goats. "At the bottom you'll find a cave. You can't miss it. No one's going to come and bother you there ... I'll say goodbye now. Enjoy yourselves."

"Where are you going, are you leaving us?" asked the queer, sulking and hunching his shoulders.

"Mind your own fucking business and don't be nosy," Alduccio told him, not at all unhappy that Riccetto was leaving them.

"What's going on?" said the queer. "What a way to behave."

"Relax," said Riccetto generously, "I'll take you as far as the cave." They went down the path hugging the bushes and found themselves in a little glade that was green and slimy, thanks to a trickle of dark effluent flowing from the cave, which was right in front of them. "That's it, in there," said Riccetto. The queer couldn't get over the idea that Riccetto wasn't staying and took him by the arm, giving him a come-on smirk, and dipping his face rather sweetly below a shoulder to smile up at him from below.

Riccetto was patient and smiled back. Since he'd been in Porta Portese he'd put on weight and no longer felt the need to be always playing smart and tough. He was a man of experience now. "Damn," he said, almost taking the queer's side, "two not enough for you, right?"

"N-no," said the queer, bending a knee like a girl playing coy to get her way.

"Damn," Riccetto said again, "you like to have a good time, do you?" And full of sympathy and a sense of his own superiority, he set off down the path with a sly wave of farewell and didn't turn around.

The path dipped along the side of the slope for twenty yards or so, then led straight to the center of Donna Olimpia. At the end you just had to jump over a ruined wall, cross a stretch of road and you were directly opposite the Franceschi School. It was still no more than a heap of broken masonry, as if it had only collapsed a couple of days ago, except that a layer of filth had gathered on the rubble, where the rain fell and the sun burned. Riccetto stood looking at it with his hands in his pockets. True, the chunks that had rolled into the road and the landslides of broken brick had been piled up more or less tidily; only a couple of blocks were still lying in the road; obviously when they had pretended to start rebuilding, for the election campaign, those two or three blocks had been left to one side, and when the elections were over no one could be bothered to come and take them away.

Riccetto looked all around with great interest; he even went behind to check out the courtyards and the big sinks in the washhouses and the toilets. Then he came back to the front, beneath the mountain of rubble and the buildings at the corners that were still standing, but empty, with slats of sodden wood nailed across the windows. He hung around for a while, after all this was why he had come to Donna Olimpia, then turned up the collar of his shirt, drew in his shoulders a little, because it was turning cold, and set off on a slow, relaxed tour of the area, starting in the center, with its cracked sidewalks and the newsagent closed, just a few people coming quietly and sleepily home. But at the entrance to the Case Nove there was a surprise: two policemen, blue with boredom and cold, were keeping guard; they would stand still for a while, then walk up and down, like two shadows in the gloom of the tenements, gun holsters on their hips.

Riccetto had nothing to feel guilty about; he was in the area for purely sentimental reasons, and he sauntered slowly by the two guards with almost a who-gives-a-shit swagger, then set off for the Grattacieli. These were four tenement blocks connected together in such a way that the horizontal and diagonal rows of the windows lined up, this way and that, without a break all the way around for hundreds and hundreds of yards, and likewise, the stairwells, which you could tell from outside by the long vertical rows of rectangular windows; while below, amid Fascist-style covered passageways, underpasses, and porches, were six or seven small clay courtyards with the remains of what were once supposed to be flowerbeds now strewn with rags and litter beneath canyons of high walls rising right to the moon. At this hour almost no one was coming from Via Donna di Olimpia to find their way home through those dark passageways and courtyards; and if someone did come by, they walked briskly along the barred windows of the semibasements, slipped through a porch, and started to climb the long flights of dusty stairs to their flat.

Riccetto wandered around the courtyards hoping to come across someone to chat with. After a while, in fact, he saw the shadow of a young man coming down the iron steps of Via Ozanam. "I've a feeling I know this guy," thought Riccetto, and went toward him. He was a redhead, all freckles, with two bushy red brows for eyes, and his hair neatly parted to one side. Riccetto watched him approaching and, sensing this interest, the redhead looked his way, keenly, on the alert. "Hey, don't we know each other," said Riccetto, going toward him, hand outstretched.

"If you say so," said the redhead, looking him up and down.

"Damn, aren't you Agnolo?" said Riccetto.

"Right," said the redhead.

"I'm Riccetto," cried Riccetto, as though disclosing an important fact.

"Ah," said Agnolo.

"So, how you doing?" asked Riccetto politely.

"Getting by," said Agnolo, who was clearly half-asleep already.

"What you been up to?" asked Riccetto, bright and peppy.

"Up to? The usual. I've just knocked off work and I can barely keep my eyes open."

"What do you do, bartender, right?"

"Right."

"And the others? Obberdan, Zambuia, Bruno, Lupetto?"

"What do you think? All working, more or less, not much else to say."

"Rocco, Arvaro?"

"Who's Arvaro?"

"Arvaro Furciniti, nickname Capoccione, remember?"

"Right," said Agnolo. Rocco had gone to live in Risano, that was the last anyone had seen of him. But Alvaro had wound up in a bad way, a grim story that ended just a few weeks ago. It was early March. Raining. Alvaro was in a bar in Testaccio where a bunch of idle youngsters were shooting pool; Alvaro was playing too, to pass the time. They were all hoodlums in that bar, including the owner, a paunchy guy, bald on top, little curls on his neck, might have been Nero, who dealt in stolen goods. The pool players were all wearing fancy shirts despite it being a regular workday, a Monday in fact, and every single one of them had two or three big jobs to his name and was living on the profits, at least as things stood. But they'd been playing all afternoon in that big damp room behind the bar, and they were bored stiff, so they decided to go for a jaunt in Rome. They'd got to Piazza del Popolo or thereabouts when there's this chance to steal an old Aprilia,* you'd have to be dumb not to go for it; there was nothing in the car, not even a pair of gloves, but they thought they'd take it for a spin that evening, then dump it somewhere. They'd had a bit to drink in Testaccio, then a bit more in Piazza di Spagna and Via del Babuino, and now they had a bit more again, driving here and there around Rome with the Aprilia they'd just picked up. They got plastered and began to drive crazily fast. They went to race round Piazza Navona, then, because the circle around the piazza was too tight, they headed for the Circuses, the Archaeological Park, and took turns hitting seventy and even eighty on the wet avenues there. Two cops on bikes went after them, but they headed down toward the Registry Office and lost them in the alleys behind Piazza Giudia; then they went back to race round Piazza Navona again and hit a

---

*Designed by Vincenzo Lancia and in production from 1936 to 1950, the Aprilia was a prestige sedan, prized for its speed and often used in motor racing.

stroller, sent it flying twenty feet or so; the thing was empty, thank God, since the kid was toddling along holding his mother's hand, but a man yelled something at them, and they slammed on the brakes, piled out and faced off with the guy, punched him out, left him with his mouth streaming blood, got back in the car, and made off as fast as the thing would go along Governo Vecchio and Borgo Panigo. They turned along the Tiber, heading north toward Ponte Milvio; but when they were passing the Ministero della Marina, they saw a classy lady out walking on her own, all dressed up, by the parapet; they slowed down, one got out, went up to her, grabbed her bag, then off; they reversed, crossed the bridge, and went back down toward Borgo Pio; they raced round Piazza San Pietro for a while and ended up back in Testaccio to drink another three or four glasses of cognac. By now it was nighttime and they decided to make a dash out to Anzio, or Ardea, or Latina, out in the country. They piled back in the Aprilia, hit the gas, heading for San Giovanni, and turned onto the Appia; half an hour later they were in a village no one had seen the name of and stopped at a bar for another drink, then raced up and down those country roads, never going less than sixty, until, almost by chance, they found themselves in a place near Latina that one of them happened to know. It was past midnight. They left the car by the road and went into some barnyards, where they stole maybe twenty chickens, shooting the farm dog dead. They loaded the chickens in the car and set off at eighty, went back on the Appia again, and, about twenty miles out of Rome, just before Marino, God knows how or why, they ran into the back of a truck. The Aprilia was reduced to a heap of twisted steel, with a tangle of bloody bodies inside, covered in chicken feathers. The only one who came out alive was Alvaro, but he'd lost an arm and was left blind.

Telling this story, the redhead had begun to feel cold, maybe because he was sleepy; his face turned pale, and, glimpsing the occasional person going into the tenement, hunched and silent, off to bed, he began to feel impatient.

"Let me go and sleep," he finally said, stretching his arms, "or my dad'll raise hell."

"See you around then," said Riccetto, who was sad to see him go, but didn't want to show it.

"Goodbye, what's-your-name, Riccè," said Agnolo, and he shook his hand and disappeared into the broad dark innards of staircase M, or maybe N, with its dusty stairs dappled here and there by the light of a lonely electric bulb.

Riccetto walked away quiet and thoughtful, crossed the courtyards, went out into Via di Donna Olimpia, passed the policemen again, hands in his pockets, whistling, and beneath Monte di Casadio took the road that went down to Ponte Bianco beyond the Ferrobedò. He had nothing to do here now and quickened his pace, still whistling away. He couldn't wait to be down at Ponte Bianco and on the tram home to bed.

The Ferrobedò or, to give its proper name, the Ferrobeton, stretched away to his right under a candy-floss moon, a fragrant dusty whiteness, all neatly ordered and so silent you could hear a guard, in one or other of the warehouses, singing in a low voice. And behind, on a kind of plateau, at the top of a few big black mounds, the immense semicircle of Monteverde Nuovo stood out stark, lights twinkling here and there under scattered banners of cloud that seemed like grainy porcelain in the silk-smooth sky. Riccetto hadn't been back here since the school collapsed and he was struggling to recognize it all. It was too clean, too neat; he couldn't believe his eyes. Beneath him, the Ferrobedò was crystal clear: its high chimneys rising from the bottom of the valley almost to the road where he stood, its store yards arranged in row upon orderly row of neatly stacked railroad ties, multiple rail lines gleaming around the occasional wagon, dark and still, then the rows of warehouses that, at least from above, looked so clean with their reddish roofs all neatly lined up they might have been dance halls.

Even the steel fencing parallel to the road on the bushy embankment above the factory was brand new; there wasn't a single hole in it. Only the old cabin near the fence was foul and filthy as ever; people passing by were still using it to take a dump; inside and out the shit lay at least a couple of inches deep. It was the only thing Riccetto found familiar, exactly as it had been when he was a kid and the war just over.

Begalone and Alduccio scampered back toward Campo dei Fiori, hands in pockets, shirts flapping open over their pants, but without singing or joking.

"So you're a thug too, are you?" Alduccio repeated, hunched over as he walked.

"Listen to the guy!" yelled Begalone, stopping in the middle of the road and stabbing his hand toward him, fingers tight together, "Were you the only one who went along or what?"

"What's that got to do with it, he said it to me, not you, out of politeness," said Alduccio cupping his hand around his mouth.

"Oh, you're so cute, aren't you!" said Begalone, setting off again. "Mongoloid," he added, banging a hand on his forehead.

"And then I never said it should only be me," said Alduccio, "idiot, I said let's flip for it!"

Meantime, bickering all the way, they'd reached Campo dei Fiori, where the flagstones had been hosed down, though there were still a few cabbage stalks and scraps here and there, and kids still playing football with a bundle of rags. At the bottom of the piazza, where the gloom was deepest, an alley opened—Via dei Cappellari—one rotting door after another, archways and crooked little windows, the cobblestones damp with stale piss. The two friends stood in the last patch of light before the tunnel of the alley, near a couple of old women sitting on a doorstep under a battered streetlamp, and Begalone pulled a coin from his pocket, turned it between his fingers, and tossed it in the air.

"Heads!" shouted Alduccio.

The coin hit the cobbles, which stank of fish, and rolled close to a manhole cover. Shoving and tugging each other's shirts till they almost ripped, Bégalo and Alduccio got down on all fours to look.

"I'm in luck," said Alduccio in a calm, loud voice and, thoroughly pleased with himself, he went ahead into the alley. Bégalo followed.

The only light on the pavement, which seemed like the floor of a cowshed, came from one or two tiny windows sunk in the dark walls, and it was hard work finding the door to the brothel. Fortunately it had been painted a bright pea green, making it one in a thousand, and then it was half open to a corridor of white tiles, like in the public baths.

They went up the stairs and came to a mezzanine landing; to one side were more stairs covered in threadbare carpet climbing under a white arched ceiling; to the other there was the door to the lounge; between the two was Madam's desk.

Since there was no one around and the door to the lounge was closed, the two friends calmly headed on up the second flight of stairs. Only to be stopped by a bellowing voice: "Yo, assholes!" It was Madam, yelling loud enough to bust her bladder. "Will you look at these two," she went on, "talk about making yourselves at home."

Her words were greeted with shouts of laughter and mocking voices from the smoke-filled lounge. Two or three customers in there even got up and came to the door to look and snigger.

Laughing themselves, Begalone and Alduccio hurried back down the few stairs they had climbed and went to speak to Madam, who had now dragged her flabby, bowed thighs behind her pulpit. But she didn't find it a laughing matter, nor did her drudge, who stuck to her like a leech, glowering fiercely.

"These cretins," said Madam, who, as a property owner, liked to think of herself as belonging to the upper classes and occasionally spoke proper Italian. "Planning to get laid without paying a cent, were you? What a world!"

"Lady," said Begalone meekly, "we made a mistake."

"Mistake, my ass," said Madam, who switched to Trastevere-speak whenever her interests were at stake, though she was originally from Frosinone. Now she held out a brusque hand. The boys pulled out their IDs and showed them; then, cheerfully enough, despite having made fools of themselves, they went into the lounge, which was full of customers, smoking on couches along the walls, red as shrimps, looking like losers for the most part, silent and horny.

Right in the middle of the room, on an upholstered stool with two or three mint-green mosquito nets around her belly, sat an old Sicilian woman sucking a cigarette smothered in lipstick.

The men watched her, mute, and she scowled in their faces, puffing smoke all around, tits hanging down to her belly button.

Walking in, Alduccio went straight up to her and, back turned to the packed room of customers, with a nod of his head muttered, "Let's go."

"What a jerk," thought Begalone, heading for a sliver of sofa, "all these guys have been here an hour and more, none of them wants her, then he's barely through the door and he takes her upstairs!" Meantime Alduccio and the whore were climbing the stairs with the threadbare carpet. Begalone started smoking, one buttock on the sofa, one off, beside two soldiers from the north, vaguely redheaded, who hadn't said a word, sitting there respectfully like they were in a church, not a brothel. "What year is he planning to come back, the asshole," thought Bégalo angrily. "If he doesn't come out with the cash next time I'll whip his ass." He took a last pull on the cigarette that was burning his fingers, chucked it under the sofa, and crushed it with his heel.

Everything was proceeding as usual: Madam in the corridor bickering with her drudge, yelling as if they were gutting her, half the words indistinguishable.

"Fat floozy!" pronounced two or three youngsters from a corner of the lounge after the shouting match had been going on for a while. And this too was the usual fare. They spoke in such low, straining voices the words seemed to come from their guts, snapping the tendons in their necks and flooding their eyes with blood; then they quickly reverted to their normal faces so that no one could tell who had spoken. Madam didn't give a damn anyway and went on yelling at her sanctimonious drudge. In short, business as usual: after a while two more girls came down; one went to sit on the empty stool, the other on the knees of one of the youngsters who had spoken up then shut up, pulling sad, suffering faces like they'd just swallowed the sacred Host. The soldiers got up and quietly slid off, followed by the insults of the two whores; the younger customers giggled among themselves, red as red peppers; the smell of smoke, sweaty clothes, and canvas shoes got thicker and thicker, and all this too was exactly what you would usually expect. When all of a sudden...

Amid the din in the lounge, over the sound of Madam's voice as she launched into the conclusion of her invective, and the whores griping about this or that, all at once, from upstairs, came a peal of laughter that just went on and on. At first no one paid it any mind. Not Madam herself, not the girls, not the huddle of customers, not Begalone. But then when the laughter didn't stop everyone began to prick up their ears. From behind her desk Madam began to raise suspicious glances toward the ceiling, then put the cash away in the drawer—cash she'd been counting over and over while yelling at her drudge—and went to the bottom of the stairs, looking up. Even the girls shut up and went to stand behind her, dragging trails of gauze behind them, rolls of flesh bouncing under skin fragrant with powder and fries. The young men from Panìgo* got to their feet and went to crowd round the door, leaning on the doorposts or on each other. The other customers gathered behind them, with Begalone at the back, everyone straining their necks to get a look at whatever was going on.

The woman laughing was still on the third flight of stairs, above the small, stuccoed arch over the staircase and beyond the landing where the threadbare carpet came to an end. But slowly, step by step, she was coming down. She had to stop from time to time to throw her head back, or bend double, the better to laugh. She laughed loud enough to be heard out on the street, but it wasn't a heartfelt laugh: for a while it went "ha-ha-ha-ha-ahhhh," then stopped, then started over, "ha-ha-ha-ha-ahhhh," but at a higher pitch, as if the slattern had something stuck in her throat. At last she reached the landing and there she stopped to laugh for the benefit of the audience who had gathered on the landing below. For a while they watched in amazement as she doubled up, more out of spite than pleasure now, louder and rowdier with every blast.

*Likely a reference to Via di Panico, about a half mile from Campo dei Fiori.

"So, are you going to tell us what's to laugh about, hey, windbag," yelled one of the youngsters. She looked at him and the others at the bottom of the stairs and laughed in their faces.

"Give me a laugh on my dick, will you!" shouted another.

She turned to look up the flight of stairs where they couldn't see and, still laughing, cried, "Hey, get a move on, or are you waiting for your wet nurse?" Then Alduccio appeared, beside the Sicilian woman, on the landing, head down as he looked for a tighter hole in the belt of his pants.

"Go get yourself a zabaglione," she went on, bursting into her mean laughter again.

"Fuck off," Alduccio muttered, finally sorting out the buckle of his belt. The Sicilian came slowly down the carpeted stairs, leaning a hand on the wall the better to laugh, and he came after, as if to hide behind her. The others had got the idea now and joined in the laughing, but not so loudly, with a little discretion even, murmuring between giggles, "Fucking hell, why so much fucking fuss?" But she went on with more of the same, roaring with laughter, to piss everyone off. "All this hurry," she turned to Alduccio, "and then you can't get it up." "I'm run-down!" Alduccio mumbled by way of justification, but so quietly he was the only one who heard. They were both down on the lower landing now, where the others were, and the Sicilian went into the lounge still laughing hysterically, pushing through the customers who had gathered at the door, while Alduccio, who was too upset and angry to look anyone in the eye, sneaked straight down the last flight of stairs, heading for the street and leaving Begalone to fork out fast for Madam, who was already protesting she hadn't been paid, then run out after him.

"We're going to have to walk as far as Stazione Termini, you know that, right?" he said anxiously to Alduccio when he had caught up with him, and the brothel door had swung shut behind.

"What do I care?" said Alduccio. He walked on without turning left or right, like a mangy wolf with his tail between his legs. They were alone in Via dei Cappellari, walking one ahead of the other, close to buildings crusted with thick, damp filth, all black, punctured here and there with small windows where people had hung rags to dry. It was so narrow that reaching out of a window you could have shaken hands with someone reaching from one opposite, and so dark you had to feel your way like a blind man. "We're going to bang our heads here," said Bégalo, "or go facedown in someone's piss." Almost groping his way along, taking care where to put his feet, he suddenly burst out laughing. "What have you got to laugh about?" asked Alduccio, turning sharply. Begalone picked his way on cobblestones that felt like they'd been smothered in grease and came out with another belly laugh. "Oh, do it again, laugh away!" said Alduccio, worn out.

Still walking one ahead of the other they crossed Campo dei Fiori, which was quiet now, and headed at a brisk pace down Largo Argentina and Via Nazionale, toward Stazione Termini, where they arrived after about half an hour. "Shall we grab a ride here?" asked Alduccio feebly. "Farther down's easier," said Begalone, his face drawn and yellow with exhaustion. They grabbed onto the 9 by the Macao barracks. Begalone was feeling cheerful. Hanging on to the buffer, he started to sing at the top of his voice, "Little clogs, little clogs!" And if maybe someone on the street turned to look, he challenged them at once: "What you looking at?" he yelled, or, depending on the kind of person and the speed of the tram: "Hey, boss, I'm riding the tram, and so?" and he raised his hand, fingers tight together, as if asking a question; or if it was a youngster: "Hey, buddy, could you be lending me a few lire?" or if it was a busty girl, "Wow, are you hot, sweetheart!" and carried away by enthusiasm, he'd start singing even louder. "Oh, give it a rest," Alduccio told him earnestly, at a stop, where they got down and loitered beside the tram, playing innocent, "you might as well phone the cops and invite them along: Hey, there's this asshole hanging on to the tram, yeah, the number nine!" "What do I care if they pull me in, you think it's any better at my place?" Begalone said, jumping back on the buffer and grabbing the rail.

In the cemetery hundreds of tiny lights shone tightly packed and quietly trembling between the cypresses beside the burial niches visible above the perimeter wall. Even Portonaccio at the end of the line, just beyond the Tiburtina station overpass, was silent, with just the odd empty tram or bus parked like a dark stain in an air so wan that the clear sky and the occasional streetlight seemed only to make it gloomier. A 309 was stopped beside the closed newspaper kiosk and not a soul was waiting at the shelter a few yards beyond.

"Let's see how much I've got in my pocket," said Begalone, turning it inside out to find his money. "Fifty-five lire," he said, "forty for the bus, and with the change we can grab ourselves a doughnut." "Sure, let's grab a doughnut," said Alduccio hoarsely. He was dying of hunger, but couldn't even think of the doughnut, hanging back hunched behind Bégalo. Bégalo bought a doughnut at an almost empty stall. "Here, eat," he said, putting the cold pastry near Alduccio's mouth. Alduccio twisted his mouth and took a bite. "Another," said Begalone. "No, enough," said Alduccio, turning his head away. "All right," yelled Begalone, "even better, I can eat it all myself." And he started to eat, laughing, mouth full. "Laugh, go on, fuck you," grumbled Alduccio, more morose than ever. "We getting on, or what?" said Begalone after a while, when he'd finished chewing, and, full of fun, he jumped on the running board. Without a word, Alduccio jumped up after him into the half-empty bus, dragging his feet, hands still in his pockets. Begalone had climbed up, whistling a Charleston tune. "Two tickets, conductor!" he shouted. "I hear you, I hear you," said the conductor, carefully tearing two tickets from his block, "no need to yell."

There were a dozen or so people on the bus, half-asleep: a blind woman who'd been out begging accompanied by a man who looked like Cavour,* two musicians with their instruments in black canvas bags, heads nodding, a carabiniere, two or three workers, a few youngsters coming back from the cinema. Bégalo and Alduccio stretched themselves out on the front seats, and since Alduccio wouldn't talk, Bégalo began to sing in a low voice. Just below them, the driver was

*Camillo Cavour (1810–1861) was one of the great architects of unification and the first prime minister of the united Italy. Statues of him are ubiquitous throughout Italy; hence, Cavour's is a well-known face.

on his feet talking to his supervisor, while behind, above its big walls, the cemetery lights flickered brightly. Amid this silence and the sad stench of poor people's clothes, a boy wearing a bomber jacket suddenly climbed aboard, a blond kid with a face that betrayed generations of poverty; he stood in the middle of the aisle and turned to face the people sitting. While no one was paying the slightest attention, he cleared his throat a few times, conscientiously, then burst into song. At this, everyone turned to look, and the boy, undaunted, went on singing in a loud nasal voice, articulating all the words of his song with great care. "Fly away! Fly away! Fly away!" he sang, and out of the corners of their eyes, Bégalo and Alduccio observed their colleague at work. Here and there some passengers couldn't help laughing and watched open-mouthed; others felt embarrassed and turned away to look out the window.

"If you don't hurry up and fly away, the bus'll be off, and bye-bye birdie," said Begalone, to break the ice, while Alduccio was taking advantage of this dummy's singing to focus more clearly on his own problems. But the boy poured out his song from start to finish into the total silence of the bus, the whole square, then went around the passengers to ask for something. Begalone shook his monkish mortician's head, puffing up his neck like a turkey, and forked out the last five lire he had. Duty done, leaving as silently as he'd arrived, the blond boy jumped down from the running board. "Scrounges his cash and he's off," said Bégalo, heart bleeding at the thought of the five lire. "Fly away, fly away," he called over his shoulder, though the blond boy was out of range now, "fly the fuck away." Then he bent his yellow face down right below Alduccio's nose: "Fly away, fly away," he went on. Alduccio rammed his elbow under Begalone's chin so that his head slammed back against the seat. His eyes were brimming with anger, ready to strike if his friend said another word. But Bégalo let it pass. Right then the driver climbed aboard, taking his time about it, but instead of sitting at the wheel he stretched out on the seat, boredom written all over his dark Judah's face; he put his hands between his legs and appeared to be falling asleep. A lugubrious voice from the back of the bus called: "Hey, driver, we settling in for the duration here, or what?" But the man didn't answer. "Fly away, fly away, fly away," said Bégalo in a loud voice. These two reactions set the whole bus talking and everyone said what they thought; when they'd all joked a bit, making comments about the war in Korea and the mayor of Rome, the driver began to show signs of life. He sat up, lazily grasped the hand brake, and the old crate began to cough and shake, until, bouncing on the cobbles, it set off along a dark and deserted Via Tiburtina.

"So long, Ardù," said Begalone to Alduccio when they reached their blocks at the far end of Tiburtino, and he started to climb the peeling stairway. "So long," muttered Alduccio, walking on toward his own block, a little farther up the empty street. But even if it had been packed with people, he wouldn't have noticed. Each streetlight spread its pool of light on the asphalt and the yellowish walls of the tenements that stretched away in rows, scores of them, all exactly the same, with their courtyards of bare earth, likewise all the same. Five or six kiddies went by playing musical instruments, a harmonica, a drum, castanets, and disappeared among the buildings until their samba was no more than a *b-bum*, *b-bum*, wandering through a city of the dead. A drunk whose face flamed red under his filthy beret was whistling to get his lover to open up for him while her husband was sleeping. Two youngsters were talking over their own stuff in low voices that nevertheless sounded quite distinct in the middle of one of the courtyards where the rows of stone supports for hanging out the laundry looked like so many gallows lined up in the dark.

Alduccio's front door was ajar and the light was on inside. His sister was sitting on a chair; on her feet at the other end of the messy kitchen, his mother was still yelling. The dishes in the sink were unwashed; the floor was strewn with food and filth, and on the table, under a light that gleamed on anything wet, there were still two or three pieces of bread, a dirty bowl, and a knife. The door to one of the two bedrooms was also half-open, and in the dark you could see Alduccio's father, still dressed, his legs wide apart on the big bed where the youngest daughter also slept. The other room, where Riccetto's family slept, was closed up, and it seemed no one was home.

"I'm going to kill myself, kill myself," his sister was shouting, clutching her head between thin bare arms, as if she was suffering from cramps. "I wish," muttered Alduccio, without looking at anyone, and he headed for his bunk along the wall in the bedroom where his father was stretched out. All of a sudden, his sister jumped up and rushed for the door. "Stop," said Alduccio, grabbing her by the waist and forcing her back into the middle of the kitchen with a shove that sent her sprawling.

She lay where she had fallen between the chair that had tumbled on its side and the table, crying, out of anger, without shedding tears, writhing on the wet floor.

"Close the door," Alduccio's mother told him.

"You close it!" he said, taking a piece of bread from the table and stuffing it in his mouth.

"Idle bastard!" shouted his mother, but not too loud, so as not to have the neighbors hear, but that only made her more furious still; she was disheveled, half-naked, just as he had left her, her sweaty breasts almost spilling from her open dress. She went to close the door, shuffling her bare feet on the tiles.

"Miserable pimp!" she went on, while from the floor the sister was making a gasping noise, muttering "God, God." Alduccio swallowed a mouthful of bread and went to the tap to drink a gulp of water. In his underpants, but still with his black work jacket on, the father came staggering across the kitchen, blind with drink, his hair sweaty and mussed on his forehead. He stood there a moment, maybe because he'd forgotten what he meant to do; then he raised a hand to cover his mouth and moved it up and down, in the air, from about the level of his heart to some undetermined point near his nose, as if to illustrate some long, complicated speech that wouldn't come out. In the end, as though realizing he wouldn't be able to say whatever it was, he hurried off back to bed. Alduccio went out for a moment to take a crap, since there were no toilets inside the apartments, and when he came back his mother again tried to have it out with him: "All day out of the house," she said. "Eats, drinks, and never brings home so much as a lira, never once."

Alduccio turned on her: "Leave off, Ma, I've had it with you," he yelled.

"And when I stop," she said, tossing her hair from her eyes and pulling away the strands stuck to her sweaty throat, bare almost to her nipples, "don't imagine I won't just start again, useless shit that you are!"

Blind with rage, Alduccio spat out the bread he'd started eating at her feet. "There," he said, "take it!" He gave the table a shove, turning to head for the bedroom, so that the bowl and spoon fell to the floor. "Is this all I get from you?" said his mother, going after him, "You reckon you've paid your debts with this?" "Fuck off," said Alduccio. "You fuck off, disgusting slob, that's what you've always been," said his mother. Alduccio lost it completely and bent to grab the knife that had fallen at his feet on the dirty floor.

8. THE GAUNT GOSSIP

> ...the gaunt
> Gossip of Strada-Giulia raises her scythe...*
>
> —GIOACHINO BELLI

IT WAS late Sunday morning. All the fine landscape you could contemplate from the San Basilio bus, during the long stretch without stops between Tiburtino and Ponte Mammolo, seemed to be made up of so many magnificent fragments immersed in a deep blue sky, from the point where the bus was now, at the foot of the slope, as far as the hazy hills of Tivoli, which encircled fields dotted with trees, little bridges, gardens, factories, houses.

Along the Tiburtina, almost grazed by the passing bus that was bowling along at forty now with a great rattling of windows and bolts, the only people around were a few young men, idle and noisy in their Sunday best, walking or cycling, or the occasional group of girls. Everything seemed freshly painted after yesterday evening's rain, even the Aniene that meandered through fields and hovels and stands of bamboo across the Prati Fiscali down to Monte Sacro.

Enjoying the view on the empty, overheated bus were two policemen, two dark men from Ciociaria,† perhaps, or Salerno, streaming with sweat, their summer uniforms unbuttoned everywhere a uniform can be unbuttoned, caps in their hands, their ex-thugs' faces gloomy

---

*In Gioachino Belli's sonnet "Il Tisico" (The Consumptive), Death appears in the last couplet in the form of a "commaraccia secca," literally a "nasty gaunt (female) gossip." Pasolini used the idea when writing the plot for Bernardo Bertolucci's first film, *La Commare Secca* (1962); the English version of the film was called *The Grim Reaper*.

†An impoverished region southeast of Rome and north of Naples.

with boredom, resentful of being subjected to this long pain-in-the-ass ride just because some kid had picked up a few burns. After the bus had raced across the bridge over the Aniene, close to the bleach factory, and come to a stop outside an old trattoria, they got off, taking it easy, lazily mopped up their sweat with their handkerchiefs, and steeled themselves to walk the length of Via Casal dei Pazzi, which led away from the trattoria, stretching off into the distance toward a horizon shimmering with heat. At the very end, like an Arab village, Ponte Mammolo scattered its little white houses over the low rolling hills.

Walking slowly on asphalt melting in the hot sun, the two policemen kept at it until they arrived at the fork in the road, where they took Via Selmi and entered the neighborhood. But the suspects they were after were nowhere to be found. They weren't in one of the last houses of Via Selmi, half built and half not, with curtains for windows and women squabbling round the washtub tap. And they weren't playing with the other kids in the road or out in the fields. Had the two men had any inkling, they could have spared themselves that interminable walk. But how could they have known! To think that, just before the bus crossed the bridge over the Aniene, if maybe they had cast a glance over the landscape and taken in the allotments just beyond the bend in the river where a swarm of kids were fooling in the water, they might just have seen them . . .

The wanted persons, in fact, were down there in the fields, or rather, in a jungle of thickets and willows, bamboo, and brambles, between the allotments and the embankment that dropped sheer down into the Aniene. Mariuccio, who was still so young he hadn't even started school, was hanging out, calm as can be, squatting with his cute little bottom on his heels, playing with two or three ants that he was poking with a stick. Borgo Antico was watching him, and Genesio was smoking, solemn-faced, a little way off and likewise crouched on the ground. Keeping them company was their small dog, Fido by name, who was also taking a little rest. He was sitting on his back paws, front legs pointed straight at the ground, and every now and then he used a back paw to give himself a scratch under the armpits. Comfortably settled, he was looking around, almost politely, to the right, to the left, into the distance, taking in the world from the housing developments of Tiburtino to the meanders of the river, with an occasional calm glance at his three little masters, who, compared to him, were mere babies, and had to be cut a little slack even when they acted plain dumb.

All of a sudden, from the depths of his contemplation, the dog stood up and went to smell Mariuccio's heels. "Here, Fido," said Genesio, but without a hint of a smile: he picked up the animal, who came running at once, put it between his knees, and began to stroke it. Letting himself be fondled, eyes closing in bliss, the dog seemed to lapse into a kind of sleepy languor, the better to savor the attention his favorite master was offering. It didn't happen often, because Genesio, who was good at heart and always troubled, poor thing, by emotions and affections, tended to keep everything to himself, speaking as rarely as possible so as not to give himself away. His little brothers kept him amused and always obeyed him, but it wasn't like they were afraid of him, and sometimes, while obediently showing all proper respect, they did take the liberty of pulling his leg a tiny bit. The little dog was just about to fall asleep in his lap; but all four of them were desperately sleepy that morning: it was their first morning of freedom, and around them in the dry grass and the bundles of flattened canes, you could still see the hollows where they'd slept, like sparrows in their nests, or little rabbits. They didn't regret what they'd done, running away from home, on the contrary, the two smaller boys were extremely happy; after all, Genesio would look out for them. And in fact Genesio sat there frowning, wondering how he would look out for them, while they played with the ants.

"Let's go," said Genesio, abruptly getting to his feet. Without asking where or why—they never did—Borgo Antico and Mariuccio likewise stood up, curious, intrigued to see what would happen next. The dog wagged its tail at their feet, happy that they were on the move again. It ran back and forth, tongue lolling from its open mouth, barking nonstop. But Genesio wasn't planning to go far. First they followed the wild and winding bank of the Aniene, jumping from one hump of ground to the next in the thick of the bamboo as far as the Pescatore Trattoria and the dredger, crossed the river on the old brick bridge, went back down to the other bank, which wasn't as overgrown, and, taking the path that ran through bushes that had lost all their leaves now, they finally came to a point exactly opposite where they'd been before, on the bend where the diving place was. And as on the day before the old drunk was there on his own, singing, "Let me poke just the point," under the arch of the bridge, a place he'd obviously taken a liking to. On the big clearing with the charred remains of the corn stubble, no one was around, not even the four black horses. But now they did hear the sound of voices and in fact at the bottom of the embankment, on the loose dirty soil by the water where they'd been the day before, there were three or four bathers who must have arrived while the three brothers and their dog were going around the dredger. They were chattering together, moving quietly about, in the still, clear light, where the rank heat was already swelling; they were stretched out in the dust, legs spread out, turning over lazily from time to time, and their voices carried loudly in the silence because there weren't many cars on the Tiburtina and the factory across the river was closed.

One of the little group was Caciotta. "If only," he was saying nostalgically, as Genesio and the other boys arrived, "that song had been popular last year!"

He meant the song Zinzello was singing; perhaps yesterday's swim hadn't been all he hoped, and he'd come back to give himself a good soaping down, without his dogs this time. Naked and thin as a rake, he was yelling wildly, at the top of his voice, from behind a bush: "Me in jail and Mama at death's door."

"Why do you wish it had been popular last year?" Alduccio asked, because he was there too, sleepless eyes red as two scars.

"Why?" said Caciotta. "Because then I could have sung it when I was at Porta Portese!"

"Great," sneered Alduccio.

"I could really have got into singing it," Caciotta insisted with maudlin enthusiasm, "when I was in jail myself! Damn! I'd have sung it every evening before going to sleep." And with all his heart he joined in with Zinzello, but each singing in his own time, one more impassioned than the other, Zinzello one side and Caciotta the other of a ragged bush, full of filth.

"They really had your ass, eh?" said Begalone, "when you were in jail?"

"What do you want!" said Caciotta resignedly, breaking off his singing for a moment.

"Well fuck him," muttered Genesio, scowling and speaking to himself, crouched just above the crumbling edge of the embankment. Mariuccio and Borgo Antico were watching him wide-eyed. It was the first time he'd said those bad words whole. "If Ma knew," said Mariuccio in a voice so low it was more a sigh, looking anxiously at his brother, "what would she do?" Genesio shot him one of his expressionless glances and went back to his contemplation of the punks from Tiburtino. The three boys' mother was from the Le Marche and at some point during the war, God knows how or why, had married a bricklayer from Andria. He slapped her around every day, poor woman; hers was worse than a dog's life. Yet, as she always told the neighbors whenever there was a moment's truce, she still wanted the boys to be brought up properly. Now she was home crying, first because she'd realized her boys and the dog had gone, and then because the police had come knocking on her door looking for them; but her three children, and they were all spitting images of her, outside and in, were too busy right then to be thinking of their mother. "Hey Borgo Antì," Begalone called from below, catching sight of him, "why don't you sing us this song!"

"I don't know it," Borgo Antico answered quickly, hardening his small brown face.

"Not true," said Mariuccio, "he does!"

Begalone flew into a rage, came up and chucked Borgo Antico under the chin with his finger. "You're pissing me off," he said. Then, with a threatening light in his Arab face: "Sing, or I'll give you what for." Sulking, head down between his knees, Borgo Antico began to sing "In Jail" at the top of his voice.

Aldo took advantage of a moment when no one was watching to slink off, as if he wanted to take a nap. He stretched on the grass that yesterday evening's rain had washed and this morning's sun had scorched, lying on his stomach, face pillowed on his arms.

While Borgo Antico was singing, Genesio went quietly down the embankment with Mariuccio and Fido scrambling after on all fours. Down by the water Genesio stopped, lost in thought, studying the river flowing by before him under the walls of the bleach factory with the whitish channel of the effluent coming down from the opposite bank. Then, taking his time over it, with Mariuccio and Fido watching with due respect, he crouched down and began to undress. He carefully slipped off his shorts, stiff with dust and sweat, his shirt, his pink vest, his shoes, his socks. He was left, thin and a little bony, shoulder blades sticking out a bit, almost naked, but not entirely, because he wasn't shameless like the Tiburtino boys his age. Not him. He'd kept his underpants on, covering up everything front and back. "Hang on to these," he told Mariuccio, carefully rolling up his clothes and buckling them up tight with his belt. "No, wait," he said sharply. He loosened the belt, unrolled his clothes, took a comb and a cigarette from his pants pocket, and lit the cigarette. Smoking, he combed his hair very carefully, asking Mariuccio if he'd got the part straight or not, and then making a kind of wave on his forehead, a black polished wave with not a single hair out of place. That done, he tied up his clothes again, gave them to his brother, and said flatly, as if this really had nothing to do with him, "Today, I cross the river." Mariuccio looked at him a moment, realizing that this was a big occasion; then he started to yell in his shrill puppy-dog voice, "Hey, Borgo Antì, Borgo Antì!" Borgo Antico speeded up his singing to get through the last words of the song and leaned over the edge of the embankment without a word.

"Hey, Borgo Antì," called Mariuccio in a cheerful rush, "today Genesio says he's going to cross the river."

Borgo Antico said nothing for a few moments, then started slithering down the embankment on his backside as far as the dry mud they used as a diving place.

"You're really going to cross the river, Genè?" he asked seriously.

"You bet," said Genesio, a half smile betraying his emotion.

"Now?"

"Not right now, later, I want to rest first."

The three of them sat together on the black sand, with their dog, who, feeling left out while they talked about important stuff he couldn't understand, wouldn't sit still and kept prancing from one boy to the other, rubbing his nose against them. Genesio, smoking and looking solemn, was quiet for a while, then told his brothers, "Listen, when we're grown up, we'll kill Pa."

"Me too," said Mariuccio at once.

"All three together," Genesio confirmed, "we've got to kill him! Then we'll go live somewhere else with Ma."

He spat the stub of his cigarette in the water, his solemn, determined face gleaming a little with sweat.

"He'll have beaten her this morning as well," he said. He was quiet a while, trying to get a grip on himself, then in his usual dull, flat voice repeated: "When we're grown up we'll show him what we're made of.

"OK, I'll try," he said then, still in the same voice.

"You're going to swim across?" asked the youngest, quavering.

"What do you mean, across," said Genesio. "Just a trial run."

"You're going to go to the middle?" Mariuccio pressed him.

"Right," said Genesio. He got to his feet and began to climb up the embankment.

"Where you going?" asked Mariuccio, amazed.

"Over there," said Genesio, without turning around.

The brothers climbed after him and scrambled down again beyond the diving place where Zinzello was just finishing up with his soap. But now another hefty figure turned up to take his place, a balding man with a straggly beard on a face burning with fever, it seemed. It was Alfio Lucchetti, uncle of Amerigo from Pietralata who'd killed himself.

"Where did these little guys pop up from?" said Zinzello, gently mocking. Still dressed, in his black pin-striped pants, holding his towel roll and soap against his thigh, Alfio looked at the kids with a wry shake of the head and a smile that plumped up cheeks rough with stubble framed by sideburns that came down beneath his protruding ears from hair combed like a teenager's, though not without a thread of white here and there. As if they weren't talking about him at all, Genesio didn't look at anyone and went to put his feet in the river. First he stood for a bit gazing at the water, then he waded in till it was up to his waist, holding his arms high, then he plunged in, swimming fast like a puppy.

"He's training to cross the river," Mariuccio informed the adults, full of naive enthusiasm, looking up at them as you might look at the top of a hill. But they were already talking about their own shit and didn't even hear. Genesio got about halfway across, to where the current formed a series of low waves, flowing faster and gathering up all the river's filth, dark streaks of oil and a sort of yellow foam that looked like thousands of gobs of spit; then he turned, eased off to let himself be carried downstream a bit, till he was near the diving place, then started swimming again, heading for the near bank. He reached it some ways farther down, toward the bridge, grabbing at the prickly bushes that trailed down from the almost sheer bank right to the water.

Borgo Antico and Mariuccio ran after him, scarcely looking where they put their feet, slithering, falling, and jumping up again in the mud, up and down over the slippery hump of the diving place, followed by their dog, who had started barking without really knowing whether he was supposed to be alarmed or happy.

"Hey, Genesio, Genesio," shouted the two younger brothers, as if he had been miles way.

"You didn't make it?" asked Mariuccio anxiously.

"You're pissing me off," Genesio said brusquely. He looked around resentfully, a quick sullen glance, then without looking at them said, "I told you it was a trial run!"

Now that he'd got the feel of it, he gazed at the river again, quietly figuring out the distances. Beyond the current in the middle there was another thirty feet or so before the far bank where the white streak from the bleach effluent dropped vertically into the water. Fido watched the river too, sitting on his haunches; he was panting, mouth open, shutting it every now and then to swallow or lick himself. He was respectful of his little masters' silence, and seemed a trifle downcast. All white except for an almost blue patch around his right eye, it looked like some bastard had whacked him there and the place had swollen up: then the ear on that side flopped down too, while the other was erect, pricked to pick up the slightest sound.

Meantime, sprawled like hogs on the muddy bank, the bigger boys showed signs of waking up. Tirillo went to stand like a statue on the diving place; he stretched out lazy and sluggish, then stood still a while, head down, clicking a sleepy tongue against his palate in a grimace of disgust. "When's he going to dive?" said Caciotta, watching from the corner of an eye so as not to have to roll over. "Don't you know I was born tired?" said Tirillo in a resigned voice, eyes heavy with sleep. Begalone had started coughing so hard it seemed he was about to bring up his lungs. "You're done for, you are!" said Tirillo, then, with a sudden burst of energy, he yelled, "Who's coming in with me?" "Oh, just do it and fuck off," said Begalone, fed up, between rasping coughs that were tearing his lungs. Making the most of the show, Tirillo raised his arms and dived in headfirst, legs spread like a duck. "Fucking pathetic," said Caciotta while the other was still underwater.

But now a sudden roar and a loud clamor put an end to all remarks. Apparently an earthquake was advancing toward them. It was pouring out of Tiburtino, and at the same time proceeding parallel along both Via Tiburtina and the banks of the Aniene. From the road came a din like something was crunching roots deep in the earth, a steady, even monotonous roar, in which, from time to time, you could make out scraping and breaking sounds, explosions of rage that came and went in a second. It approached like an immense steamroller grinding the whole horizon from the developments of Tiburtino to Monte Pecoraro, crushing and shattering everything in its path, like a blanket bombing. From the other side, along the bank of the Aniene, it was as if a swarm of monkeys and parrots had been let loose, or were being chased from the forest by a terrible fire, all shrieking wildly, whether out of fear or from exhilaration, it wasn't clear. In the end it was an army of kids, half of Tiburtino on the move, running like crazy, in their best pants, waving shirts and vests they'd stripped off as they ran. You couldn't make out what they were shouting, all at the same time, one group calling to another, as they spread out and scattered along the bank; but they kept coming, along with the roaring sound along the road, and as the one became more distinct, so their shouts began to make sense: "The Bersaglieri, the Bersaglieri!"* they yelled, and already the first boys came pouring round the bend where the diving place was, and you could see they didn't really give a damn about the Bersaglieri, it was just a chance to kick up a din. Up front, running like ponies with their manes in the wind, were Sgarone, Roscietto, and Armandino, faces full of a fun and mockery that belied their wild cries and the mad effort of the run. It was an impromptu stunt on the part of the kids, who, being in such a crowd together, felt tough and grown-up and were all playing smart-ass. The swarm passed by at top speed, raising a heavy cloud of red dust along the bare ground of the bank, then, following the bend of the river, yelling "The Bersaglieri!" as loud as they could, though absolutely without a scrap of interest, they turned up the bank toward the Tiburtina. Here an army column was already in sight, with Bersaglieri outriders on motorbikes and in armored cars, alternating with trucks full of Bersaglieri in combat uniform, machine guns between their knees, then tanks with caterpillar tracks that sank into the tar as if it were butter. The first kids were already scrambling up the embankment to the road, near the bridge, while the last, a bunch of tough nuts, albeit only five or six years old, had arranged themselves in a line, stepping forward in time, singing a mocking version of the march of the Bersaglieri, "*Papparappa pappa para, papparappa pappa paara.*" Caught up in the general enthusiasm, Caciotta started running after them, likewise Tirillo, who'd remerged from the oil slicks and the spit. Borgo Antico and Mariuccio strained their necks to shout to

---

*The Bersaglieri, famous for their black feathered hats, are one of the most highly trained corps in the Italian Army. They are popular for their spectacular parades and lively band music.

Genesio, "Are you coming, Genè? There's tanks!" But Genesio shrugged his shoulders and sat down where he was among the bushes, as if he hadn't heard. "Are you coming, Genè?" the others went on calling anxiously. Then seeing that Genesio really wasn't planning to come, they set off just for once on their own, trotting after the two big boys toward the embankment up to the Tiburtina, with poor Fido chasing after, utterly in the dark.

The only ones left at the diving place were Alfio Lucchetti, who was withdrawn and grim now that Zinzello had gone; Alduccio, who kept his face buried between his arms to protect it from the burning dust; Genesio, solitary as a hermit the other side of the diving place; and Begalone. Begalone couldn't stop coughing and hawking up phlegm with a noise like a ladle banging in an empty can. His yellow skin was covered in a coating of red that hid his freckles, to the point that his crucifix ribcage seemed to be wrapped in boiled meat. Going to look in the pocket of his pants, he pulled out a handkerchief already spattered with red stains, coughed into that, and pressed it against his mouth. No one paid him any mind and he went on coughing, on his own, cursing and swearing. Finally the fit was over and, taking it slowly, he put his handkerchief back in his pocket and tossed his clothes back under a bush as if they were rags. Since the cough had left him with his head swimming and a sense of nausea, no doubt partly the result of exhaustion, having hardly slept the night before, he decided maybe a dip in the river would do him good. He dragged his weary bones up from the ground and tightened the piece of string he kept tied round his head like a frayed ribbon to hold his hair in place, lifeless yellow hair that he wore loutishly long, down to the first bones in his back. Then, very slowly, since there was no one watching, he went to the spittle-like edge of the water to take a simple, ordinary dip, the way old folks do when they paddle, or like Alfio, standing close by, who'd long since set aside youthful ambition and thought of the river only as his bathtub. He put his dirty feet in the water but the sudden sensation of cold had him pulling them out quick, one then the other, treading like a hen, and grinding his teeth. "Fucking shit." Then he got used to it a bit and, feeling bad, stepped into the river, taking it slow until the water was up to his nipples, which stood out like two bits of red sealing wax on his rib cage. At last, he launched into a swim, a leisurely sidestroke in the middle of the river, but now he felt even worse; his head spun like a top and he had the impression there was something like a dead cat in his stomach. He was about to faint. Frightened, he began to swim frantically toward the bank; no sooner had he set foot on the ground than he found he couldn't stand up and went down on his knees in the mud to vomit. That morning, not having had anything the day before, he'd eaten a half a basket of bread and pork rinds. The poor guy hadn't digested them and now he was retching up his soul.

That was how the others found him, after running to the road and watching the tanks passing until the last one had turned off to Ponte Mammolo. "Begalone's sick!" shouted Caciotta, seeing him stretched on the ground with his mouth in the mud. The others ran up, but Begalone didn't seem to notice, eyes half-open, staring into emptiness. Caciotta and Tirillo grabbed his shoulder and shook him: "Hey, Bégalo, Bégalo, what's up?" they asked, but nothing, Begalone didn't speak, his face so filthy it turned your stomach. There were at least thirty little kids around him now, all scruffy and sweaty and shoving and shouting to see him. Alduccio came down too, his face flushed with sleep, and started to yell, "Keep away, scram, idiots, can't you see he needs air?" He shook Bégalo's shoulders too, in the middle of the circle that had formed around him again. Bégalo muttered something to himself, grimacing, nauseous. "What did he say?" asked Caciotta. "God knows," said Tirillo, a bit frightened. "Let's wash him," Alduccio decided, and got down to it. Cupping his hands, he took some water from the river and threw it into Begalone's face; the boy started a moment, the way drunks do, then plunged back into his torpor. "Come on," said Alduccio. The other two helped him, and with three or four carefully aimed splashes they had all the filth running off his face and chest. "We're really fucked," muttered Caciotta, "if we have to carry him home." Tirillo signaled his agreement with a move like he'd been punched in the head, pulling a face that said, "Fuck that, Caciò." But there was no alternative. They dragged Begalone a bit further up the bank onto dry ground and left him lying there while they got dressed. Then, with all the little kids around watching excitedly, they dressed Begalone as well, and he let them, occasionally retching to bring something up. Then Caciotta grabbed him by the armpits and Tirillo by the feet and they started the long walk to Tiburtino, stopping every ten yards or so to rest, followed by the swarm of kids who fought and shoved to get close. Alduccio only helped for the first stretch, along the path, occasionally taking turns carrying him. Then, when he was about to turn back, he saw Riccetto in the distance, coming toward them, obviously in a good mood, all dressed up and walking carefully so as not to get dust on his smart white brogues; neatly folded in his hands he held a new pair of trunks, and his blue shirt was flapping over his butt.

So Alduccio ran ahead a bit, making up the ground he'd lost behind the procession of kiddies, and was just in time to hear a solemn-faced Riccetto questioning the others and them saying what had happened. Caciotta and Tirillo were taking a rest, with Begalone laid out on the ground like Christ pulled from his cross, but right when Alduccio arrived he began to move a bit and, with the others holding him under the armpits, he slowly got to his feet. Riccetto looked him over with a pessimistic grimace, but when he saw Alduccio he thought, fuck Bégalo, and turned to his cousin, grinning: "Hey, cuz, what's up? Busy night you had, right?" Alduccio lost it, his nerves snapped: "You dick," he told Riccetto, "you think I'm in any mood for jokes? Fuck off and play the fool somewhere else." Face twisted with rage, but you could see something was eating him and he was on the brink of tears. Alduccio turned and made to walk back to the diving place. "Rubbed you the wrong way, did I, cuz?" said Riccetto, following with springy steps, full of cheerful mockery. Alduccio turned like a snake: "Fuck off!" he yelled. "OK, OK," said Riccetto, shaking his head, "but I reckon you'll end up like Lenzetta! Just like Lenzetta!" he repeated. It was a while in fact since anyone had seen Lenzetta, for the simple reason that he was doing a year's solitary in some place outside Rome, Volterra or Ischia maybe, after they had sentenced him to no less than thirty years inside...One day—very likely he was drunk, or God knows what had got into him—he'd hailed a taxi, got himself a ride out to some deserted place near the Grottarossa, pulled out the gun he'd stolen from Cappellone, and killed the driver to take the five or six thousand the man had in his pocket...

Riccetto was quiet for a while, watching his cousin walking with his head down, then he decided he'd had fun enough and said, "Hey, come on, nothing's happened! Calm down, cuz, cheer up and go home, it's about time, I reckon..." Alduccio looked at him skeptically, but with a glimmer of hope in his eyes. "What do you mean nothing's happened," he asked. "Nothing, nothing's happened, come on," said Riccetto. "I was just joking. Your ma hasn't gone to the police! She made up a story, said she'd slipped and hurt herself, I don't know!" Alduccio was quiet for a bit, still walking toward the swimming spot, deep in thought. Then he turned around and without a word to Riccetto set off back toward Tiburtino, almost running to catch up with Bégalo, who was on his feet, walking now, his arms around Caciotta's and Tirillo's shoulders.

"So long, cuz," called a wise Riccetto, waving a hand but not bothering to turn.

He went on alone, in no hurry, toward the bend beneath the bleach factory. He launched into a song and by the time he was through with it he was at the top of the embankment above the diving place. The three kids from Ponte Mammolo were down there, off to one side, but he couldn't see them; on the other side was Alfio Lucchetti, who'd finished washing up and, as if nothing special had happened that morning, was pulling on his old striped pants.

"Now who's that?" wondered Riccetto at the top of the embankment. "God knows!" He looked a little longer while the man, unfathomable, shoulder blades protruding sharply and chest a rug of curly hairs, continued to dress. "Riiiiight!" Riccetto said to himself, remembering he'd seen the man at Amerigo's funeral, and found him pretty disturbing. "Of course, now I remember!" And very calmly he began to get undressed, without thinking anything of it, just giving the man a last glance as he left, telling himself, "He's a loser."

While he was taking off his pants, lifting each leg high so as not to get dust on the legs, he whistled away complacently, chattering to himself, remonstrating under his breath with the holes in his socks or congratulating himself on the smart T-shirt he'd picked up. "It's a winner," he told himself with conviction, looking it over as he folded it up.

"Now I'll just go and see that asshole of a boss," he said when he was down to his underpants, "get him to give me my cash, eat, and after lunch do some living. Go for it, Riccè!"

With this cheerful plan in mind, he stood at the high point of the diving spot, hands on his hips, and from here was finally able to see, to his left, in the bushes, his boss's three little boys. Fido ran to greet him, wagging his tail, crazily excited, jumping right up to his chest with his paws stretched out. But Riccetto barely gave the creature a distracted pat: he was so pleased to have seen the three boys down below. Now he felt even more cheerful; he hardly wanted to take a swim on his own, in that deep lonely silence that seemed to grow as noon approached. But there was another reason for the good humor that had brightened his already bright face under its cropped curls. He watched the boys. They had realized he was there but kept quiet. Riccetto went on watching them. They didn't respond. He stared at them, and the boys turned their backs to him, throwing him a sidelong glance from time to time. Then, catching a moment when all three had turned to look at him, Riccetto broke the silence, raising a hand, fingers tight together, and moving it up and down, the way you do when you're threatening to give someone a good slapping. The three little boys looked at him angrily, shaking their shoulders.

"Right, right," said Riccetto, "keep on just as you are!"

"What's up with you?" Genesio let out, then shut up, silent and prickly as a hedgehog.

Riccetto was having a whale of a time and instead of answering at once began to stare at them again, nodding and making faces.

"Nice stuff you guys get up to," he shouted after a while, loud as he could.

"What have we done?" Mariuccio spoke for all three, feeling less responsible no doubt, being the smallest.

"What have you done?" yelled Riccetto, with wide eyes. "Damn, what a brave little boy you are, wow!"

"Right, so what have we done?" the child repeated candidly.

"Well, fuck all three of you!" cried Riccetto severely, hitting them with a loud, stern voice like it was a fatherly telling-off, "and you even have the nerve to deny it?"

Genesio was getting interested too and, scratching his foot with a stick, all hunched over, asked, "Deny what?"

"Whaaat!" said Riccetto, and despite the almost tragic thought he was thinking, he was overcome by a great wave of laughter that had him bubbling like a kettle.

"Roasting roaches, that's what," he shouted, shaking with laughter, at the expression he'd come up with, "and then you have the nerve to ask, 'What did we do'!" He went on laughing to himself, even rolling around on the ground, *roasting roaches* was so smart: even if Piattoletta hadn't been roasted exactly, more like lightly toasted. The three brothers didn't understand a fucking thing.

"What are you talking about?" demanded Genesio in a hoarse voice.

"You know very well, smartass," said Riccetto, getting up and calming down a bit.

"OK, we left home, so what?" admitted Genesio without batting an eyelid. Riccetto looked at him; this he hadn't known.

"Oh," he said, "left home as well, have you! So you did know that the police are looking for you!"

Now it was Genesio's turn to be surprised, but crouching down with his chest against his knees, he kept his amazement to himself, quickly casting his mind over what Riccetto had said. Not so Borgo Antico and Mariuccio; Mariuccio chirped, "Not true, the police aren't looking for us!"

"If you say so," mocked Riccetto playfully, "but you'll see when they come for you if it's true or not."

"Oh, piss off," said Mariuccio.

"So why are the police after us?" asked Genesio, like nothing was up.

"Why? Why?" asked Riccetto sternly. "You have the nerve to ask me? What were you doing yesterday evening on Monte Pecoraro, eh? Tell me that!"

"What did we do?" said Genesio, looking Riccetto in the eyes now with an air of defiance almost.

Riccetto frowned as though offended by such obtusity. "Who was it," he said, "that burned Piattoletta on the pylon up on Monte Pecoraro?"

For a moment Genesio was astonished; then he shrugged as if to let the whole thing drop and said quietly, "How do I know?"

"You, you did it," exclaimed Riccetto with a cry of malign triumph.

"Bullshit," said Genesio, shrugging his shoulders and looking away, eyes burning under his black curls.

"No, no, it wasn't us," said Mariuccio.

"It's no good denying it," said Riccetto, who was finding this funnier and funnier, "there were witnesses, for God's sake."

"What witnesses!" said Genesio.

"Oh, come on," insisted Riccetto, "at least sixty people, yesterday evening! Roscietto, Sgarone, Armandino, all the kids from Block II, don't bullshit me!"

"It wasn't us," repeated Mariuccio, almost desperate now.

"Well, you'll see when they put you in prison if you have the nerve to deny it," said Riccetto solemnly. Indignant and choking with emotion, chin beginning to tremble, Mariuccio blubbered, "It wasn't us."

Seeing that he was crying, Riccetto left off, and, still standing at the top of the diving place, he sang to himself a bit, crushing the three small boys under his good humor.

"Go ahead and cry," he said from time to time to Mariuccio, breaking off his singing for a second. Though he did feel a bit sorry for the kid; he'd remembered when he was like them, how the bigger boys at the Grattacieli would beat up on him, and he would slink away looking for cigarette butts with Marcello and Agnoletto, spurned and despised by the whole world. He remembered the time they'd stolen money from the blind guy and gone to swim at the Ciriola barge, how they'd taken that boat out and he'd saved the baby swallow that was drowning under Ponte Sisto...

Far away the noon sirens sounded.

"Let's take this swim, come on," he said to himself out loud, "otherwise the boss'll get drunk, damn him, and then like hell I'll get paid. That's all I need, to be broke today of all days."

So saying, he dived headfirst into the river, without heeding Mariuccio, who had already got over his tears and was shouting after him, "You know Genesio's going to cross the river too?"

"Shut up," Genesio told him, and rather than getting in the water, he immersed himself in thoughts about these latest developments. But then his attention was caught by what Riccetto was doing in the middle of the river, and he started to watch as intently as Mariuccio and Borgo Antico. He went down to the water's edge and, half turning toward his brothers, who were fascinated by Riccetto's antics, said in a low voice, "Afterward we'd better go home, or Ma will be upset." Having announced this plan for the day, he was free to concentrate on Riccetto, who was putting on quite a show in the middle of the river. On and on, he flapped and banged his arms like paddles, slapping the water and raising sheets of foams, then he plunged his head under, pushing up his ass and legs like a duck, then he played dead on his back, belly up, singing at the top of his voice. With sudden brusque energy, he swam back to the diving place, climbed out of the water, dripping wet, and then, strutting about and puffing himself up for the benefit of the kiddies, who watched open-mouthed, he dived in again, headfirst, arms outspread.

When his head popped up, he began to swim with big, strong strokes toward the other side. Without a word, splashing through the mud, Genesio hurried to a point below the diving place where the water came up to his chest and launched himself into a lively doggy paddle.

"Are you crossing the river, Genè?" Mariuccio and Borgo called after him excitedly. But he didn't even hear them, couldn't hear them, swimming after Riccetto with mouth held high and tightly shut, head twisted to one side, so as not to drink the river water.

He reached the current, which carried him down a few yards together with all its filth, then, hands still moving rapidly back and forth underwater and head turned to one side, he crossed the other half of the river. Riccetto in the meantime had reached the other bank, beneath the white streak of the bleach acids, and was already diving into the water again, swimming back as fast as he had swum across. He made it in just a few strokes, occasionally playing dead along the way, belly up, singing again; then he climbed up the bank under the diving place, and, still singing, began to do a few exercises to dry off. The sun was at the zenith, scorching; all around, below the bleach factory, it was so hot it seemed the very air was burning, while far away, over the fields and the roads, now that the tanks were no more than a distant rumble, a blinding noonday silence had settled. In a few minutes Riccetto wasn't just dry, he was sweating.

But Genesio was still on the other bank. He had crouched down, the way he did, under the little stream of bleach in the slimy white mud. Behind and above him, like a landslide in the circles of hell, rose the bushy embankment and the big wall of the factory with its green and brown tanks and silos towering above, a great pile of metal containers shimmering in an air that was almost black in the dazzle of so much light.

Mariuccio and Borgo Antico looked at the brother crouched there like a bedouin. "Aren't you coming back, Genè?" called Mariuccio in his shrill voice, clutching the bundle of his brother's clothes tight against his ribs.

"Coming now!" replied Genesio from the other side, without raising his voice, crouching still with his face between his knees. Riccetto was taking it easy getting dressed, sorting out his socks, taking care he didn't put them on inside out. "I'm going to tell the police you're here," he shouted cheerfully to Genesio, who was almost ready, "and your pa too!"

Setting off, he felt full of optimism again, but this time he made no more than the usual threatening wave of the arm toward the kiddies who were watching anxiously from below. While he was walking away, though, half turning back to wave his arm, he happened to glance over at the factory walls and, up above, in a small, lonely window in the midst of the big steel-plated cylinders of the silos, caught sight of the custodian's daughter, vigorously rubbing the glass pane. "Hot stuff!" said Riccetto, immediately horny. He walked on a few steps, then changed his mind and looked at her again, then walked a few more steps toward the bridge, then changed his mind a second time. She was still up there, rubbing away at the glass that dazzled like it was melting in the bright air. "Fuck it, let's hang on a bit," he said. He stopped and slipped between two bramble bushes and a bed of nettles, so that neither the boys down by the river nor the kids walking by on the Tiburtina could see him. Though actually no one was going by at that time, in that heat; all you could hear were a few cars and, in the distance, the rumble and revving of the tanks.

As soon as he was between the bushes, he slipped off his pants and, pretending his underpants still needed wringing out a bit, stood there nude, half-hidden, admiring himself, and trying to get himself admired by the girl in the window.

"Genè, aren't you coming back?" Mariuccio went on calling, voice drenched in anxiety. Genesio heard and didn't answer, then ran into the water, swam to where the current flowed, but turned straight back and sat sullenly under the embankment and the high wall.

"Aren't you coming back, Genè?" Mariuccio called again, disappointed.

"I'm staying here a bit," said Genesio from the other side, "it's pretty nice here!"

"Come on, come back!" Mariuccio kept at it, neck swollen with the effort of shouting across the river. Borgo Antico started shouting too and Fido was barking and prancing about, nose pointing at the opposite bank, as if he were calling Genesio too.

So Genesio got to his feet, stretched a bit, something he never did, and shouted, "I'll count to thirty, then dive in." He stood still, in silence, counting, then stared hard at the water, eyes burning under the dark wave of his still neatly combed hair, and finally dived in with a belly flop. Swimming fast, he was soon almost halfway across, at the point right below the factory where the river began to bend toward the bridge where the Tiburtina passed. But the current was strong here and pushed him back toward the factory bank; coming the other way, Genesio had had no trouble crossing the current, but getting back was a different matter. The way he was swimming, doggy paddle, kept him afloat but without making any headway; meanwhile, holding him in the middle of the river, the current had begun to take him downstream, toward the bridge.

"Hurry up, Genè," his brothers shouted from under the diving place, not understanding why Genesio didn't just come toward them, "come on, it's time to go!"

But he couldn't cross the strip of water that raced along, full of foam and waste oil and sawdust, a separate current in the yellow mainstream of the river. He was still there in the middle, and far from getting nearer the bank, he was being dragged down farther and farther toward the bridge. Borgo Antico, Mariuccio, and the dog scrambled headlong down from the mound of the diving place and began to run fast, and even crawl where they couldn't run, falling and getting up again, along the black mud of the bank, after Genesio, who was being carried faster and faster toward the bridge. So it was that Riccetto, still showing off for the girl, who was little more than a smudge rubbing away at her windows, saw all three pass by beneath him, the two little ones tumbling and yelling in the bushes, frightened, and Genesio in the middle of the river, never letting up his rapid doggy paddle with his thin arms, but never advancing so much as an inch. Riccetto stood up and, naked as he was, walked a few steps toward the water, between the prickly bushes, and stopped there to see what was happening before his eyes. At first he couldn't get his head around it, thought they were joking or something; but then he understood and he rushed down the slope, slithering as he went, yet at the same time realized that it was too late: to dive in the river under the bridge was tantamount to saying you were tired of life, no one could survive it. He stopped, pale as death. Genesio, the poor kid, had run out of energy, flapping his arms wildly, though still without calling for help. Every now and then he sank under the surface of the water, then reemerged a bit further away. Finally, when he was almost at the bridge, where the current broke and foamed on the rocks, he went under for the last time, without so much as a cry, and for a few seconds you could just see his small black head under the surface of the water.

With trembling hands, Riccetto pulled on the pants he'd been carrying and without another glance at the little window of the factory, he stood there, not knowing what to do. He could hear Borgo Antico and Mariuccio screaming and crying under the bridge, Mariuccio still clutching Genesio's vest and shorts against his chest; and they were already beginning to climb up the bank, scrambling on their hands and knees.

"Best split," Riccetto muttered, almost crying himself, and he set off fast along the path toward the Tiburtina, almost running, so as to be above the bridge before the two boys got there. "I love you, Riccetto, you know!" he thought. Slipping and grabbing onto the stumps of the bushes, he clambered up the steep slope with its burned stubble and thick dust; then he'd made it, and without looking back he set off across the bridge. He was able get away without anyone seeing because right then there was no one about, no one in the empty fields stretching away toward the clustered white houses of Pietralata and Monte Sacro, no one on the Tiburtina. Not a single car passed, not a single old bus. In the vast silence, all you could hear was the occasional tank, far away, beyond the sports grounds of Ponte Mammolo, a low rumble plowing the horizon.

OTHER NEW YORK REVIEW CLASSICS

For a complete list of titles, visit www.nyrb.com.